MUSKOKA MIRACLE

CAROLYN MILLER

CHAPTER 1

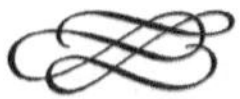

Toronto

"And I'm going to close with what I always like to say, we can trust God with it all, yeah? Yeah!"

Sarah grinned as she wrapped up the podcast. "Thank you, dear friends, for taking time out of your busy lives to pause, connect, and remember God's faithfulness. I'm Sarah Walton, and you have been listening to *Time Out with Sarah*. Until next time, keep trusting!"

She pressed the cued outro music, a sample from one of her independent singles, and waited the requisite five seconds until it was time to end and save. Nearly two years of doing her podcast and she was finally getting the hang of it. She placed a hand on her stomach. "Just in time for you, huh?"

Her eyes closed as a wave of thankfulness rolled over her. God was so good. So very, very good. Who would have thought six years ago that she'd be married and living in Toronto? She'd expected to be married, yes, but not to Dan. Her heart panged a little as she remembered Stephen, whose death in a car crash on New Year's Eve had precipitated her exodus to Canada all those years ago. Sometimes she wasn't sure whether she should admit to Dan that she still occasionally thought about her former fiancé. Not in any betrayal way, which was why she hadn't said anything. But completely wiping all memories of her dead fiancé seemed impossible.

She blew out a breath, then pushed away from the desk, in the soundproofed second bedroom she'd commandeered in their high rise apartment. Half the room held an assortment of music and recording equipment and this desk where she did her podcast and connected with the other musicians from Heartsong Collective who lived around the world. The other half held an assortment of baby paraphernalia, ready for six months' time.

Six months' time. She shivered. No-one, apart from Dan and the doctor knew. After the doctor's visit the initial elation had diminished as he'd examined her results and studied her previous medical records, warning that her hCG levels were low, and there was a possibility of miscarriage. But her other symptoms seemed to indicate her body was adjusting as it should. But even with the first ultrasound showing a little heartbeat she'd been reluctant to say anything to anyone, wanting desperately to get to twelve weeks, which the doctor had indicated was the best time to determine true viability.

But the doctor's cautions were falling on deaf ears. She and Dan had just looked at each other in wonder. After all that they'd gone through, this was an absolute miracle; God would certainly not let anything happen to their miracle. But they hadn't told anyone else yet.

Sarah delighted in hugging her secret to herself. Each day that took them closer to the twelve-week mark was brighter. The birds seemed to sing more sweetly. Even the sickness and tiredness were okay now she knew they were signs that her body was doing everything it could to help this baby along.

Dan was so excited. He tried to downplay it, of course, but she could tell. He'd become even more gentle, his caresses were more tender, and the light in his eyes was something she'd never seen before. Who knew such a tiny sac of cells could be responsible for so much?

Her prayers of thankfulness came from the very depths of her being. She'd never imagined—never dared to imagine—this possibility.

Please Lord. She placed a hand on her abdomen, her prayers for this one near constant. After the past two miscarriages, surely God would let this one live. *Please Lord.*

A faint siren stole through the window, and she got up to peer outside. Blue skies were always welcome for a transplanted Aussie, and the fact that Dan's season was soon ending, and summer was on its way meant they'd finally get the chance to return to Muskoka. She couldn't wait. It was her favorite part of the world.

The sound of keys clattering on a table outside drew anticipation, and she hurried to open the door. Then nearly slammed into Dan's broad chest.

"Whoa." He laughed, holding her upper arms to steady her.

Clumsy was as much part of her DNA as the vibrant color of her hair.

"Someone seems eager to see me."

"Oh, you know it." She slid her hands up behind his neck and tugged his face lower. "Hi."

His eyes darkened. "Hello, Princess."

His lips met hers, sending tingles shimmering across her skin. Who said marriage sucked away the sparks? Nearly three years of marriage and their relationship was just as hot as in the beginning.

A satisfyingly long smooch later, and she leaned back in the cradle of his arms. "You're home earlier than I thought."

"I was hoping you'd have finished your podcast by now."

"Yep, all done, and ready for next week."

"Organized as ever."

"The only way to be." Especially with their crazy schedules. Him with hockey, which meant six months of the year she barely saw him, between his training, road trips and games. Coupled with her own trips for recording sessions and tours with Heartsong Collective, time spent together that wasn't snatched or planned to the nth degree was a rare commodity. He'd talked about being one injury away from retirement, and while she prayed daily for his safety, she couldn't wait for the chance to slow the hectic pace of their life, as his retirement from hockey would do. Her heart sparkled. And allow for other things.

"And," he continued, "I might've thought that hanging with my wife was better than hanging with the guys."

She smiled, tracing a hand down his rough cheek. "You thought right."

His lips curved higher, then he drew nearer, as if for another kiss, but she pulled back. "But I'm guessing someone also might've just remembered that his mom is expecting us for dinner tonight, and hates it when we're late."

"Do we have to go?"

"You know we do."

"Do we?" he asked, dropping a kiss on her jaw.

"They're your parents," she murmured. And while things were much easier than when Sarah had first met them, it still wasn't as relaxed as with her own. Even Dan often said the same.

"Why are we talking about dinner with my folks when that's still a few hours away?"

"Exactly." She raised her eyebrows.

He smiled and lifted his. "Oh, I like how you think, Mrs. Walton."

"I thought you might, Mr. Walton. Come on."

"You don't have to tell me twice."

LATER, they drove the twenty minutes from his apartment to Sunnybrook, and the Tudor-inspired house his parents had bought when they'd made their millions on the stock exchange.

Hard to believe that just over the parkland was where Drake had his mega mansion, with some reports putting the rapper's house at costing $100 million. How insane. And while she might've had her share of travel and meeting famous people, sometimes it still seemed crazy to her just how disparate the world could be.

"Are you okay?" Dan asked, as they drove along.

"Absolutely." She grinned. "Never better."

He reached across and caressed her belly. "Everything feeling good?"

"Yep." She placed her hand on top of his. "Nothing to worry about." *Please Lord.*

"Do you think we can tell them?"

She pressed her lips together, holding in the protest. She didn't want to tell them. Not when she hadn't told her own parents yet. Her own parents, who had prayed with her, believed with her, for just this miracle ever since the accident five and a half years ago.

"I'm gonna take that as a no."

"A not yet," she amended.

"That's probably wise."

She winced. She hated letting practicalities get in the way of what should be unfettered joy. But the last two times when she'd felt this rush of excitement had only resulted in devastation. She couldn't bring others into it, not until they'd reached twelve weeks. *Please Lord.*

Her parents had been so supportive, flying from Sydney both times, comforting her and Dan. Part of her clung to the fact that at least she'd been able to get pregnant, which, considering the accident and all the subsequent surgeries, felt miracle enough. But it seemed like the miracle of conceiving life was a different one to that of being able to carry a child to full term. *Lord, let this time be different.*

It wasn't her fault, the doctors had assured her; Dan and her parents, too. She peeked across. He caught her gaze, smiled, and held out his hand.

Lord, let this time be different for his sake, please.

Maybe she was the only woman in the world who wanted a child more for her husband's sake than her own. But she knew he had regrets from the past, regrets she suspected would only truly be resolved by the birth of his child.

They held hands until he pulled into the drive of the house with its mock Tudor facade, then she internally braced.

He chuckled.

"What?"

"It's funny how you still seem wary about meeting them."

She exhaled. "I still give that impression?"

"Only to me."

"I hope so. I don't want them to feel like I'm uncomfortable around them." Even if it was sometimes true. She'd often wondered how Dan and his younger brother Sam had managed to escape the stiff and starchy personalities epitomized by Helen and Andrew Walton.

"And I only notice because I know you so well, Sar Bear."

She rolled her eyes at the nickname, a new one he'd started with its reference to a bear encounter from her first summer in Muskoka, when she'd complained about him calling her 'Princess' all the time, because it just sounded too… princessy.

She wasn't precious, or pompous, or pretentious. Far from it. She was still normal, clumsy, mostly unfiltered Sarah. The girl who dropped food on her clothes and tended to overshare.

They knocked then entered, and were met with a, "You're here!"

"Hi, Helen." Sarah hugged her, then moved to hug her father-in-law. "Hi, Andrew."

"You're looking well."

"Thanks." She smiled, thankful Dan was near. He found encounters with his parents draining sometimes too.

"So, let's eat. I'm glad you're here on time."

Sarah smirked at Dan who rolled his eyes back at her.

Helen served the meal—brisket and roast vegetables. Not usually what Dan ate during the playing season, but Helen never seemed to pay attention to the subtle and unsubtle hints about what an NHL player's diet should consist of. Variations of pasta and chicken weren't favorite meals of Helen, it seemed.

Sarah soon relaxed, and enjoyed the meal, even though Helen kept looking at her. She refused Andrew's reiterated offer to have wine, covering her glass. "Thanks, but not tonight."

Or any time in the next six months. She would not let anything happen to this precious bundle inside.

Dan clasped her hand under the table, his touch instantly bringing ease. Oh, she loved how this man was always so attuned to her moods and needs.

"So, just one more week of the regular season, then playoffs, huh? How do you fancy your chances against Florida?" Andrew asked.

Sarah squeezed Dan's hand. He'd tried his best, but the Leafs' offense had been hit with injuries lately, and they looked destined to scrape into playoff contention, rather than steam-rolling their way to the top of their division as predicted a month ago. They required only one more win.

"It's a bit early to say," Dan hedged. "We have to get there first."

"Here's hoping you do." Andrew lifted his glass.

Sarah lifted her glass of water too. Smiled encouragement at Dan. "You'll make it. You make that team great."

He relaxed. "And this is why I love you." He pressed a kiss to the back of her hand, then murmured for her ears only, "and for other reasons."

She smothered a laugh, glancing up to see Helen's eyes on her again.

"You seem happy, Sarah."

She half-shrugged. "It was a good day." She shared about recording her podcast, and that she'd had some inspiration for a chord progression for a new song.

"No, it's not that." Helen's head tilted. "I don't know what it is. But you seem to be glowing."

Glowing? Sarah instantly dialed down her smile. No. She didn't want Helen putting two and two together. Not until she'd told Mum and Dad, at least.

Helen's eyes rounded. "No."

Oh no.

"Don't tell me." Helen's voice hitched. "Are you... are you pregnant?"

Sarah's grip tightened on Dan's. "Um..."

"You are! Oh my goodness! Why didn't you say anything?"

Sarah cast Dan a pleading look. He mouthed a "sorry" then turned to his mom. "We haven't told anyone yet."

"Why ever not? This is what you've been hoping for, isn't it?"

"Yes." Dan's attention returned to Sarah, and he kissed her hand again. "Praying for, for years."

There. That proud yet tender, hope-filled look was why she couldn't deny the man anything. Couldn't even be too upset that his parents—the ones who had everything—had this information first.

She glanced back at his folks. "We wanted to wait until twelve weeks."

"Especially after..." Dan stopped.

They hadn't told his parents about the other miscarriages. They'd told her parents though. She cringed. She could imagine just how well this would go down.

"After what?" Andrew asked.

Good to see he was paying attention.

"It's good to wait until twelve weeks so the baby is more viable," Sarah said carefully.

Helen's eyes widened. "Are you telling me you've been pregnant before?"

Hopes at keeping their previous experiences with pregnancy a secret deflated. But she couldn't lie. "It was only twice."

"Twice?"

God bless her ability to overshare. She gestured for Dan to take the lead. They were his parents, after all.

He fumbled his way through explanations, bravely taking the verbal bullets when Helen asked if that was why Sarah's parents had visited last year.

Sarah studied her hands, now in her lap, tension rippling over her, through her. She forced herself to relax. This was exactly what the doctor had warned about. She needed to be careful not to let pressure build up, not to let herself get worried. She tuned out the conversation as best she could. She really needed to contact her parents. She glanced longingly at her phone. Maybe she could do so now, before Helen took it upon herself to spill the beans. Given the mood she was in she likely would, too, as payback for being out of the loop. Ugh. How awful to think Helen would be so petty. Ugh, and double ugh. She was an awful daughter-in-law to even think that.

"Well, Sarah, I can't pretend not to be a little miffed that you didn't choose to tell us about the previous pregnancies—"

"I'm sorry, but it was so new, I could barely get my head

around it myself," she rushed to explain. Especially when she'd been stunned by the fact she could even get pregnant. "Then when we lost them—" Her heart panged, her throat filled.

"It wasn't an easy thing to talk about," Dan said, coming to her rescue.

That's what he did. He might be the Leafs' top defenseman, but he was her protector too. She reached across and held his hand. Oh, she loved this man.

"I can't believe you didn't tell us," Helen grumbled again.

Heaven forbid Helen hold this against her. Sarah knew she would never measure up to Helen's other daughter-in-law, Marguerite, who often seemed like she was Helen's mini-me, albeit a nicer, younger version, and now a mother of two. The gold-plated daughter-in-law.

"It was only six and eight weeks, Mom," Dan said tiredly.

"And how far along is this one?" Helen asked.

"Ten."

"Well, practice makes perfect, huh?" Andrew said.

Sharpness stabbed her chest, and she blinked back emotion. How could he dismiss their agony in such a callous way?

He hadn't seen their tears, hadn't seen his son's anguish, didn't know the atomic bomb-sized emotions they'd experienced. Ecstasy at finally believing God had granted the desires of their heart; then agony when it was ripped away. The hopes, the possibilities, the future they'd dared to dream, then the doctor's words in that examination room. "I'm sorry, but you've lost the baby."

How crazy that it was a baby when it was wanted; a fetus if it was not.

"Dad, that comment was uncalled for."

Sarah glanced at Dan. She'd seen that hard expression a few times. Usually when it was directed at an opposing player with a bad attitude. Dan glanced at her, his eyes softening, his eyebrows arching as if asking if she wanted to leave.

Boy, did she. She nodded.

He stood, then helped her up. "I have a big day tomorrow, so we need to go. Thank you for the meal. It was delicious."

"Yes, thank you," Sarah murmured.

The next minute passed in mumbled apologies she wasn't sure she believed, then they finally exited, and were safe in his car.

He reversed, and only when the house could not be seen did she relax. "I'm so sorry."

"You? What for?"

"I didn't mean to say anything."

"Honey, you've got nothing to be sorry for. I've always loved how your face can't hide a thing."

That made one of them.

"Besides, my mom guessed, and we couldn't lie, could we?"

She shook her head. "It's just that I really wanted Mum to know first," she confessed.

His chin jerked. "They'd at least understand. I can't believe my parents sometimes."

"I think they just felt left out." Regret shafted her chest. Maybe they should've told them about the previous pregnancies. Even if they hadn't because of exactly that reason, with their tendency to make things about themselves. Dan's parents weren't much in the way of emotional support, or any kind of prayer support. They weren't believers, despite Dan and Sarah's best efforts to share—and show—the good news.

"Well, they should know that if they're going to react like that then of course they won't be told." He glanced at her. "What's the time in Sydney?"

"Mid-morning. You think I should—?"

"Tell your parents? Yeah."

She sighed, then tapped a message on her phone. *Are you free for a chat?* Ideally, she would've liked her sister, Rebekah, as part of this conversation too. Oh well.

Her phone was ringing by the time they reached the apartment's parking garage, which meant there'd be guaranteed glitching until they were actually upstairs and in their home. She had to wait to return her mum's call as the elevator took its sweet time to reach the sixteenth floor. Then, when it finally did, they were forced to make small talk with some neighbors. Lincoln Cash was an actor, who just so happened to have moved two doors down from Dan's cottage in Muskoka, then had bought an apartment in this very building, on Dan's very floor. He was working in a TV show being filmed here, so they'd bumped into him a few times. Jackie, his wife, was nice, and they'd recently had a baby, which had caused no small amount of envy.

Finally they were able to escape inside their apartment and she returned her mother's call. "Sorry about that. We had to wait until we were out of the elevator."

"Is it true?" her mum asked.

"Is what true?" Sarah glanced at Dan, who shrugged.

"I just got a message from Helen Walton, congratulating us on being grandparents again."

"Oh, Mum." Sarah sank into the leather lounge and closed her eyes.

Dan murmured, "My mom messaged her?"

She nodded, her eyes still closed. Dan muttered something under his breath. "I'm sorry I didn't tell you," Sarah murmured. "We were waiting until—"

"Twelve weeks, I know. It's okay, Sarah."

"I really wanted you to know, too." She sniffled. "Especially after what happened the last time."

"It's okay, honey. Is Dan there?"

She opened her eyes. "Yes."

"Then put this call on speaker."

She did, and Dan sat beside her, his arm around her.

"Congratulations, you two," her mother said.

"Thanks, Mum." Sarah pressed her cheek into Dan's chest. His heart ticked reassuringly.

"Thanks, Lindy."

"So how are you feeling, Sarah?" her mother asked.

"Good. A little tired, but nothing to complain about."

"I'm glad, *so* glad for you both. Oh, look, James is back. Can we tell him?"

"Of course." Excitement filtered past the previous regrets. Helen and Andrew's reaction didn't need to sour this special time.

And sure enough, her father was thrilled, calling it a "real answer to prayer."

Their encouragement soon led to a call to Rebekah, who was just as excited, then a call to Sam, then Luke, so all the siblings knew too.

"We should call John and Ange too," Sarah suggested. "I know Mom will be itching to talk to her, but she won't say anything until we give her permission."

He grimaced. "Unlike some."

"Hey." She hugged him, as a twinge of guilt at not telling his parents demanded she be gracious. "Let's put it down to your mum being excited, okay?"

"Hmm." He lifted her chin. "But nobody does excitement quite like you."

NOBODY DID DO excitement quite like Sarah. Since meeting her in Muskoka she'd brought a sparkle to Dan's world, a zest and energy that was the perfect complement to his more laid-back ways. They were a perfect match. God-ordained, some might say.

He glanced across at where she slept, and traced her

features. Fair skin, red hair, pink lips, dark lashes. He smiled. She must've got them tinted recently, and not said anything.

He shifted his pillow and settled on his side, watching as she rested. He should be asleep too, his game tomorrow demanded he be on full alert, but he much preferred this. It was funny how his priorities had changed since getting married. Once, hockey had been his all-consuming focus; now, the thought of retiring from the game he loved tantalized. Hockey defensemen often had longer careers than forwards, and some played into their late thirties, but he didn't want that. As soon as this child was born, he wanted to be a full-time dad. And that might be a little awkward, seeing he hadn't told his agent or anyone on the team about their family plans. But as he was on the last year of his contract, and his agent was already murmuring about negotiating for the future, then he probably needed to say something soon.

Fatherhood. His heart glowed. It still stunned him to think that God was gracious enough to allow him to experience this deepest desire of his heart. Especially after—

No. He was forgiven. He knew that. *Knew* it. God didn't hold his unsaved self's sins against him, not now. But sometimes it was harder to believe that. Like when the miscarriages had occurred, and he'd had the awful thought that perhaps it was God's punishment for his previous actions. But God was a God of grace, and Sarah was full of grace, too, which was why she'd instantly refuted him any time he'd dared murmur some of his doubts.

"You are *not* your past, you hear me? Don't let the devil lie to you. Don't believe him. Believe God's promises, okay?"

She could be fierce, his wife. That passion was part of why he loved her. That, and the way she overcame her grief, possessing a strength he'd needed, that he'd clung to.

He remembered the first time he'd seen the two pink lines

on the pregnancy test. His heart had kicked at the impossibility. "Is that saying what I think it is?"

Sarah had nodded, then talked about a babymoon, then she'd taken another test. Two lines, one slightly fainter than the other.

The doctor had confirmed that her hCG levels were low, but they'd believed, they'd prayed. Surely God wouldn't give them this miracle just to take it away?

Then she'd started bleeding, and they'd lost it. The same myriad of emotions had occurred several months later. Hope-filled dreams of answered prayers crashing into the reality of blood and loss. For him, the second time was worse than the first. The first time had been so quick. A pregnancy test then two weeks later it was gone. The second time, hope had lived a little longer, grown roots and gotten a little more established. So when that was ripped away the loss felt all the greater.

And while he'd chafed at his father's insensitive comment, part of him had wondered if this process was helping Sarah's system flush out the bad and prepare for the miracle of new life. He'd seen the doctors' reports. He knew that the accident had scarred her internal organs, which meant getting pregnant was a miracle, especially as she only had one fallopian tube. He didn't know all the ins and outs of what that involved, but Sarah had been blunt that marrying her came with the strong possibility that they might never have children she could carry to full term. He'd known that. Had prayed about it and felt God reassure. So the fact she had gotten pregnant at all was a miracle. But now it had fed fresh hunger to be a dad.

He reached a hand across, and gently laid it on her belly. She didn't wake, but smiled.

And he prayed for their child, that God would bless this tiny person, and have His way in their life. And that God would bless his beautiful wife, and lead them into His purposes.

CHAPTER 2

The anguished cry of a loon ripped through her dream, startling her awake. What? Beside her, Dan slept, his breath slow and easy. It was a dream. Everything was fine. She closed her eyes, and placed a hand on her stomach. *Stay safe, little one.*

She drew in a deep breath, then released, forcing herself to relax, to not worry. God was with them. He loved them, had good plans for their lives. They could trust Him. She knew that. But trusting God with their child's life felt almost like a step too far, like she was stepping out into a chasm with no visible bridge, like in an old Indiana Jones movie. And while she knew faith required stepping into places unseen, the fact she'd been here before, trusting God that He'd bring His miracle of new life into fullness, and seen that crumble, had eroded some of her faith.

Not that she'd admit that to anyone. Not that she'd ever admit that on her podcast. She was trying to encourage others to trust God. What would it say if she admitted that God had let her down? Twice now? She couldn't. Which was why nobody knew about their miscarriages. Apart from the doctors, and now their parents.

She exhaled. She hoped Helen and Andrew wouldn't mention that to anyone else. She didn't think they'd be so insensitive. Would they? No.

Amid the churn of such thoughts—she *didn't* want to believe it—she grew aware of another sensation. She kept her eyes closed, forced herself to relax. Be calm, be still, and know that—

Her stomach tightened, then released. *No.*

Her body tensed again, as a trickle of fear wove past her prayers. No. Not again. Not when she might finally give her husband his dearest wish.

Lord, she silently prayed, not wanting to disturb Dan sleeping beside her. *You know we love this tiny person already. Please keep him or her safe.*

For a moment hope bobbed higher, just above her fears, before the memory returned of Dr. McKinnon's frown and thinned lips when he'd seen the wavery pink lines and examined the blood test results. But God was bigger than a test result. God was bigger than her fears. She knew that. *Knew* that. She'd even written a song used in churches worldwide about how God could do anything. So surely it stood to reason that if God could do anything, then He wouldn't want her to suffer more loss. Not again…

She drew in another deep breath then slowly exhaled. Relax. She needed to relax. Stress led to higher blood pressure which wasn't good for the baby, and after the tense moments last night she'd known she needed to forgive and let it go. Which was hard to do, especially when her heart had always felt a little prone to picking up offense like a magnet collected nails. *Lord, I forgive them*, she prayed. *Forgive me, for all I've done wrong, and—*

Another pang hit. *No!* This cramp was more intense, like a heavy band around her stomach. It subsided, then resumed, gripping her in a tight squeeze until the hope she'd been praying with fluttered away, broken. She knew what this meant. *Oh God...*

She hurt. But the pain in her body was nothing compared to the pain in her heart. Listening to Dan's even breathing she stilled, wanting to absorb the last moments of his peace before it too broke. *Oh God, be with him....*

Tears heated the back of her eyes. She quietly slipped from the bed and padded to the ensuite bathroom, closing the door before turning on the light. If this was what she feared, Dan needed to sleep as much as he could, because he likely wouldn't after.

And this, on such an important game day. Why—?

"Oh!" Her stomach squeezed, and she inched to the toilet, sat down, tears sparking. "Lord, please no, please no..." she whispered.

But it wasn't long before she faced the same result as nine months ago, staring at clotted blood as she tried to believe that God was good, and this wasn't her nightmare back again. *No, God, no.*

This was her child! He or she was not supposed to be brought into the world like some dismembered, unidentifiable blob! *Oh God, where are You now...?*

Tears trickled down her cheeks as Sarah gasped and silently moaned her way through the next hour, propping herself against the cold, white tiles, watching, heartbroken, as more tiny clumps escaped. *Oh God... Oh God... No, no, no...*

When the cramps and flow had ceased, she slowly eased her way to the shower, washing away the bright red stain. Sorrow felt like a heavy presence that was waiting for her to stop so it could explode; she had to keep moving to prevent that from happening. Mechanically she dried herself, pulled on fresh underpants, attached a pad, refusing to look down, thinking, thinking ahead to what to do.

Tears leaked as she cleaned up. Should she wake Dan? He

had a game today. The team's last chance to make the playoffs, no less. But he'd want to know. Not that there was anything he could do. It was just like last time, and the time before that. She'd started bleeding, and when she'd presented at the doctor's clinic, they'd said there was nothing anyone could do.

The doctors. She probably needed to make an appointment. But they'd be closed right now. After pulling on warm pajamas, she wrapped a robe around her and stole out to the kitchen to her phone. She composed a text to her mum: *I'm bleeding again.* Then hesitated before pressing send.

Was it bad to be telling her mother when she hadn't even told her husband? But the thought of telling Dan, of having to help him deal with his loss when she could barely even process hers, felt like a weight too heavy.

No. Instead of telling her mum first, she needed a moment to recalibrate her emotions, to get herself calm. Her body would do what it did, and she couldn't change that. But she could do something different to what she'd done the last few times tragedy had struck. When Stephen had died, she'd locked herself in grief for eighteen months. It was only by going to Muskoka that she'd finally come to terms with things and found a way forward.

And while Muskoka was only two hours away, it wasn't like they could go there today. Dan had a must-win game to play first. Thank God it was here in Toronto and not an away game. But would he even want to play if he knew this?

No, she couldn't go to Muskoka, but she still knew things had to be done differently to the last two times, when their disappointment had paralyzed, sending her into another of those emotional tailspins she was all too prone to, while Dan's grief had hollowed him into becoming a shell of the man he usually was.

"Lord, help us," she whispered.

She boiled the kettle, taking care to switch it off before it loudly beeped its boiling duty was done, and made a cup of tea. After retrieving her Bible, she stole to the second bedroom and the baby paraphernalia there, stroking a teddy bear blanket that lay waiting for the baby who seemed destined to never live. Her heart wrenched. *Why God, why?* She wiped her eyes, snatched a tissue, and gently blew her nose. She didn't want to wake Dan.

The bedside clock's illuminated hands had shown three a.m. when she'd exited the bed. She knew she couldn't sleep now, but also knew she couldn't do what she'd done in the past and just wallow in sorrow.

God, help me, help Dan, help us.

Her mind flashed back to the hospital ward when she'd woken in the early hours of the morning, and had to start dealing with the previous night's news about her fiancé's death. Her body felt the same now as it had then. Fragile, like she was made of glass, like she was barely tethered to this earth.

But unlike that time, instead of running away from God, this time she wanted to run *to* Him. Despite everything, something deep inside could sense this was another defining God moment in her life, and after the years of resentment she'd had to overcome from making the wrong decision when Stephen died, she knew she couldn't go down that same bitter path again.

Balancing her Bible and cup of tea she moved to the comfy lounge chair near the window, where the open curtains revealed Toronto's night lights. She sat there for a moment just watching, the lights blurring and shifting as she blinked away the tears.

Oh God, why? Why did this happen? Everything was going fine...

The storm descended and she wept an agony of tears, trying desperately to muffle them so Dan wouldn't wake up. She didn't know what to say, what could help him. She barely had enough reserves to breathe let alone comfort him.

Oh God, help...

Grabbing another tissue she blew her nose, thankful that Dan wasn't up to see her puffy red features. He'd seen that before; not pretty. Then wondered how vanity could even be talking right now. Unbelievable.

Exhaling a long, shaky sigh she looked at the Bible, recalling the many stories of lost dreams and sorrow intertwined amidst the hope. She picked it up, the pages falling open automatically at the start of Job. Two days ago her uncle had been preaching about Job's trials, and the church bulletin still marked the page. Familiar with the story, Sarah read it again.

God, help me understand...

Dawn's pink fingers were stretching across the sky by the time she finally looked again. Her head was swimming, the tiredness she'd been living with for the past few months making her weak, but still, something in her didn't want to stop. Psalms were next, and she slowly began reading.

Psalms had always been one of her favorite places to go. Singers usually could find things to appreciate about other people's songs. Scanning the happy praise ones, she searched for answers, just as Uncle John had said to do.

As she read so many of David's songs, fragments of sermons and Bible verses she'd heard all her life melded into a fuzzy certainty. Somehow, God was still God. He still loved her and Dan, He still had good plans—her heart caught at that—and she still needed to trust Him. *Live in the opposite spirit*, cried another faint voice. *Put on the garment of praise for the spirit of heaviness!*

Praise? Praise God at a time like this? Everything in her wanted to cry and weep and blame and throw accusing words at God. Not praise Him. How could she do this? Another memory surfaced, a verse Dan had reminded her about, back in Muskoka when she was still depressed. "I can do all things through Christ who strengthens me."

Well, this was one of those times to prove whether the writers of the Bible really did know what they were talking about, stop questioning, and just do.

With a voice raspy from tears, wet cheeks from hours of

sorrow, and a spirit that hovered too close to despair, Sarah opened her mouth.

"Lord, You are good, You are faithful, You have good plans for me."

The whisper broke, and she hunched over, grief threatening to overwhelm again, before she took another deep breath, trying to regain control.

"Lord, I love You, I praise You, I want to honor You..."

As she softly spoke the words aloud, it felt like her soul was trying to stand up, no longer crouching, cloaked in despair.

"Lord, You are the creator, You are Jehovah Jireh my provider, You will provide for me and Dan..."

She even managed to sing a couple of lines from the song she'd been working on yesterday. "I know You love me, I've seen Your grace so many times."

She continued on with the rest of the verse, then sang some choruses from church, faith-building words that sounded nothing like the last time she'd led them from the front. No, this was definitely real now. Who cared about harmonies or trying to stay in pitch when it felt like a battle for her soul was taking place? So she sang, raspy, broken phrases as she shuddered through tears. "Lord, You are our deliverer. You are our strength. You are our comfort."

As she repeated and reiterated the verses, swatting away the hopelessness that hovered, it felt like a spiritual battle was taking place, God's truth fighting a dark force. Demons of despair and condemnation were not going to be entertained. Not this time. Instead, they were going to be excised, eliminated. They were not welcome here, in her life, or Dan's, or in their marriage.

And by the time the first streaks of sun gold illuminated the city, Sarah felt a strange peace surround her, despite the deep grief that still lay in her heart.

"God," she whispered, "I know that You are faithful. Help me to trust You."

~

A FAINT SOUND WAKENED DAN. He rolled over, stretching out a hand. No Sarah. Instead, the sheets felt cool, a sign she hadn't been in bed for ages. He stretched, then slowly made his way out of the bedroom, grabbing his robe as he saw the faint light shining under the second bedroom from the end of the hall. That wasn't unusual. He'd woken in the past to find her in here, writing a song she said had come in the middle of the night.

But Sarah wasn't at the keyboard, headphones in, smiling to herself as she composed a song, or chatting quietly on the computer while she connected across crazy time zones with her family or Heartsong Collective colleagues. Instead, she sat in the chair near the window, staring out as Toronto's morning lights gleamed, ready for a new day. Her Bible was open, and a full cup of tea sat abandoned nearby.

"Sar?"

She turned, hastily rubbing a hand over her face, before gazing at him, deep sorrow in her eyes.

Oh God. Dan's heart started beating double time as he moved past the furniture to kneel at her feet. "Sar, what is it?" He held her cold hands, praying desperately that she wouldn't say—

"I've started bleeding."

No. He shook his head, trying to remember what the doctor said. "It doesn't mean it's a..." His throat clamped. He couldn't get the word out, couldn't go back to before.

Sarah peeked at him. "Dan, it's serious."

No. *No.* Why was she telling him now? How long had this been happening for? "We can go to the hospital." He stood. He needed to do something. But Sarah just sat there, her green eyes glimmering with tears, gently shaking her head.

"It's no use. I've seen…" Her voice broke, she hunched over and put her head in her hands.

No, God. No.

His chest cracked open with a now-familiar kind of ache, one that threatened to swallow him whole. Emotion pricked then welled, from the seemingly never-ending well of grief that existed just below the surface of his soul these days.

He slowly moved to wrap her in his arms. Her tears were all the proof he needed. God had let them down. Again.

THIS HAD TO BE A NIGHTMARE. Who stuck screaming infants and happy round-bellied pregnant people in the same waiting room as a couple who'd made an emergency appointment because they feared a miscarriage? What kind of insensitive jerks ran this place? Ever since they'd arrived at the medical center an hour ago, he'd tried to blot out the little kids, tried to blot out the people living their best lives, all of them oblivious to the couple whose lives had likely shattered. They might be unaware, but he'd noticed a few people sneak looks at them. He hunched down, a baseball cap pulled low on his head, doing his best to hide his face. This was no time to be recognized.

Sarah, too, seemed determined to act like normal, flicking through a few dumb magazines even as her tears wouldn't stop falling. He'd cried with her this morning, but had to be brave now for her sake. He'd phoned the club, his voice breaking as he briefly explained his need to be absent for a few days to take care of a family emergency. The Leafs had a must-win game, but when he'd explained about the miscarriage, he was told to take as much time as needed. That was something at least.

But hockey seemed pointless. Not compared to helping his wife in this moment. He grasped her hand again, gripping it tighter, wishing he could infuse what little strength he had to her.

"Shh, Princess. It's gonna be okay." Not today, or tomorrow, not even next month. Maybe never. Not if this really was another miscarriage. A tiny part of him still clung to hope; it wasn't officially over until the doctor said so. God was supposed to work miracles, wasn't He? God could still make this baby live. Even if He had let the others die. But Dan knew he had to say the words, for her sake, even if he wasn't sure if he believed them. Not anymore.

"Mommy?" A little boy poked his pregnant mother.

Why did that family get two when they couldn't even have one?

The little boy pointed at Sarah. "Why is that lady crying?"

Sarah ducked her head as the mom murmured something. Dan shifted to screen Sarah, to give her more privacy, even as he burned with frustration. Why the heck were they still out here? Hadn't he explained this was an emergency? What was wrong with the people who ran this place? *God, help us!*

"Sarah Walton?"

Finally. Dan wrapped an arm around her and helped her stand. His heart wrenched in fresh sympathy. For all the grief he felt, she was feeling it too, only it was actually happening inside her body. She'd continued to cramp throughout the morning, and the mild gasps signified pain that was hers alone. He picked up her bag and coat, then reached out for her hand, and they followed the nurse like lambs to the slaughter.

Once seated, Dr. McKinnon leaned over the desk and began a gentle interrogation about the last twenty-four hours. Dan sat silent. So much of what Sarah was saying was news to him. Why hadn't she told him earlier? They might've gotten here sooner, found something to save the baby. The doctor made notes, took another blood sample, nodded, felt around her stomach area, checked Sarah's latest clotted pad, then sent them off for another ultrasound. Yet another hour later—this time speedily processed by a silent sonographer who'd looked at them with sad eyes—and they were back in the office.

Dr. McKinnon looked over the results, pursing his lips, before glancing up at them. "I'm sorry, but this confirms it. You have lost this one too. I'm sorry."

Dan blinked back the burn of tears, gripping Sarah's hand, more for his sake than hers. "Is…was there any reason why this happened?"

Sarah stiffened, like she thought he might be blaming her. Man, he didn't want that. "Sar, I'm not—"

"No. We all knew from the start that the hCG levels weren't high, and that like the last times, that miscarriage was a risk." He studied Sarah seriously as she wiped away tears. "Chromosomal abnormalities cause about fifty percent of all miscarriages in the first trimester, and nobody knows why, so this is not your fault. There was nothing you did wrong, and nothing you could have done." He glanced at Dan. "Nothing."

Dan dipped his chin, tightening his hold on Sarah's hand, even as he felt a ping of relief. Since the last two miscarriages, he'd read up on some of the causes, and while much of a miscarriage seemed shrouded in mystery, there were always some anecdotal studies or myths that suggested certain things were triggers, like stress, or exercise or lifting things. Helplessness washed over him to be the one unable to do anything but watch his wife go through this.

"Sarah, I'm going to schedule you for an immediate D&C, and with your permission, we'll test any tissue for chromosome irregularities."

Tissue? Their child was now tissue?

"Have you had anything to eat or drink in the past seven hours?"

As Sarah shook her head, Dan listened as the doctor explained what would happen over the next few days and weeks. The previous miscarriages had resolved naturally, not requiring any medical intervention, nothing like the horror awaiting her. How could a child be scraped from a womb? It seemed so barbaric. The doctor finally packed them off with his deepest sympathies.

Later that day, as Sarah finally awoke from the anesthesia, Dan took her hand, smoothing her hair as her eyes filled with tears. He so loved this woman; he'd hated today, feeling so help-less, watching as she suffered and being unable to relieve a single part.

"Hey, Sar Bear."

Her bottom lip trembled. "I'm so sorry."

"Princess, it's not your fault. You heard what the doctor said. It was likely chromosomal abnormalities, not anything else. So please don't start worrying about what you could have done differently." He kissed her hand, then sat on the recovery room's plastic chair.

She looked at him steadily, weariness rimming her eyes. "I'm not worried about that."

Dan had a strange sense that she suddenly wasn't talking about fault or blame, but that in the midst of this horror she was concerned for him. Oh man… Tears prickled quickly, and he glanced down at the floor, trying to pull himself together to face her scrutiny.

"I love you, Daniel." She touched his hair, her hand lying on his head, like she was praying a benediction.

He glanced up. The brave smile she gave him might wobble a little, but still had the power to make his insides turn to jelly.

"I love you, Princess." He tried to force a smile that only got halfway. *God, where are you?*

CHAPTER 3

Sarah woke from a too-short sleep. She blinked. Where —? What—? Oh.

Afternoon shadows splayed across her bedroom, and she peered across to where Dan sat in the corner, on the comfy chair she'd bought for his birthday last year. He was hunched over, head in his hands, staring at the floor, grief etched in his features. He'd cried with her yesterday morning; she'd felt his tears in her hair and the way his body had gone rigid when she'd told him about her night. He sat still, too still for her to think he was normal. Which she couldn't blame him for. This wasn't normal. And while the doctor might disagree, it still felt like her fault.

Oh, guilt was a game she knew only too well how to play. If only she hadn't gotten worried, hadn't allowed herself to stress. Would their baby have been saved?

Coupled with this was the fear that her sickness had contributed to Dan's team being eliminated from playoff contention. He hadn't played; his absence had been noted; and she knew from some of the concerned texts she'd received that people were worried. But she had no strength to reply. No strength to even formulate an answer. And while part of her knew that shouldering responsibility for the Leafs' loss was foolish, the fact remained that if Dan had played, they likely would've won. And now she suspected there would be talk of the coach being fired, of Dan's contract value being diminished, all because he'd insisted on being at her bedside yesterday.

But looking at him now, the strength she knew existed in him seemed far away, and she wondered just how much time Dan was going to need. Her eyes filled with fresh tears, and she tried to gulp down a fresh bubble of sorrow.

He startled, and glanced up at her. Then stood, drew near. "You're awake."

She tried to smile. "So are you."

"How are you feeling?"

Her throat closed at the tenderness in his voice. She swallowed to clear the rocks. "I've been better."

He clasped her hand, and she threaded her fingers through his. "Do you need anything? Tea? Food? Pain meds?"

She shook her head. "Just you."

He finally smiled. Well, his lips lifted a little, but there was no light in his eyes. The effect was eerie.

"Your mum would like to speak to you."

She tried to calculate the time difference. Couldn't. Her brain was too fuzzy. "What's the time there?"

He glanced at his phone. Probably at the world clock app. His brow wrinkled. "Nine in the morning."

A wave of weariness washed over her. She yawned. "I'll call her soon. What… what have you said?"

His lips tightened. "That we lost it."

It. How awful that all their hopes and dreams could be disposed of in a detached, impersonal two-letter word. Her eyes filled, and his face crumpled as he knelt beside the bed, and wrapped her in his arms. Shuddering breaths didn't convince her that he wasn't crying.

Yesterday's silent drive home from the hospital had been followed by a night of agony. The physical pain, the cramping and bleeding wasn't pleasant, but she'd been through months of pain and rehabilitation before, so she kind of knew her body enough to be able to recognize when she needed to sleep, and when she needed to pop another pain pill. No, the agony had been internal, a thousand pin pricks a day that had necessitated escape.

On arrival home they'd discovered a huge bouquet of flowers 'congratulating them on their exciting news'. Dan's face had gone black as he read the card. While it was nice his parents had sent the flowers, she couldn't look at them, and neither could he apparently. She'd discovered the flowers in the kitchen bin this morning.

Their special secret had turned septic, into a rotten shock, and she wondered how Dan would cope with the phone calls still to be made. He wasn't doing well. But then, who would be? He was always much quieter than her, but he was reverting to the shell that she'd seen before, hollowed out, as if something deep was bothering him. Was it the past? Or was he newly aware of what their future would be? Despite the tenderness and concern he showed, she still wondered if he did blame her, still wondered if there was something she could've done differently.

So many things should have been done differently. Like the drama with his parents, which had only worsened this morning when his mom dropped in. She'd never done so before. Sarah had listened through a fog and eventually gathered that Helen had called in to see if they'd received the flowers, and had wondered how poor Sarah was feeling.

"I was in the neighborhood, anyway. Andrew was back at work, and I spoke to Luke and Marguerite and darling Adam and little Lucy on a video call this morning. Oh, it will be wonderful to have a little grandchild nearby! With Luke living so far away I never get to see Adam and Lucy as much as I should. So, you can imagine how excited I was to hear your news."

"Mom…"

Sarah glanced across at Dan's tired face. *Lord, please help Dan and his family cope…*

His mother ignored her son, trilling about something she couldn't resist buying this morning. Fearing the worst, Sarah forced a smile as Mrs. Walton handed her the little gift bag, opening it to discover a tiny yellow jumpsuit with matching bootees.

She'd tried to hide the tears, but her mother-in-law was too quick.

"Why, Sarah, whatever is the matter? If you don't like it…"

Dan interrupted roughly. "We lost the baby, Mom. Sarah had a miscarriage yesterday."

As she'd lowered her head into her hands she tried not to hear Dan's quiet quarrel with his mom about why they didn't let them know this piece of information either. So much for sympathy.

How many other family members were still in the dark? How many other random presents were headed their way? How could she explain—again—that she was not going to bear a child, especially when she'd only just told them she was? Oh, this was too hard.

After faintly thanking Helen, Sarah had wandered off to bed, thankful to hide away and try and escape her pain for a few more hours of sleep.

Dan now touched her hair. "So, how are you feeling?" he asked again.

It was hard to shrug with sheets and quilts tangled around her chin. "Better."

He studied her for a moment, then nodded. "Mom said she'd

inform the rest of the family. I spoke to your folks. They're telling Bek. There's no-one else is there?"

"Only John and Ange."

Dan sighed. "Great. So we'll be in for some counseling from them, too."

"Too?"

He looked over at her again. "Your dad. Thinks the answer to everything is a sermon."

Wow. Even if it was kind of true, it was so unlike Dan to say something like that.

He sighed. "Sorry, Princess. But I just feel like we're at the mercy of anyone who wants to drop in, give unwanted advice, then leave."

What was it he'd once said to her? "People care."

"I know, but…"

There was a world between knowing something was true and experiencing the unexpected cuts and bruises of real life.

Through the bedroom's window came a baby's cry.

She flinched. Anger surged. She tamped it down. It wasn't Jackie and Lincoln's fault if that sound was like fingernails screeching down an old-fashioned blackboard, reminding her of what eluded Dan and herself.

"Man." Dan groaned. "I don't want to let it get to me, but Lincoln's little baby just brings it all back. I'm starting to hate that sound."

"I know." She didn't wish them harm, but what she'd give for just *one* child…

He thrust his hand through his hair then clasped his head. "I wish we could be elsewhere, just us, and not have to worry about who's going to call or send flowers or drop in."

She closed her eyes as tiredness flooded her again. "What about Muskoka?"

"Muskoka," he repeated. "Yeah, maybe…"

· · ·

Usually the drive north to Muskoka was filled with anticipation. This was the place she'd found healing and hope, after all. But today she felt numb. Part of her was glad to be escaping the city, and all the questions, all the guilt. Another part just wanted to sleep, to hide, to burrow under layers of blankets and never emerge again.

She'd called her parents, sobbed her way through explanations. She probably sounded worse than she actually was, for they'd offered to come over, but she'd refused. She couldn't keep asking them to disrupt their life to travel all that way and babysit her. Besides, she had Dan, whose season was almost finished, and spending time in Muskoka meant they'd be next door to Aunt Angela, who had cared for her during that first time when she'd arrived from Australia. She didn't want—need —anyone else. Especially Dan's family.

Sarah stared out the window, tears trickling down her face. Why did she have to have the type of personality where emotion always bubbled close to the surface? She was definitely Dan's opposite in that regard. But it was like her tears needed to escape, even as her heart still felt strangely protected from the ravages of grief she'd experienced before.

Trees flashed past, blurs. She swiped at the moisture on her face, but refused to make a sound to further add to Dan's upset. He wasn't doing well.

She peeked across. He drove, brow lowered, lips firm, a muscle throbbing in his jaw. She knew he didn't blame her, but it didn't stop her guilt. Oh, how she wished she could be the wife who was healthy and could bear the child he desperately wanted. He might've known what he was signing up for when he asked her to marry him, but she suspected he hadn't really known what that actually entailed.

She closed her eyes, refusing to let more tears seep out. The taunts hovered in the air: *You can't give him what he most wants. You're a failure. You're broken.* But even as her heart wrenched, she recognized these held the hiss of the pit of hell. She wasn't a failure. God said she wasn't. And the devil could try to lie and make her feel less than those women who could bear children, but that didn't make them any better. She was loved by God just as much as they. She knew that. *Knew* it. She hoped Dan knew that too.

She dozed a little, startling awake when his Jeep hit a rough patch of road. She shifted.

"We're almost there," Dan said.

"Thanks for driving," she murmured.

"Of course." He peered across at her. His grim expression softened a little. "How are you feeling?"

"Tired. Achy."

"The doctor said that was to be expected."

The doctor. As if reminded by that last word her abdomen tightened again. She groaned, placed a hand on her midriff.

"Oh, Princess."

Dan's shadowed face held gauntness, like he hadn't eaten in days. She hoped he'd find a way to get back to some kind of normality now. She winced. Normality. Childless. That was their normal, it appeared.

But no. She refused to live defeated. This might be their normal now, but God was able to do anything. God had blessed the barren with children. Look at Hannah in the Bible. Look at Rachel. Look at Sarah, her namesake, for goodness sake. Sarah had been an old woman when God had blessed her with a baby. God hadn't changed. He could still do such miracles today.

She hoped this retreat to Muskoka would help her soul remember that. And remind Dan of that truth, too.

THE TREES WERE SILENTLY DANCING, their branches swaying to the breeze as the sun edged its way past the heavy clouds. Since arriving two days ago, Sarah had barely moved from the easy chair in front of the huge picture windows that overlooked the lake. Lake Muskoka had always been a place of healing, and right now that was exactly what was needed.

Escaping T.O. had been a godsend. Coming here to Muskoka was always good, but the hoped-for healing was taking longer than he'd hoped. He only had another day or two before they'd have to head back. He'd missed two more games. Fortunately, they'd been away games, which meant for the next few games he'd be around, but still, the compassionate leave would only extend so far.

At least Muskoka was doing Sarah good. She'd barely moved from her sunny position overlooking the deck, the chaise lounge good for lying on, listening to music, reading, or sleeping. These past few days she'd been amazing, a pillar of strength, despite having had most of the stuffing knocked out of her. He didn't know why she was so strong, and he felt so empty and weak.

Maybe it was because she'd been down this road before, had suffered more recently than he had, when Stephen had died. Sarah had been depressed for months, and the girl he'd first met out here had been a shadow of who she was today. She'd had to learn a lot about overcoming, so maybe that had helped her deal with the grief now.

That made one of them. He knew he wasn't coping. He was keeping things together by the skin of his teeth, and he suspected he wasn't fooling Sarah any, but he couldn't break down in front of her. Not like he really wanted. Still, the fact he wanted to break down and she was teary, but still seemed to possess an unlooked-for strength made other questions rise.

Horrible thoughts that taunted and jeered. Like, maybe she was glad to be over the pain. Or maybe she hadn't wanted the baby as much as he did. He guessed it would be hard for anyone to feel quite like he had, for she sure hadn't done any of the things that still sometimes made him doubt God's love for him. It wasn't like she had ever prayed for the death of her son.

His skin prickled. God had forgiven him, but still... Was this part of God's punishment? If so, how much did he need to be punished before God deemed it enough? That 'practice making perfect' thing his father had said made him wonder if God did the same. Give and take away, then give and take away. How many more miscarriages would they have to go through before God finally deemed Dan penitent enough?

He grimaced. These were stupid thoughts, and not what he believed. But still, the temptation to think like that grew. God might be good, but He'd let them down. Again. Again and again. And it was getting harder to believe that this was a promise that would ever come true.

Muskoka's beauty filtered through the windows, a promise of peace that allured yet fell short.

Dan slumped on the lounge, bare feet propped on the coffee table, and glanced down to where Sarah slept, his lap as a pillow, blankets tucked up to her chin. His lips lifted, fell. Today had been much like the others, quiet, just them, their phones switched off, few distractions, except for a couple of movies Sarah had watched, before falling asleep partway through each time. He'd watched the three hours of *Anne of Green Gables* before, and should've realized the scene where Matthew died would hit hard. Fortunately, she'd already been asleep when that scene played, and she hadn't seen his tears.

He had to remain strong for her. Even if part of him itched to get out and do something. Anything. Too much quiet left too much time for questions, questions he could barely formulate, let alone articulate aloud. Questions—mostly to God—starting with *Why*. He sat here next to Sarah to be with her in case she needed anything, but his mind was edgy, restless. Anne and Gilbert didn't do it for him. Five hours of *Pride and Prejudice* hadn't done much to distract him, either. He wondered if *Die Hard* even could.

Sarah stirred, and he shifted, stroked her hair. "Hey, Sar Bear."

She yawned, and rubbed her eyes. "Was I asleep again?"

"Yep."

Her nose wrinkled. "I feel bad that you're here missing games to keep me company while I sleep."

"I don't mind." He much preferred this to fielding explanations from teammates.

"You're a good husband." She reached up and stroked his jaw.

"You're a good wife."

Her face crumpled. "I just wish—"

He bent and kissed away the protest he could feel forming on her lips. "I love you. I chose you, remember?"

She nodded, another tear slipping from the corner of her eye.

He wiped it away, as tenderness washed through him. He might wish to have a child, but he wouldn't want any other woman as his wife. It had taken so long for him to find the perfect woman that any thought of another needed to be firmly batted away.

"What do you want to do for dinner?" she mumbled.

Food? "I'm not hungry."

She shifted in his arms. "Are you for real?" She reached up and touched his jaw. "That's got to be a first."

He only gently squeezed her by way of reply. How could food help a broken heart? "Are you hungry?"

"A little."

That was a first. "What do you want to eat?" He'd get her anything. Especially if it could be gotten by phone. He had little energy to make something, especially when the cupboards were close to bare.

They hadn't had time to contact anyone to fill the fridge, and while Ange had made a lasagna, he hadn't yet replied to her message to let her know if there was anything else she could do. He wasn't up to a sermon from his pastor, or trying to keep it together while he dealt with their sympathy. Him and Sarah was about all he could deal with.

"Pizza?"

"From Muskoka Shores?"

"That's nearest, right?"

He phoned and placed their usual order, and they continued to watch the sunset meld through the trees. Pink tinted the lake, bathing it in beauty. Once upon a time they might've gone out on the back dock and lain on the boards to watch it; today he suspected she'd prefer to be cozy and safe from the elements. Which was perfectly okay with him. He didn't want to do anything that brought her a moment's discomfort. She was in obvious pain still.

"It's so pretty, isn't it?" Sarah murmured, as if she could read his thoughts.

"Sure is." He pressed a kiss to her head.

"Are you okay?" she asked softly.

"As okay as you are," he lied.

"Are you sure?" She inched around to look at him, then winced.

"Hey, don't move. You need to take care of yourself, okay?"

"I am. But I also need to know that you're doing okay. I love you, you know."

"I know. And I love you too."

"I know," she whispered, wrapping his arm around her more tightly. "I just hate to think that you're sad."

He forced a smile. "So, you're allowed to be sad and I'm not?"

"No, I don't mean that. Just that…" She paused. Yawned. "Oh, I'm so tired I barely know what I mean."

"It's okay. I'm okay. And we'll be okay."

"Promise?"

"I promise." *Lord, help me.*

CHAPTER 4

"Go. I promise I'll be fine."

"But—"

"I'm sorry, babe, but the longer you sit next to me watching all these girly shows, the more I can feel your muscles withering away."

His mouth tweaked up. "Wow. Harsh."

She offered a smile as fake as his. "Go catch some fish. I can always call you if I need you, but I'll be fine."

"You sure?"

She nodded. "I'll be okay."

He kissed her, and she watched as he exited onto the back deck then down to the dock.

Dan wasn't okay. She'd sensed that a little more each day. Sure, he was grieving, and Sarah knew not everybody grieved the same way, but she sensed he was distancing himself from God. She understood that only too well, and was determined not to make the same mistake again. God was the only thing she could cling to right now. Dan was great for reassuring hugs and cuddles, but right now, despite his muscular physique, he seemed to have little else. She hoped fishing, something he'd always loved, would help, even though he'd be alone with his thoughts. Maybe God could speak to him on Lake Muskoka. Heaven knew Dan needed God. Just like she did. She really needed God to be her strength, because neither she nor Dan had much of their own.

She moved to the living room, to the piano placed in the corner. She sat on the piano stool and placed her phone on the top of the piano. After opening her recording app, she swished through until she found the recording of the song she'd started to sing at the apartment's mini studio in Toronto. Oh, how poignant were the words now. How much more did her spirit now need those words to be true. She pressed play, closed her eyes, and listened to the song she'd begun a week ago.

"I know You love me. I've seen Your grace so many times.

Your faithfulness surrounds me. You gave me this hope I feel inside.

I will not worry. Because I know that You're always there.

Nothing can come between us. Because Your love is…"

She listened to the joy in her voice, recorded only a few days ago when everything had been going well. Were these truths still true today?

Of course they were. Technically. But she didn't *feel* like it was true though. Her heart was like a stubborn rock that refused to move. Not encased in ice like it was the first time she'd escaped Australia and come to Muskoka. Things weren't that bad yet. Which was exactly why she needed to sing these words again now.

She pressed pause, then played the recording from the beginning, this time joining in, in a tentative, raspy voice. Then she sang it again, this time without the music, just her voice, in a version that was slower, more raw, more real, where every word felt like another sword against the emotions that threatened to sink her to the bottom of the lake.

"I know You love me." She did know that. She *knew* it.

"I've seen Your grace so many times..." Oh, how true. She had seen God's grace, over and over again. Grace with her salvation, grace with the accident, with her family, with Dan, over and over again.

"Your faithfulness surrounds me—" Amen.

"—You gave me this hope I feel inside." Well, maybe she didn't *feel* much hope right now, but she knew it resided within her all the same. That's what the Holy Spirit did. He lived inside her, feeding and fueling hope when she had none of her own.

"I will not worry." Her voice sounded so weak as she said that. But it was true. God said in the Bible not to worry, to be anxious for nothing. *Lord, I give You all my worries. Worries for Dan, for our marriage, for my health. Take it all.*

"Because I know that You're always there." *Thank You God. You never leave us or forsake us.*

"Nothing can come between us..." According to Romans chapter eight, neither death, nor life could separate believers from God's love, so not even a miscarriage could.

"Because Your love is..."

She paused at the as-yet unwritten chorus. How could she describe God's love?

God's love hadn't changed just because her circumstances had. God's love remained sure, secure, wide, and immovable. How could she describe it in a song that could be sung by believers around the world?

"Lord give me words to describe Your love."

She closed her eyes, her heart catching as she recalled past conversations and past vistas, here in Muskoka and elsewhere. Discussions about the height and breadth of God's love, how His mercy was like the stars in the heavens, vast and immeasurable. God's love was so huge, yet tender and so personal, like right now, as if God had gently pressed His finger on her soul as words sprang to life.

She pressed record, and played through the song again, and

this time when she reached the chorus she kept going, those images still in her mind, stirring her spirit.

"Because Your love… is great. Your love is beautiful." Her throat caught. "Your love so undeserved. Your love stretches out forever to me." *Yes, God, yes God, it does, I know it.*

"Your love is not contained, I see the evidence each day. Your love means all the world to me."

Her eyes pricked, moisture sliding under her closed eyelids. Her hands moved into the chords as if they knew where to go. Oh, she loved it when music just flowed, like a ribbon from heaven through her soul and out onto the piano's keys.

She went back to the start, tweaking the chords as she went. It was important to make worship songs like this singable for a congregation, not just for her. A few more adjustments, and she played it through again.

"…Your love means all the world to me."

She paused. She could end it there, or add something else. A bridge was always a good way to reinforce the most important message of a song. And right now, she needed to reiterate this part, especially when her emotions still felt all over the place.

She pressed record again. "There is nothing I can do, to make You love me more or less." She didn't have to be good enough to deserve God's love. Neither did Dan. They were imperfect people, made righteous because of Jesus.

"I'm created as Your child." Her eyes blurred. God's child. She pressed a hand to her stomach. Wanted. Loved. Designed by God for His purposes. Not an accident. And because she was God's child, that was why she could sing with sureness, "So You love me. Yes, You love me."

She repeated it, as an image of her child, her lost child, swelled in her mind.

Oh, she might have lost that child, but God was with her reminding her that she was God's child, and nothing could take that away. She was loved *because* she was God's child. As was everyone else. For if God so loved the world that He gave His only Son, then surely that meant He loved all people, that He'd created them, that He wanted a relationship with all?

If people only knew that God loved them, that He wasn't some scary ogre in the sky, then surely more would turn to Him and live His way. People like Helen and Andrew, Luke and Marguerite, even Dan's brother Sam, who didn't seem to be walking with God too closely these days. Oh, how they needed to know God's love.

She exhaled, and bowed her head. "Lord, I don't know what You want to do with this song, but let it be a blessing to others."

After swiping away yet more tears, she sang the bridge again, reminding her soul of the truth of God's word. There was nothing she could do for God to love her more. Writing great songs sung by Christians around the world wouldn't do it. Being a good Christian wouldn't make God love her more. He just loved her. And similarly, there was nothing she could do that would make Him love her less. Nothing, death nor life, nor tragedy or triumph. She could walk away like the prodigal son and God would still love her. God's love didn't change. Because God's love wasn't based on her actions, but on His character. And God was love. "God, You *are* love."

She exhaled shakily. Oh, how powerful were these truths, powerful that she needed to hear them now, needed to be reminded of their truth. God was so good.

She might still be crying at her loss, but loss didn't change the fact that God still loved her, and He was here right now, holding her up, restoring her soul. Oh, praise God that praising God was like a balm to her spirit, and could set one free from the depths of pain.

~

DAN TIED UP THE BOAT, surprised to hear faint music coming from the house. Sarah was playing the piano? It felt like years since he'd heard her play. Fishing had been pointless. He'd tried to tell Sarah that, but she must have wanted him out of the house or something. He'd been concerned about leaving her alone, but she'd insisted, so he'd given in. He didn't want to be the cause of any more angst for his wife.

These past few days he'd tried to be super careful, taking care of the meals, the cleaning, doing whatever she wanted and letting her rest, taking care of everything so she could concentrate on getting better. But he got the feeling that despite his efforts, she was still worried about him, which might be why she'd suggested he have a break. That'd be just like her, still trying to put his needs above hers. But he didn't want her worrying about him. Not when all her energies had to be on getting better.

The music drew him forward, just as it had all those years ago when he'd first heard her sing next door at John and Angela's, and he hadn't been able to stay away. Sarah might've sung in stadiums and arenas where he'd played games, but she never seemed to understand the magical pull her voice possessed. She just shrugged and said singing was just part of who she was. Which was what made this moment significant.

Thank You God that she's singing again. He moved slowly up the path, listening to the stops and starts of the stilted music, like she might be crafting a song, or in tears. He stopped on the deck, the open sliding doors allowing the sound to fill his ears. Then he heard Sarah, talking to herself, as she scribbled something on a piece of paper. He entered, not wanting to disturb her, knowing from experience that if she knew he was here she'd clam up.

He lowered onto the walnut dining chair, watching his wife look more animated than she had in days. Eventually she nodded as if satisfied, leaned back then began the piece from the beginning.

"I know You love me, I've seen Your grace so many times. Your faithfulness surrounds me…"

He stiffened. How could she sing this song at this time? God wasn't faithful. He'd abandoned them. Again.

"Your love is beautiful. Your love so undeserved. Your love stretches out forever to me. Your love is not contained, I see the evidence each day. Your love means all the world to me."

As Sarah sang the chorus again Dan felt his throat thicken in protest. Right now God's love felt far away. He'd seen Sarah's tears, knew she felt that way too. Didn't she? Or was this more evidence that she hadn't wanted the baby as much as Dan had?

He shut down that thought. No, this was a declaration of faith, a faith song, for sure. She wasn't finding this easy. Those catches in her voice as she struggled to sing said so.

Then the music changed as she sang another section.

He closed his eyes, listening to Sarah's beautiful voice struggle through the rest of the song, feeling a faint something whisper an invitation to join her in seeking God.

Nope. Couldn't. Not yet, anyway. He sat still, ignoring those little promptings, waiting until Sarah finally finished and sat, shoulders slumped. Was she praying?

Her stillness seemed almost unworldly. Concern creased his chest, and he carefully got up and slowly made his way over to the piano stool, touching her gently on the shoulder.

She jumped.

He nearly smiled. "Hey, Sar."

"I didn't know you were here."

Good.

She reached up and grabbed his hand, pressing her face into his palm. "You know He does, don't you?"

His heart tightened.

"Dan, you know that God loves us right now?"

No wonder she'd turned what should be a statement of fact into a question. He hadn't been acting like it. How could a good God allow such a bad thing? How could the Creator God allow the tiniest, most innocent part of creation to die? How could a God who said He was Love do something so unloving as let their baby die? How could God ignore their prayers?

She stared up at him, green eyes watchful, piercing through his confusion to the truth.

He cleared his throat. "I know He's supposed to be."

She pushed up one side of her mouth. "You *know* that God loves us right now."

Statement. Truth. Fact. Part of him still did believe.

She gingerly moved around on the seat to hug him, and he leaned over, burying his face in her hair, before her gentle tug on his t-shirt pulled him to the seat. She wrapped her arms around him, and he could feel the old tingly rush at their touch.

She pressed his head into her shoulder, then whispered in his ear, "Dan, I need you to hold me, but I don't need you to hold me up. We can be as weak as we need to be right now, as long as we know God loves us. God *does* love us. His love is the full stop, the period, the end point, regardless of our circumstances. But if we don't know that, if *you* don't know that, you'll keep trying to be Superman, but will come crashing down. And I don't want you to fall. I need you, Dan. Please don't fall."

Trying to hold back the tears was futile. He tucked his face into her neck, and clung to her like a life preserver. She might say she needed him, but right now he felt like he was drowning, and he needed her. Oh, he needed her. Her words, her touch, her faith, her prayers had reached that part of his spirit that was still alive, touching a chord that now hummed. He could feel her fragility, emotional and physical, as the shoulder of his t-shirt dampened, and her brokenness encouraged him to finally be real. With a sudden sob that seemed wrenched from his gut he let the wall fall, as they held each other and wept.

No, he didn't have to have the answers. He didn't have to be strong for her. He just needed to be real, to admit he was struggling and needed God's help. *Oh God, help us. Help me to trust You again.*

Finally, when it seemed his emotions were wrung dry, he released her, swiping his hands across his face. Man. His wife might be the emotional one, but he'd never cried as much as he had in the past year. Good thing nobody apart from her was here to see him now.

Outside, a sudden breeze sang softly through the trees, as inside, a sweetness borne of shared pain, flowed between them. He felt closer to her again. The two were one again, thanks in no small part to the reminder that the third strand of their union—God—was here too, reminding them of His presence, and His power to bring healing and restoration.

He drew in a shaky breath. Released it. "I love you, Princess."

"I love you too." She squeezed him tighter. "And God loves you even more."

He hung on, his soul wrestling with her words. It might be true, but he still struggled with believing it. Sometimes he wished he had his wife's certainty. Maybe that came from a lifetime of putting scriptures into song, that the verses dug deeper into her heart so she knew them on a deeper level than he ever could.

Regardless, he knew he was going to need it for when they resurfaced in the real world.

The topic of returning to the real world was one she broached that night over dinner.

"I think we should return to the city."

"What? No. It's too soon."

She shook her head. "Hiding away as we have has been good, just what I needed, but we can't hide here forever."

"But the season is almost done. Me returning now won't make any difference."

She winced, like she thought he was blaming her for missing games.

"Sar, no. It's not your fault. Please don't think I'm blaming you."

"The fans will blame me."

"No, they won't—"

"They always do."

"They won't," he repeated firmly, "because they won't know why I wasn't there."

"Exactly. It doesn't matter how it's described, as soon as the team says you're away on personal leave they'll think it's something to do with me, and—"

"So what if it is? You're the most important part of my life. You're more important than hockey."

"You say that, but they don't agree."

"Who cares if they agree?" he said roughly. "This is my life. You, our baby, this is our real life. And if the team agrees that I need personal leave, then it's for a good reason, and the fans need to respect that."

She pressed her lips together then nodded. "I know that. It's just I think explaining a few things might help people understand."

Uh uh. He was in *no* way ready to spill their personal lives in that way. His wife might be on every social media platform known to man, but Dan stayed away. Bad things happened to people who spent too long on their phones looking to be entertained by other people's lives they judged better—or worse—than their own. "No. We don't owe anyone anything."

"But it could be important. Especially as you're looking for an extension on your contract."

"I don't care about that."

She arched her eyebrows.

"Okay, I do, a bit. But honestly, the people who need to know, know. Those who are making those decisions know why we're here and not there. The team is the one who gave me leave."

"I know."

"And to be honest, right now I don't even care if I don't get an extension. I could retire and I'd be happy."

"Really?"

The skeptical lift to her brow echoed his heart's protest. Okay, so maybe that was an exaggeration. He might pretend to be happy, but he'd rather leave on his own terms, rather than feel pushed to do so because of this unexpected tragedy.

"So what would you do if you retired?" she asked, ramming the point home.

He didn't know. His future felt as nebulous as any hope of a child seemed to be. He'd completed a year of a business degree, so he could finish that. But that wouldn't take too long, and then what? Coaching? No. Working with the team in some other capacity? Maybe. But that would mean more time in the city, and he'd half promised Sarah that when he retired, they could leave the city and raise their family in either Muskoka or investigate living in Australia. And while the idea of living in Sydney appealed—imagine living somewhere with that much sunshine —something about Muskoka kept drawing him.

"All I'm saying is that it might help the fans understand and be supportive if they knew."

He shook his head. "Nope. I don't want people talking about us, which is why I don't want people knowing."

"But don't you think us talking about it would help others who have had a similar experience?"

So? he wanted to say, but didn't. Right now he didn't care about anyone else. "Look, Sar, I don't know how you can even suggest such a thing. Just in case you haven't noticed, I'm nowhere near being ready to talk about this. I'm not over this, and I sure as heck can't think that anything I have to say would help anyone else right now."

He'd be more likely to turn people away from God if they truly knew his thoughts.

"Maybe I'm just taking longer to process this, because I didn't have a missionary for a dad, and I was never a pastor's kid —"

She flinched.

Man, he hadn't meant to sound so harsh. But the honesty, now stirred, kept on gushing out. "But I'm in no way able to give advice on how to move on or move forward or whatever the correct term is. I've got nothing, Sar. I honestly can't even think about it without tearing up."

He winced. He hadn't meant that to slip out. But exposing his vulnerability stirred further honesty. "I don't want to tell others about this, because that means talking about it, and I have no words to say. I've got no answers for myself let alone anyone else. Maybe you're a better Christian than me, but I can't just let it go. Not yet."

She lowered her head.

His chest panged. He was such a crap husband sometimes. "I'm sorry. I didn't mean to sound angry."

Except part of him really was. He was angry at people feeling they had the right to comment on their lives, to pass judgement on Sarah. How dare people do that? But deeper than that, he was also angry at God for allowing this to happen. He was even a little bit angry with Sarah for obviously not caring about the miscarriage as much as he did. Maybe the baby wasn't a 'real' baby in anyone else's eyes, but he felt the loss.

She pressed her lips together, then drew close. "I'm not a better Christian than you," she whispered.

Oh, she was. Way better. Still, this crap husband knew the right words to say. "I'm sorry for saying that."

"I forgive you," she whispered.

The room drew quiet again, the moment of tension cooling like the remains of their meal.

She propped her head in her hand, weariness etched in her features. "So are you saying you don't want to return to the city?"

He sighed. "Honestly? What difference will me playing in a game or two make? Not much. The results don't matter, seeing we're out of the playoffs now."

Her forehead pleated. "I'm sorry."

He shook his head. "It's not your fault. I would've made the same decision a million times over."

She moved around to his side of the table, and wrapped her arms around his neck, pressed her face into his jaw. "I love you."

"I love you," he said automatically.

He did. And loving this woman meant acknowledging when she was right. Like now. Because she *was* right. He needed to return, they couldn't hide in Muskoka forever.

He sighed. Maybe it was time they returned to face the music.

CHAPTER 5

"You'll be pleased to know that everything is looking as best as can be expected."

Sarah nodded, then asked the question she wished Dan was here to hear. "Um, so when do you think we can try again?"

Dr. McKinnon frowned. "Like the previous two times, you need to give your body time to heal. I'd advise that you wait until at least your next cycle before you resume intimacy again."

She withheld a sigh. "Thank you."

Dan's patience was one of the things she loved about him, but he'd chafed at the doctor's restrictions last time. Mind you, the way she was feeling right now, she'd be happy to put off anything like that for months. The distance between them was growing. He had optional training yesterday, which seemed pointless with only two games to go, but when she'd tried to tease him about that he'd simply frowned at her then opted to go anyway. Then he had an away game this afternoon, which meant he wouldn't return until much later tonight. Things between them felt so strained.

"And don't be surprised if there is more spotting over the

next week or so. Ideally, you want to allow as much time as possible before engaging in such encounters. Allow your body the time it needs."

She nodded.

"But Sarah."

Oh. A 'but' was never good.

"Seeing as you now have had three miscarriages in a row, we need to do some genetic tests. The testing of the tissue was inconclusive, so we'll need to do some blood tests on you and Dan to check for genetic conditions that might be causing miscarriages."

Fear clanged across her chest like a loud gong. Genetic conditions? "What do you mean?"

He eyed her seriously. "There are certain autoimmune or hormone conditions that can contribute to infertility issues, including chromosomal incompatibilities."

She blinked. "Are you saying that Dan and I might be incompatible?" The idea was laughable. He was her perfect match. He often said she was his. God wouldn't have brought them together in this way if that wasn't true. Would He?

"I'm not saying that, no. But there are some couples whose genetic screening means they are more likely to, ah," he cleared his throat, "have a child with significant health issues, if indeed they are even able to be carried to full term."

Breath was suddenly hard to find. "Are you saying that even if I was to carry a baby to full term that it might have birth defects?"

"We don't like to use that kind of terminology," he said. "And that is why we advise for the screening."

"I don't understand how this can happen."

His mouth tweaked in a non-smile. "I wish your husband could've been here so we could discuss that."

Oh, she wished that too. "He had a game. But I'm sorry, I

don't understand. Why would we need to have screening for birth defects?"

He clasped his hands together on the desk. "We like potential parents to be aware of all their options."

Options? Like what—terminating a pregnancy? The fear hovering around her swooped low, clawing her as she tried to grapple with what the obstetrician was saying.

"So, Sarah, can we do this now?"

"Sorry, do what?"

"Your blood test," he replied patiently.

"Oh. Uh, sure."

"Good. We can do yours now, and we'll schedule Dan's when he's able."

A few minutes later he was pressing a sticky band-aid on her upper arm. "In addition, I'd like to conduct a hysterosalpingogram, where we test your uterus and fallopian tubes with an X-ray dye."

"When?"

"When you've stopped bleeding. So if you like we can schedule that for two months' time."

She didn't like, but if it helped… "Okay."

She exited his office, made the new appointments, paid, then moved to her SUV. The vehicle with its extra safety measures made her feel a bit like she was encased in a bubble in Toronto's city traffic, like nothing could touch her. Which was just what she'd needed after the car accident back home had made her fear driving again.

Home. How funny she still thought of Sydney as home, despite having lived here for nearly three years.

Twenty minutes later she drove into their apartment's parking garage, praying she wouldn't come across any babies. Muskoka had been a great escape from that, but here there were too many triggers for envy, fear, and tears.

Fortunately, God was kind to her, and she rode up to the

sixteenth floor without encountering anyone. Which was good. She needed to get her mind focused on the things that she had to do today. Like cancel her music commitments at church. And contact the Heartsong crew and tell them she'd be available to tour later this summer after all. Not that she'd spoken to Dan about that yet. They'd talked about visiting her family in Australia, but the latest pregnancy had put paid to that. But now it was an option, especially with the tour.

Dan always preferred Muskoka, and had a camp for city underprivileged kids this June as he always did. But so much needed to be talked about. Like what his future retirement plans might be. It was one thing to have vague discussions about things; quite another to imagine what their lives could look like if he was home all the time, instead of chuffing off to play games for half the year. Especially if there was no baby, like they both had dared to hope for their world to revolve around.

The door opened, and she exited, then stilled. Jackie Cash stood outside her apartment door, her sweet little bundle poised on her shoulder.

No. She didn't want to say hello. She didn't want to pretend she was okay. She could hop back in the elevator, or maybe try for stealth moves across the hallway to access her apartment, but Jackie might see. Darn, Jackie *had* seen, judging from the relief on her face.

"Hi, Sarah."

"G'day." The Australianism still slipped out occasionally. There was nothing for it, but she'd have to suck it up and pretend seeing her neighbor didn't hurt.

"Hey, I'm sorry to ask, but would you mind holding Charlie for a moment?"

Yes. Yes, she minded. But saying so would only make her look petty. Quick, could she fake a cold? She coughed. "I'm not sure you really want me to. I've just been at the doctor's." That was true enough.

"Oh. Okay, then. I appreciate you letting me know."

Sarah nodded, faked a smile, and hurried inside, closing the door, and rushing down the hall in case her neighbor felt like being neighborly and wanted to talk with her.

Once inside the sound-proofed room she closed the door, her movements stilling at the sight of the box holding a cot. Oh, why had they thought to buy it? Her eyes filled. She knew exactly why. It was a faith statement, something that said, 'one day, in God's good timing'.

Her knees buckled. Which was when? "When, Lord?"

She sank onto the soft rug, heart sorrowing as she gave into tears.

Was the doctor right in suggesting she and Dan were incompatible? Was a child of theirs destined to have health challenges? How did others deal with this? Where was God in the midst of this? Oh, she *wished* Dan was here, but was also perversely glad Dan could not see her now. He didn't need to see her being weak. Not again. She'd been so emotionally weak these past six days he hadn't wanted to leave her today. But she'd insisted.

Her cheek brushed the soft lamb's wool, and she closed her eyes. Oh, she was tired, so tired. She really needed to sleep.

HER PHONE REMINDER WOKE HER. She cracked open a gummy eyelid, her face sticky with tears and snot, her back aching. Where—? Oh. She pushed herself upright, glanced around. Why was she on the floor in here? Had she fainted? She'd fainted before with one of her pregnancies. Maybe that was why the doctor was so concerned.

Her eyes filled, as the memory of her miscarriage surged, then fears screamed again: *Incompatible. Birth defects. Health issues.* Her heart buckled. "Lord, where are You? I need You." Her faith felt so feeble right now.

More tears threatened, but she blinked them away. No. She

wouldn't give in. God gave her strength, she could do this. She rubbed her eyes, no doubt smearing more of her makeup. Her makeup mask was the armor she'd needed for her brief scurry out into the world earlier.

She switched off the phone alarm, set to alert that her podcast had dropped. She opened the app, saw she had comments to reply to. Comments she didn't want to reply to. How could she have been so blithe about trusting God last week? It was so much harder now.

Echoes of the prayers she'd prayed recently whispered to her, but thanking God for His love felt so false. Maybe God had buoyed her in those initial moments, but her spirit felt gouged out right now.

The doorbell rang. She froze. They weren't expecting visitors. How she hoped it wasn't Jackie again!

After tiptoeing to the front door, she peered through the peephole, then waited for Davis, the apartment's concierge, to leave. When she judged the elevator door had closed, she opened her door and snatched up the parcel. The Express Post label and Australian markings must have made him think it was urgent. Most parcels were left downstairs for collection.

She closed the door and moved to the living area, using her fingernail to pierce the bag. It had to be from her family. It felt too soft and squishy to be from Heartsong.

A few seconds later she was reading a card from Bek, pressing her lips together to hold back a sob. Her sister had meant well. The 'Congratulations! We are so thrilled for you! We love you!' showed that. After hearing their news Bek must have rushed straight to the post office in order for it to arrive so quickly.

Sarah eyed the paper-wrapped gift. Did she dare open it? Heart quivering, she slid aside the tape and was soon staring at a toy koala, the stitched smile unable to raise one from her. Oh. Her eyes filled, as she caressed the oversized gray ears that the little one this was intended for would never touch. Her baby. Her lost baby. Dan's lost baby. Their broken baby, their broken dreams, dreams that—according to the doctor—might never come to life. Bek couldn't have known how much something intended to bless would hurt.

She drew in a desperate breath, but new sobs clamped her chest. She couldn't do this. So she abandoned the stuffed toy on the dining table and stumbled to the bathroom.

THEY MIGHT'VE WON, but the locker room held a heaviness similar to a loss. That's what happened when they won games while they were out of playoff contention. He'd heard the murmurs, heard the disgruntled fans, knew people weren't happy with him, but still the truth refused to spill. He was counting down the hours he had to interact with people before their season was officially done and they could escape to start their summer. Part of him wished he hadn't returned. He couldn't escape the feeling that people blamed him for not showing up last week, for letting them down.

He still hadn't told anyone. Management had only said, "Family emergency" to his teammates, while he still hadn't responded to messages from Brendan Jordansen and Marc Valesky, those he considered closest to him on the team.

Marc sidled up to him. Stripped of his goaltender gear he looked half his size. "Good to have you back. Everything okay?"

Dan nodded.

"Is Sarah alright?"

His throat clamped. She was doing better than him, a power-house of strength. Maybe that was because she didn't care as much about the loss of the baby.

"Dizzy?"

Dan refocused at his nickname. "She's been sick." He coughed as if to reiterate it.

Sure enough, Marc backed away. "Are you sure you should be back?"

He shrugged, tempted to shake his head. Then figured that was hardly the way to alleviate concern. "Apparently you guys need me," he tried to joke.

"Yeah, we needed you last week, man," Matt Reynolds called, obviously eavesdropping.

Guilt strung his chest tight. He knew he couldn't blame himself, but the barb stung all the same. "And here was I thinking you'd be able to manage just one game."

One of the team's rentals, brought in to improve their chances at making playoffs, rose. His eyes narrowed as he muttered something, before Matt told him to shut up.

Dan's stomach tensed. Fighting with his teammates was no way to solve anything. They'd probably back down if they knew the reason for his absence. But still, another part of him didn't want to expose himself to their pity. How could he play the role of top defenseman for his team if they caught him crying, like he probably would after that admission? No. He braced, his jaw tense. He just had to tough it out, get through these last games, clear out his locker for the season and come back next year to try again. He hoped.

He kept his eyes closed and feigned sleep during the plane trip home, avoiding conversation. When it landed, he gathered his stuff, and soon escaped to the parking lot. Among the BMWs, Audis and Mercedes, his Jeep stood out as one of the more humble vehicles. But utility as well as comfort was important, and he didn't like to change his car in the winter like some of those driving more flashy vehicles did. Especially when he had so many trips to Muskoka.

"Dizzy, wait up."

He paused, keys in hand as Brendan, his defense partner, hurried to his side. "Yeah?"

"I didn't want ask inside with the others listening. But *is* Sarah okay?"

He closed his eyes, pressed his lips together. *God, give me strength.* He hadn't even told the other guys in the online Bible study yet. Admitting it to Brendan felt fraught with difficulties.

"She's not, is she," Brendan said. Statement. Not question.

He shook his head.

Brendan's breath hitched. "It's not... cancer, is it?"

His shoulders eased. "No. She, ah..." He cleared his throat. "She had a miscarriage last week."

"Oh, man. That sucks."

"Yeah."

"I'm sorry," the father of two said.

Dan really didn't want to hear sympathy from someone who couldn't know how he felt. Owning the truth felt like an impossible tightrope to walk along. One wayward word, one misplaced hug, and he might slip into the yawning abyss of anger he could feel swirling so close, ready to consume him. He needed to get out of here.

"Gotta go."

"Is there anything we can do?"

"No. Unless you want to pray for us," he goaded. They'd had a few discussions about faith in the past, and Brendan had always been reluctant, so that was an easy—

"Sure."

Huh?

His surprise must've shown on his face because Brendan shrugged. "Hey, it can't hurt, can it?"

"No," he rasped. "Thanks."

He managed to drive away without letting any emotion escape, but was glad for his tinted windows as he sat at a red light and angrily wiped away moisture. His heart was a mess of conflicting emotions. He was glad that Brendan was even going to pray, but seriously? God better not be using his loss to touch Brendan's heart. That seemed so harsh.

By the time he parked next to Sarah's SUV he was steaming. He probably should've gone to the gym at the club to burn off some of this energy. But if he had, he'd likely be forced to confront some of his teammates, and he had no patience for that. He had to calm down. Sarah didn't need this. Anger wasn't something he did too often—passionate outbursts was her domain—but he could feel himself on the verge of losing it.

His white-knuckled hands unclenched from the steering wheel, and he lowered his head. "Lord."

So many things he could pray. So many things he didn't know how to say. It felt overwhelming, a riptide of emotion that threatened to suck him out and drown him in the deep blue sea.

"Lord, I need You." He knuckled away more stupid tears. "How do I do this? How do I love her when I feel so broken? I've got nothing."

You've got Me.

His skin prickled. For a second, that actually sounded like God was talking to him.

"I might have You," he prayed aloud, just in case it was. "But honestly, it doesn't feel like You've got me."

There was no bolt of lightning, so maybe God was okay with raw prayers like that.

"Lord, I really need to feel You right now." Oh, man he hated these tears. "I can't keep it together. I don't want Sarah to feel like I'm letting her down."

Rest in Me.

Rest in God? What did that mean? They'd slept enough in Muskoka that his body had been itching to return.

He waited, but there wasn't anything else that implied God might be speaking to him, so he rubbed his eyes, prayed his nose wasn't red, and exited the vehicle.

Three minutes later he'd entered his apartment. It was quiet, but Sarah's handbag on the dining table suggested she was home.

"Sar?"

No response. She was probably in her mini studio. He knocked gently, then opened the door. Huh. Still no Sarah. Where was she?

Another sound met his ears. He frowned. Moved to the bathroom. Opened the door.

Then saw his wife crouched on the bottom of the bathtub, her hands over her face, her sobs muffled by the overhead shower's running water. He felt the urge to help her, but with what? Empty platitudes? Promises of God? Why would God give them such a miracle, only to take it away again so soon? What was with that? Wasn't God supposed to be into giving good gifts to His children? So why had He allowed this to occur? It didn't make sense.

He closed the door. He had no answers. God felt so far away.

CHAPTER 6

Sarah shifted on the leather lounge, taking a moment to savor the apartment's quiet, and the warmth this pool of sunlight bathed her in. Some of the agitation from past days eased. She glanced at the clock, counting down the minutes until she could expect to see Dan again. Not that she had any certainty that he'd be rushing home to see her.

Her heart ached, as she wished she knew what to do. She hated this distance that seemed to be growing between them. What time they spent seemed to consist of silence, shortness, and unspoken words. She hadn't talked to him about what the doctor had said. She hadn't mentioned she'd emailed Tisha and the other Heartsong head honchos about the possibility of joining the upcoming tour. She hadn't admitted how much she wanted to return to see her family in Australia. Those conversations felt too big, and hard, and raw, with potential for explosions she didn't have the capacity to face. Once upon a time she'd reveled in the fact that she and Dan could tell each other anything. Now, the unspoken weighed between them, and her heart seemed to be collecting new aches by the day, a speckled place of damaged hopes and dreams.

How could she have ever thought she was getting better? It didn't take much for something to trigger her back to grief. A teddy bear. A mother pushing a baby pram. A TV advertisement that showed a happy family.

Her heart clenched. "God, I know You're faithful." Even when her own faith felt feeble. "Lord, have Your way."

The tension eased a fraction, as it did each time she tried to combat her pain by speaking out God's truths, the words about God's love cocooning her, wrapping her in reassurance like strips of linen around a mummy.

A mummy. The words lingered in her mind, flicking her thoughts from Egyptian tombs to those words recalled from her childhood. Oh, how she longed to be a mum, to hear the word "Mummy" spoken to her.

"Lord, help me trust You. Help Dan trust You."

Her gaze fell to the huge black and white photograph that Sam's photographer girlfriend—or former girlfriend, she no longer knew—had taken at their wedding. Back at their reception at the resort at Muskoka Shores, when Dan had kissed her hand and looked at her with eyes filled with intense love. Sorrow clanged. He hadn't looked at her like that in weeks.

"Lord, bless him. Bless us. Help us find our way."

Her prayer sparked more for his family, her family, for healing and reconciliation, at least on Dan's side. Her own mum had called, and she'd finally managed some more conversations with her and Bek. But tiredness still swamped her. She'd used weariness as her excuse to miss Dan's last two games of the season. He was clearing out his locker today, having been excused from end-of-season media availability, then they were heading back to Muskoka.

And while she was relieved to go—hopefully, Jackie and her baby would stay here—part of her wished she could return to Sydney. To be with her family at her real home.

She blinked. Really? She still thought that way? Dan was her family now. And home was where he was. It'd been a while since she'd returned to Australia, but she shouldn't be missing it like this. It felt disloyal, a betrayal of their marriage vows to wish to be with her parents. But he'd been so distant lately, like he blamed her for the miscarriage. He might say he didn't, but she couldn't help but feel like he thought he'd made the wrong choice, in choosing someone who'd said she likely couldn't have children. That was the reason why after dating for six months she'd broken up with him briefly and returned to Sydney on New Years' Day. She'd been sure he could find someone who could give him what he truly wanted in life—a second chance at fatherhood. Until she'd finally believed he meant what he'd said in his emails and messages, and they'd reconciled—long distance—before he'd made his feelings obvious in April of that year.

And here they were, another April in, and she was feeling a sense of loss again. Except this time Dan was hardly speaking to her.

He was a quiet man. She knew that. Hers was a personality and temperament more inclined to big feelings and talking things through. But he had withdrawn, become even more introverted. And now with all these things she needed to say but somehow couldn't, she didn't know what to do. Some moments it felt like sadness had worn down their marriage until it was hanging by a thread.

The front door opened. She pasted a smile on her face and stood. "You're back!"

His lips tweaked up, and he accepted her hug and kiss perfunctorily.

"How was your day?"

He shrugged, the movement dropping her hands from around his neck. Okay.

"That good, huh?" she teased.

"I'm glad it's over."

"That bad, eh?"

He shot her a glance. "Matt was still hassling me about my absence."

"He doesn't know, does he?"

"*I* didn't tell him."

Oh. "But someone else has?"

He sighed. "Brendan. I told him the other day."

He had? A spike of resentment flared. "I thought you didn't want anyone to know."

"He kept at me, so I had no choice. He was asking if you had cancer."

In that case… "Well, I'm glad you could set him straight."

"Yeah, except he's now blabbed things."

"He's your friend."

"Not if he's telling people like Matt."

"Oh, I'm sure he was just trying to shut him up."

He grunted.

"He cares about you, Dan."

He exhaled heavily. "Brendan did say he'd pray for us."

"He did? I thought you said he wasn't a believer."

"He's not."

"Oh. Well, still, isn't that good? If nothing else, then it's good that this has caused him to talk to God, don't you think?"

He leveled a gaze at her.

"You don't think that?"

"Are you packed?"

His ignoring her earlier question meant it took a moment to catch up. "For Muskoka?"

He nodded.

"Yes. I packed your stuff too."

"So we can go now?"

"Yes. Well, almost. I was just going to get the perishables from the fridge."

"I'll dump this then we'll go, okay?"

"Um, sure."

THEY HAD to stop by the clinic on the way, Dan needing to give a blood sample to test for those irregularities that Dr. McKinnon was concerned about. A short time later they were heading north on the 400. This trip usually took two hours, but the minutes seemed to stretch, no doubt thanks to the tension she could feel emanating off Dan.

She wasn't used to this. She could count on one hand the number of times she'd seen him look so tense. One of the things that made him so good as a defenseman was his ability to stay relaxed, cool, and calm under pressure. And while this was a different pressure to what he experienced on the ice, he was not carrying it well. She hoped Muskoka would help him find some peace again.

She peeked across at him.

"What?"

She flinched.

He appeared to notice, as his shoulders slumped. "Sorry. I didn't mean to snap."

"It's okay." Not really. But she had to keep the peace.

"Then why do you keep looking at me?"

"Because you're my sexy husband?"

He huffed.

"It's true."

"You sound like you want something."

"I want you to be happy."

"Happy?" He glanced at her. "It's a little too soon for happiness, Princess."

She pressed her lips together. She didn't mean happiness exactly. Oh, she might write songs sung by people around the world, but sometimes she was so bad at saying what she really meant.

He sighed again. "Sorry I'm so grouchy."

"It's okay." Her voice was small.

He reached across, tangled her fingers in his. "I just feel like I'm getting everything wrong all the time. I hate feeling like I'm hurting you."

"You're not."

He shook his head. "I wish I hadn't told Brendan about what happened."

"Why?"

"He asked us if we wanted to join him and Candice on a cruise this summer."

"That was nice." And unexpected. And could be fun.

"I said no."

Oh. But how did that relate to him knowing about the miscarriage? "You think he asked because…?"

"Because he felt sorry for us, yeah."

She winced. "I think he might've asked because he thought it might help, and be a distraction."

"I don't want to be on a cruise surrounded by people, especially lots of kids and babies everywhere. I get that you're stronger than me—"

What?

"—but being around babies and kids is not good for my mental health right now."

Wow. A real conversation at last. She concentrated on the latter comment, which was a heck of a lot easier to address than the first. "I don't want to be around babies either," she confessed. "I find I get so envious all the time."

His grip tightened. "See? And that's why I don't want people to know. Because they keep making suggestions on what we can do. They don't know what we're going through."

True. "But they won't know unless we tell them, and if we're honest about how it feels."

He scoffed. "Don't tell me. You want to tell the world."

"No."

"You do. I bet you want to tell your podcast listeners."

What? She studied him, but he kept his face averted.

He didn't mean it to sound like that, surely. Guilt grew. She'd always tried to be encouraging on her podcasts, sharing snippets about real life and revelations she'd had about God. People liked to know she didn't find life always easy. But this past week or so had knocked the stuffing out of her, which meant comments about this week's episode had gone unanswered, when usually she would've replied by now. The fact she hadn't was probably already worrying them. "I would like to tell them sometime," she murmured.

"Are you serious? I can't believe you would want to tell people. This is our private business, Sarah. Not anyone else's. Why does anyone else need to know?"

Always his argument whenever she wanted to share personal stuff on the podcast. He'd refused to let her say anything about this latest pregnancy. And even though she was a twenty-first century woman, she was also trying to be a God-honoring husband-respecting one, so she hadn't shared, even though every atom in her being had wanted to share this most wonderful news. Until their wonderful news was destroyed.

She glanced at him. He kept his gaze averted. She bit back a sigh. If they were arguing about this, then imagine what he'd say about some of the bigger things. "People can't relate if we don't say anything," she said carefully.

He finally looked at her, his chocolate eyes, usually so warm, were glittery and cold. "I don't want people feeling sorry for me."

"They won't." They might. They probably would. In a flash she could see their apartment littered with flowers, cards, and tiny bears. She pushed it aside. "They will feel listened to, related with, seen."

"Do you even hear yourself?" He shook his head. "It sounds like you just want more followers."

~

As soon as the ugly words escaped, he felt sick. "Princess, no, I didn't mean that." He peeked across.

She'd inched back, her face pale. "Do you really think that's why I do this?"

"Of course not." She was nothing like those influencers who would do anything for a quick buck. "I'm sorry."

She faced out the car window, as if she didn't believe him.

And fair enough. He'd already apologized several times today. He wouldn't believe him either.

"Sarah, you know I didn't mean that."

She shook her head, her face averted. "I don't know that. Not really. I feel like you're blaming me for all this." She sniffled. "And yes, I understand why you would, because no matter what that blood test you had today says, we both know that I'm the reason why I can't stay pregnant. But you knew that when you married me."

"I know. And I truly didn't mean to imply that I blame you."

"Do you blame me?" She faced him then, and he caught a glimpse of her eyes, sparkling with sorrow.

His heart wrenched. "Princess, I—"

"Don't you dare say you're sorry. Tell the truth. Do you blame me? Is there a tiny pocket of your heart that is blaming me for this?"

He concentrated on the road. He couldn't face her. "No." Was that a lie? No. He didn't blame her. Instead, "I blame God."

She exhaled. "I knew it."

"How?"

"You've just seemed so distant lately. You're not yourself. I can remember the time when you would've been ecstatic to hear that Brendan was praying, and now you don't even seem to care."

"Because I don't. Not when it's at our expense."

"But what if it's our expense that is the thing that gets him saved? Doesn't that make this whole awful experience worthwhile?"

No. Nothing could make this worthwhile.

Ever.

He wasn't used to driving to Muskoka with a silent Sarah. But this made two times in the space of ten days. But unlike last time, illness wasn't the excuse he could use. She was mad at him, and he didn't like it. At all.

The afternoon sun was glinting off the lake as he pulled in. It felt weird to be here, less than a week since the last time they'd stayed. Usually when he came it was for weeks on end in the summer. He could only manage the occasional day here and there during the season.

He parked, and she exited and moved to the back.

"Let me get the bags," he said, as she moved to collect hers.

She tugged, and he grasped her hand.

"I said, let me."

She shook his hand off, then reached in, then winced.

"Sar."

She shuddered in a breath, then shook her head, and spun away from his reach, leaving the suitcases while she collected the eco-bag of perishable food items.

Great. This was exactly how he wanted his time here to go. Sarah angry at him, and it was all his fault.

He hefted the bags from the garage up the stairs, unsurprised to see she'd switched the kettle on and was opening the curtains.

"Sarah?"

"Yes?"

"Please don't be mad at me."

"I'm *not* mad at you."

Her insistence drew his lips up. "Are you sure?"

"Oh, so it's funny now, is it?"

Any hope of breaking this tension with humor faded. "I just didn't want you straining yourself. You need to be careful."

"Thank you, Dr. Dan."

He bit back a sigh and carried the bags up to their bedroom. He hoped she'd still regard it as their bedroom. He wouldn't blame her for wanting to sleep somewhere else. Maybe he should be a gentleman and ask if that's what she would prefer.

He deposited their bags inside, then returned. The orange light of the coffee machine indicated Sarah had switched it on. But she already held a mug of tea as she leaned over the wooden railing of the deck.

Irritation flared. So he'd have to make his own beverage then. He pressed his lips together and did just that, using the excuse of the coffee machine's whine to pretend not to hear her. Mature, he wasn't. But right now he barely cared. He needed to do something to work off this tension, and the thing he loved to do since getting married was no longer available to him, not for another month at least. Which meant he probably needed to work off some of his pent-up energy in the basement gym, and hope that his frustrations would be burned off before he said something else that they would both regret.

IT WAS GETTING dark by the time he returned. The house was cool, dim. He could smell his sweat, but no trace of her fragrance. "Sar?"

No reply.

He glanced out on the deck. Nope. No sign of her. Man, this was growing old, playing hide and seek, looking for her. Maybe she was asleep. Or maybe she wasn't here. She'd probably gone to her Aunt Angela's next door and was complaining about him. Not that he could blame her. Because while he might be able to lift impressive weights, she was the one who was really strong. He was weak, definitely the weaker Christian right now.

"Sarah?"

He went up the stairs. After that workout he really needed a shower.

But when he opened the door to the bathroom, he discovered through the steam that Sarah was once more crouched on the bottom of the bathtub, her sobs muffled by the running water of the shower overhead.

"Sar?"

She didn't turn, didn't acknowledge him. Oh no, something must be really wrong.

"Sarah?"

He reached in, turning off the shower taps, getting his sleeve wet. "Princess?"

He grabbed her towel, wrapping it around her as the sobs continued. "Princess, what's wrong?"

She didn't face him, didn't answer for the longest time.

Had she gotten more bad news? A call from the doctor? *Lord, help her*, he prayed.

She sucked in a shuddery breath, then her breathing steadied, like she was trying to get it under control.

He tucked the towel around her and gently scooped her up, cradling her against his chest. He tugged free another towel to keep her warm, and moved to the low, sturdy chair in the bathroom as he cradled her close.

Her wet hair trickled water down his shirt. He barely noticed, too intent on this beautiful, sad woman who was his wife. "Sweetheart, I love you."

She turned then, pressing her damp face into his neck.

Moisture slid down his skin, but it felt hot, like tears. How could he have thought her strong? She was as good as him at playing pretend. When she started shivering, he gently rubbed her back. "Sar, I love you so much. Please tell me what's wrong."

The wet tendrils of her hair swung as she shook her head.

His heart wrenched. He could barely remember a time when Sarah hadn't wanted to talk to him. "Sar, I'm sorry. Please tell me what I can do."

She gulped, then lifted her head. Her face was blotchy, her eyes red-rimmed.

His heart grew sore. Oh, he hated her feeling this way.

She studied him, searchingly, until he felt he could no longer hide.

"What is it?" he whispered.

"Dan, I can't do this." Her breath shuddered. "I love you, but it feels like you don't love me anymore. You might say it now, but you haven't been treating me like you do."

His gut wrenched. Yeah, he could understand why she'd think that.

"I can't take this coldness from you anymore. What is it? What have I done that makes you dislike me so much?"

Huh? He didn't dislike her at all! "Sar—"

"No." She shook her head. "Here we are, coming up to our third wedding anniversary and you don't even act like you want me around. You don't even seem to want me anymore."

Yeah, their sex life had certainly taken a beating in the past year. From the bliss of being newly married, the pregnancies and losses meant she'd gotten so sick and tired she couldn't. Her work also made her tired, which coupled with his busy schedule of late games and away matches and his depression in recent months had meant he hadn't wanted to. Their pre-marriage counselling had suggested that maintaining a healthy sex life was important, as it worked like glue to keep them together. They certainly needed more glue.

"I know you're still sad about the baby, but honestly, what did I do wrong?"

Nothing. That was the problem. He sighed. "You haven't done anything wrong."

The eyes were sparkling now with angry tears. "No, that can't be true. You think I have. So what is it?"

He didn't even really know anymore. He shrugged.

She leaned closer. "Talk to me, Dan. I hate this silence."

So did he, if truth were told. "It's just been a lot tougher than I imagined."

"What has? Our marriage?"

He shrugged again. "The past couple of years have been tough." Three miscarriages in eighteen months would do that.

The hard, green gaze softened slightly. "It has."

He lowered his gaze, unable to look at her anymore. Just nodded.

"So the miscarriages, the uncertainty about your career, I get that all these things add up to frustrations, but that's not enough to cause this much misery."

"It's just…"

"What?"

He clamped his lips.

"No, tell me. I want to know. Is it the podcast thing?"

"What? No. I shouldn't have said that about followers. I'm sorry."

She shook her head. "If you want me to stop it I will. And I won't tell anyone about what's happened to us. Not if you don't want me to."

His heart broke a little more for her. "One day, maybe. I don't want you to stop it. Because I know that what you share has been really helpful to lots of people." He'd seen the comments, knew Sarah was ministering in a way through her words and music to a far bigger audience than even her missionary parents had ever dreamed. "You're amazing."

"Then what is it?"

"You never seemed to show much emotion after," he swallowed, "after—"

"Are you seriously asking me whether I was sad about losing the baby?" She looked at him incredulously, pointing to the shower. "What did you think that was?"

A woman breaking down. And the second time he'd seen that. He pressed his lips together. How could he accuse her?

He knew how. He wasn't coping with his emotions, didn't know how to continue to be strong for her when it felt like all strength was lost. He didn't know how to fake it long enough to make it. Her emotions pulled on his, and tugged him to want to help her, yet drew shamed awareness that he couldn't, that he was drier than a desert of forty years with no rain.

"Dan, did you ever think about how I might feel?" The flash was back. "Part of my depression after Stephen's death was knowing I'd never have kids—do you remember that? How do you think I felt when I found out I was finally pregnant—with your child? It was a dream come true! A miracle! I couldn't believe it, it was so amazing. Here I was, married to the man of my dreams, and going to have his child."

She swallowed, and reached out for his hand. "You saw me now, and you've seen me before. I've cried so much, especially when you weren't here, because I didn't want to be upsetting you even more."

Just like he had. His grip tightened.

"I know in the past I have allowed grief to settle inside me until it became almost impossible to dislodge," she continued. "And I knew I couldn't allow that again this time. So I've tried to be conscious of connecting with God, and it's not been easy, but it's definitely helped, even if at times I feel like I'm dangling by a thread. But you… you don't seem to have tried to connect with God."

No. That was so true. "He's been far away."

She shook her head. "No, you have. I know, because that's how I lived for way too long when Stephen died, blaming God for stuff."

What could he say? It was true. He looked up, into her beautiful green eyes, tinged with a violet rim around the iris.

"Daniel, I love you so much. Please don't shut me out." She moved closer, wrapping her arms around him like she used to.

His arms automatically went around her. "I love you too, Princess." He tucked the towel around her closer. "I'm really sorry," he murmured into her damp hair. "I'm really, really sorry."

"I forgive you. And just so you know, I'm sorry too."

He hugged her, and the room filled with a new sense of peace. They might not have it all together, but God was with them, His grace and forgiveness wrapping around them like the faintest perfume. And somehow in Muskoka he was going to trust God to bring them together. And help them find a future, even if it seemed destined to be without a child.

CHAPTER 7

The first week in Muskoka passed in quietude, much like their time before. It was good to switch off, to exist in their bubble of just them, especially now Dan seemed to have come out of his shell and was talking to her again.

She wished she was physically able to show him her affection, but even that seemed too hard. And while her heart was willing, her flesh remained too weak, as evidenced by more spotting.

Dan was good though. He'd gone fishing a few times while she'd read and slept. It felt like her body was slowly trying to resume normality, and she couldn't wait until she stopped bleeding, and the weather was warmer, and she could swim again. Swimming and reading had proved two of the biggest enjoyments of her time here over the years. Mind you, the lake would have to be a lot warmer for her to enjoy a dip. But the hot tub could be nice.

Dan returned from his trip and cooked the walleye he'd caught, and she was reminded of back when they'd first started hanging out.

"What's that look for?"

She shrugged. "I was just remembering when Mr. Fit and Healthy had to have moussaka made with sour cream."

He chuckled. It was nice to hear. "I'm happy for you to make that again any time you like."

"With no Rob and Jason?" she teased, referencing his friends.

"Definitely not."

"Whatever happened to Rob?"

"Are you asking your husband about a man you once dated?"

"*Once* being the operative word. We went out one time, Dan. I didn't think you were so insecure."

His low laughter came again. "I don't think I'm insecure. Am I?" he teased.

She wrapped her arms around his neck. "That sounds like a comment from a very insecure man. Someone who needs reassurance."

His eyes darkened, his lips twitching. "And just how do you plan to reassure me?"

"Like this." She tugged his head down and pressed her lips to his, and showed him some of the passion the rest of her body could not yet. He made a noise at the back of his throat and clutched her closer, dragging her hips flush against his. Soon all thought of food was consumed by a different hunger, something that was only stopped by the scent of—

"The fish is burning!"

He dropped his arms and tried to salvage the meal, but the charred remains suggested it was destined for the trash.

"I'm sorry," she said, as meekly as she could.

"I'm not." He faced her again. "I'd much rather kiss you than fry fish."

"In that case..." She tilted her lips invitingly.

They ended up eating cheese and crackers for dinner, ice-cream, and canned peaches for dessert. Now his off-season was here,

Dan didn't have to be quite so vigilant with his diet, which made a nice change from the chicken, vegetables and pasta that seemed to make up most meals between October and April. Maybe she could treat him to a five-star degustation at Alphonse's at the Muskoka Shores Resort. Or maybe she could investigate a nice foodie getaway for their anniversary in two months.

She tucked her head into his chest. From their position here on the two-person lounge on the deck they could see a few stars twinkling above the trees.

"Do you think we could have dinner with Ange and John soon?"

"Sure."

Good. She snuggled closer. "I think they'd like that. I know they've been praying for us."

"They're good people."

"Yes."

The minutes passed, and she wrapped his arm around her tighter. "What about asking Sam to come stay?"

She felt his nod. "It'd be good to see him."

"Where is he with his journey to finding God?"

Dan's chest inflated then sank. "Last we talked he's still on the journey."

"I really thought that your missions trip with him to the Philippines had helped."

"I did too. But I think he's not wanting to have things packaged up nicely for him, he wants to find it for himself."

"We'll keep praying then."

"Amen."

It was nice to feel like they were back to being them. Comfortable, at ease. Their fish-burning kiss in the kitchen was the first time of real passion in nearly two weeks. Funny how honesty and passion could bring something good. She hoped the rest of the things that needed to be said would lead to a similar result.

She shifted on the lounge. "Have you heard anything more from your agent?"

"I haven't checked my phone yet."

Her chest tightened. Neither had she. This time of peace was exactly what she needed. No stress. No obligations. No decisions—apart from what to eat each day. The bigger questions that faced them—Dan's future playing contracts, her potential travels with Heartsong, hearing their blood test results, telling their friends and fans about the miscarriages—had been shelved for the moment. Allowing this sense of… peace.

"We should probably do that soon," he murmured.

"Do what?" she asked sleepily.

"Check our phones. Deal with the real world."

"I don't want to," she admitted.

"Neither do I."

She slipped her hand under his shirt, her fingers traveling to the smooth skin just above his heart. "Besides, this feels pretty real to me."

He glanced down at her, eyes dark, heated. "In that case…"

"Ready?"

Dan wrinkled his nose. "Are you sure about this?"

Nope. But apparently adulting meant interacting with the wider world, much as she'd prefer to stay in this cocoon of love. Last night had seen more stirring of that heat in the kitchen. "After three." Sarah braced, holding her phone in her hand. "One, two, three."

She pressed the power button, and it zipped to life with scores of notifications. Her heart sank, and she scrolled through the emails, deleting the ones that didn't require a response. Sure enough, there were some from Heartsong, and a couple from Dr. McKinnon. She left those to deal with later, and quickly scanned her social media comments. She should probably follow the advice of some of the other Heartsong peeps and employ a VA, an assistant she could deal with virtually, to reply to her social media. She'd always resisted, as that felt a little inauthentic. But right now, she realized she had little emotional capacity to reply in a genuine way. So she simply hearted some of them, replied with a "thanks" for others, and "God bless you" for others.

She closed the app. Glanced at Dan. He was frowning at his phone. "What's wrong?"

He peeked up. "My agent wants a meeting."

"By phone or online?"

"He's suggesting in person. He's in Toronto tomorrow."

"Tomorrow?"

He winced. "This is what happens when I don't check my phone."

"Why would he want it in person?"

"Probably so he can talk to the team bigwigs at the same time."

Which meant Dan would have more chance to extend his career with them. "Do you want to work there again?"

"And finish my career a Maple Leaf? Yeah, I've been praying about it, and I think I do."

"Is he certain that there's no way this can be conducted online?"

"It shows I'm more committed to another contract if I'm there in person too."

True. She drew in a breath. "Then in that case, go."

"Are you sure? I didn't want to cut our time short here."

"Our time? No, I'll stay here." And avoid any more baby sightings. "I'll go see Ange or something. Why? You don't plan to stay in T.O. do you?"

"Not a second longer than I need to."

"Okay, then. I'll be waiting for you when you return." She smiled. "But first you probably need to reply so he can set it up."

He nodded, and moved away to make the call. Leaving her to check her own emails from Heartsong and Dr. McKinnon. Oh, she hoped it wasn't bad news.

She opened the Heartsong one first. Yes, they'd love to have her in a tour that would start in Sydney. Sydney? Her heart leapt. Go see her family? Oh, she'd *love* that. She checked the date. Her heart sank. Except that would be in October, just when Dan's season was starting. She chewed her lip. What would he think about her not being there for that?

Since marrying him and becoming a team WAG, she was conscious of trying to support him as much as possible, which meant saying no to some tours. Yes, she was an independent woman, but she also wanted her husband to feel like she had his back. They had fans in very different worlds, and while he avoided social media, they both knew his fans were way more passionate about him than hers were about her. Which was probably just as well, because her job meant she was supposed to be pointing people to loving Jesus rather than loving her. But balancing fame was yet another of those weird things that made their relationship knotty at times. Like his comment about wanting more followers. Her heart pinged. She knew he'd said that in the spur of the moment, that he was sorry for saying that to her, but the mouth only spoke what the heart entertained, so he obviously must've thought that to some degree. Hmm. It was probably wise to talk to him about this tour soon.

She peeked up. He was still on the phone, now out on the back deck, one hand on the railing. *Lord, have Your way with his contract.* So that meant she should be brave and open the doctor's email. Oh, what would they do if he'd written to say the blood tests had showed they were chromosome incompatible? "Lord?" she whispered. "Help me be brave."

She winced, and opened the email. Stared at the words. Her chest released. The reports hadn't come in yet. It was simply a reminder of what they'd talked about last week, with advice regarding looking forward. Along with something new: That if the results came back as incompatible, then maybe they should consider alternatives like IVF.

IVF? That seemed a step too far for right now. She couldn't even think about that. She closed the email, stared out at the lake shimmering through the trees. What was the point of thinking about IVF if her body couldn't hold a child?

She placed her hands on her abdomen. "Lord, You are Jehovah Rapha, our healer. Please heal me." She might've prayed for healing like this hundreds of times before, but she was going to be like that persistent widow in the Bible, knocking until God gave her an answer.

She dropped her hands as Dan came in, his forehead creased. No need to add to whatever concerned him. "Is everything okay with your agent?"

"Kris is a little mad that I took so long to reply, but says he'll set up a meeting tomorrow."

She nodded. Different agents handled their clients in different ways. But extensions like this could be delicate, especially considering Dan had missed a crucial game that knocked them out of the playoffs. Showing he was committed meant it was important to be there. "So, are you still okay if I see if John and Ange are free tonight?"

"Are you sure you don't want to be just us?"

Just us. What a powerful combination of two small words. "Much as I'd like, I think it won't hurt to have some more praying people committing this to God."

"You know it's not about the number of people who pray who twist God's arm, right?"

"Yes. But I also know that people pray about different aspects, so it won't hurt to have two people who love us know about some of these things."

He sighed. "Then set it up. If they're free."

"Dan." His agent shook his hand. "Long time, no see."

"Thanks for making the time today."

"Thank you. I realized after the call that Sarah hasn't been well, and you were probably up in Muskoka, eh?"

Dan shrugged. "I'm heading back there after this, so let's get to it."

Kris talked, and Dan listened, the sounds of the quiet restaurant dimming. He'd had meetings with Kris before, and knew several other hockey friends had signed him as their agent, people who had garnered huge endorsements, like the Porsche dealership. He wasn't quite a Porsche man, but the terms and numbers that Kris was offering made his eyes widen. And while he wanted to be as authentic as the next guy, the fact was that with retirement looming, this was his final chance to capitalize on his playing career before the offers would dry up. He wasn't quick with his words like some retired players who went into sportscasting. He wasn't about to go against his values and endorse casinos or sports betting companies, like some others did. He'd always hated attending those fundraising nights organized by the team, when all team members were expected to show up in a suit at a casino event, like his presence was giving a big fat yes to people losing their money. But the things Kris kept saying swirled around him, tantalizing possibilities, almost like he was the devil offering temptation.

Lord, show me the right way, what You want for me. And for Sarah. For this wasn't about him anymore. If the Leafs didn't extend the offer Kris wanted and Dan did retire, then suddenly the world could be theirs. The world, meaning they could move to Australia, so she could be close to her family. She'd always been a lot closer to them than he had with his. To be honest, he often preferred her family to his, too. She'd sacrificed a lot to live here, to be by his side during Toronto's miserable winters. But if they lived in Australia, and visited Canada occasionally…

"What do you think of that?" Kris asked.

He blinked. "Sorry. You'll need to repeat that last part."

Kris's bleached smile reminded Dan of a shark. He was suddenly extremely glad that John and Ange had prayed for them both last night, praying that Dan would have wisdom for the future—and for this meeting right now.

Which meant Dan wasn't alone right now. God was with him, the Holy Spirit giving wisdom. *Lord, thank You for giving me wisdom.*

"Dan?"

Darn. He'd missed it again. But suddenly it didn't matter what Kris was trying to say. Dan knew he needed to make it clear exactly what he wanted, what he was about.

He straightened in his seat. "I think I've made it very clear in the past that I want nothing to do with any gambling company, so you can take that off the table right now."

Kris opened his mouth, but Dan plowed on.

"I want to support family-friendly initiatives, and I don't care if they pay less than what the sports betting company does. I know you want me to choose the bigger paycheck because that's a bigger cut for you, but I'm not going to support something that goes against my principles."

"Principles?" Kris scoffed. "How can providing for your family be against your principles?"

"When it involves people who gamble away their income and destroy their families in the process, then yeah, I have a problem with that."

Kris's mouth sagged. "I think you're being hasty—"

"I don't care if you do. Sarah and I have talked about this, and I don't want to be supporting anything like that. So don't mention it again. Now, have you got anything else?"

His agent's face turned red and splotchy, like he was

desperate to argue, but Dan wouldn't let him. Maybe some Christians out there didn't mind a flutter, but he'd seen teammates who had been addicted to gambling, and how it could fuel foolish dreams and lead to family and marriage breakdowns. He wasn't about to endorse anything that encouraged that.

Kris made several other suggestions, which he promised to think about, after discussing with Sarah. He loved having her as a sounding board for decisions, to have an excuse to defer some of these things Kris pushed for. Sarah often brought such a different perspective to him. But then, growing up as a missionary's daughter in a remote village in the mountains of Papua New Guinea would do that.

"So, have you heard anything from the club about an extension?"

Kris explained about how the negotiations were tracking, most of which Dan knew. "It didn't help that you missed the playoff-spot game, of course."

"I think the fact that I've been a valued member for the past nine years should override that. Especially given the reason."

"Your wife being sick?"

He clenched his hands. "My wife suffered a miscarriage."

Kris winced, then offered his sympathies. "But I'm sure there will be other babies."

"This is our third miscarriage, Kris, and there are no guarantees."

"Oh. Sorry. I didn't realize that."

No. There was a reason for that. Because Dan had never told him about them. Regret at his quick temper melded into understanding for why Sarah had thought it wise to share a little more openly about their situation. For how could anyone know or understand or give grace to a situation when they didn't know the most important parts? It was unfair of him to assume people would be understanding when they didn't know the most relevant things.

That thought kept him company as he made a quick visit to the team's front office, doing his bit to be 'seen' by the organization's staff, and—as hoped—allowing for a not-so accidental encounter with the general manager and team owner.

"Dan! We didn't expect to see you back so soon."

"Can't keep me away from the place," he joked, shaking their hands. "But I'm glad I got the chance to thank you both for your understanding about why I had to take time away when Sarah needed me."

"We're glad she's on the mend."

Dan shrugged.

The GM peered more closely at him. "She is on the mend, right?"

Perhaps this was another time to be open and honest about things. "It was our third miscarriage, and to be honest, it's been a little overwhelming."

"I'm sorry to hear that." The team owner—a father to three daughters—clapped him on the shoulder. "Truly."

"I have to say the results when you were away weren't what we wanted," the GM said.

"But perhaps proof that we need him around," the owner said.

The GM nodded. "I hope you'll be signing on again, Dan."

"I hope so too."

And an emotion he hadn't felt for a long time—something that felt like hope—buoyed his spirits on the drive back to see Sarah. Maybe they could discuss this tonight over dinner in Muskoka.

CHAPTER 8

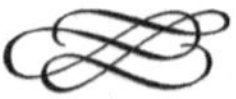

"This is so nice." Sarah glanced around the restaurant that was often heralded as Muskoka's finest. Alphonse, the Paris-trained chef whose name graced the resort restaurant, had a flair for cooking Canadian produce with a French twist. And even though it wasn't a special occasion, the fact that they were out socializing again made it feel special enough. Especially with Dan's encouraging news from Toronto.

"Thanks, sweetheart."

"I figured a positive conversation like that deserved celebrating."

He smiled at her. "I think from Kris's latest email the negotiations are heating up now."

"I'm not surprised." She reached across the table and held his hand. "The team management are fans of yours."

His lips tweaked higher, the sparkle back in the golden glints of his chocolate eyes. Her heart spasmed. He seemed so much happier than two weeks ago.

And while she'd like to celebrate with him properly, her bleeding had started again, which put a dampener on their reunion earlier. Still, maybe that meant it was just her cycle reasserting itself, which meant the time for true reconciliation wouldn't be much longer. She hoped so, anyway.

"So did Kris have anything good to suggest regarding sponsorship?"

"A few things. Nothing that grabbed me."

"But if you've got another year then the pressure is off a little, isn't it?"

"A little. But it's still something to be aware of. I can't pretend to be living the high life when I'm no longer playing."

"But you've invested wisely, and it's not like we're lacking money." It still amazed her how different her life was now to how she'd grown up. Strangely enough, there wasn't a thatched hut to be seen in the big smoke. "We'll just have to keep praying that God will open the right doors at the right time."

"Amen." Dan clasped her hand and gently squeezed.

She used the last of her dinner roll to mop up the remaining sauce. "Hopefully you can get this sorted soon, and then go do your camp and have fun there."

His brow lowered. "I can't believe I forgot that."

"I can't either. I know I'll never forget my one and only time." Camping *Survivor*-style in the Canadian wilderness with a bunch of city teenagers. There was a reason she had a vintage-styled magnet on the fridge that declared, 'I love not camping'.

"I need to get onto Boyd and see where he's up to with it all."

She nodded. Boyd was one of Dan's long-time friends who worked as a youth minister in Toronto. They'd started this camp for underprivileged youth together a bunch of years ago, and it was one of the highlights of Dan's year.

"He's usually pretty organized, isn't he?" She grinned as he nodded. "Gotta say, rather you than me."

He groaned. "I have to admit that I can't see me doing this forever."

"You let me know when you'd rather 'camp' at a place like

this," she waved a hand at their surroundings, "then I'll reconsider."

He chuckled, drawing her grin. Oh, she loved this man.

"Is everything satisfactory?"

She glanced up. Startled. "Oh! You're Alphonse, right?"

He inclined his head. "When I heard that a Leaf and his charming wife were visiting, I thought I'd say hello."

"Everything has been delicious," Sarah gushed. "My only problem is how I'm going to manage to fit dessert in. Especially when it all looks so good."

"That's never proved a problem in the past," Dan teased.

She wrinkled her nose at him.

"If you like, we can prepare a dessert sampler, then you'll know what to order next time."

"Next time." She winked at Dan. "I like the sound of that."

Alphonse nodded. "Then I'll speak to Camille, our dessert maestro, and we'll send it out soon."

"With two spoons?" Sarah asked.

"Naturally."

Alphonse excused himself to return to the kitchen and she smiled at Dan, who snickered. "What?"

"It's fun to see you back with your enthusiasm."

She mock-sighed. "I can't help it. Chocolate does that to me."

But it was good, after so many weeks of tears and grief, to feel this small spark of hope and life again. Maybe God didn't have a baby in their future, but that didn't mean He didn't have other good things. And no, not just chocolate desserts, but good plans for them to walk in. Which reminded her. She needed to talk to Dan about Heartsong. But there was time enough to do that.

Later, after enjoying delectable desserts that guaranteed a return visit "in the very near future" as she assured Alphonse, they exited through the resort's main entrance, only to spy a familiar face.

"Serena?"

Their wedding coordinator turned, eyes wide as she beamed. "Dan and Sarah! Hello! How are you two?"

"Full." Sarah patted her stomach. "Alphonse is a master, isn't he?"

"He's a wonder." Serena smiled. "You're both looking well. Here for the summer?"

"For as much as we can." Sarah was again reminded to mention to Dan about the Heartsong tour. Not that it was happening in summer, but it might affect their plans.

"Serena? Oh, excuse me." Another face that was vaguely familiar drew into view. The brunette glanced between them, her eyes widening. "I know you."

"This is Dan and Sarah Walton," Serena said. "Toni Vandenburg is the sister of my husband Joel, and our resident artist here at the resort."

"That's it! I remember now. We have one of your pieces hanging in our house," Sarah said. "Does 'resident artist' mean you have a gallery here?"

"Yes."

"Uh oh." Dan's lips lifted.

"Oh, come on. Just for a moment? Unless Toni has already closed for the day."

Toni chuckled. "I could be persuaded to reopen for potential repeat customers."

"Then can we see? Pretty please? I just *love* your paintings."

The gallery proved to be a wonderland of artistry, with all kinds of watercolors, acrylics and oil paintings lining the walls. Many were scenes evoking Muskoka, which made it very hard to choose. "But we should choose something, shouldn't we?" she murmured to Dan. "It'd be rude to insist on coming here and not buy anything."

His lips curved up one side higher. "I knew what was going

to happen when we walked through those doors. Besides, I'm sure there's a spot somewhere that needs a little something."

"How little?"

He chuckled and shook his head. Okay, she'd take that head shake to mean size didn't matter.

But it was good to feel like they could bless others. And the painting she chose—which looked as though it could've been painted from Dan's deck—obviously was the result of many hours of work, so it was justly deserving its price tag.

"Where is that going to go?" he asked, as Toni wrapped it.

"In the apartment. We need the reminder to return to Muskoka as much as possible."

"Okay then."

He placed it in the Jeep, and she squeezed him tight. "Thank you."

"Is that all the thanks I get?"

She winced. "It is tonight. And for this upcoming week. But after that…"

His eyes lit. "Really?"

She nodded. "Really."

He kissed her, and her heart skipped several beats. She couldn't wait to show him how she really felt. In one more week.

"Thanks for doing this today, Ange."

"I'm glad we've got the time, especially with the men out fishing today."

Today, the perfect Muskoka day for fishing, according to Dan. Their dinner together two nights ago had seen an invitation from Dan to John about fishing, which had resulted in John's instant yes. This had resulted in Sarah joining her aunt for afternoon tea, as Ange called it, eating scones and drinking hot tea here on the back deck of the little cottage where Sarah had stayed when she'd first come to Muskoka all those years ago.

The lake glinted through the trees, the sandy beach promised fun for warmer days, the peace she'd always found here only further enlarged by spending time with one of her favoritest people in the world: her aunt Angela.

"I'm glad for John's sake that Joel could take today's meeting at Golden Elms."

"Golden Elms?"

"The retirement home just outside the town." Ange sipped her tea. "Joel's always very obliging, which is just as well, considering he's the assistant pastor."

"Oh!" The dots were being joined together. "He's the one married to Serena, right?"

Ange nodded. "John plans to hand the reins over to him soon, but he needs a little longer, considering Joel has a young family."

Young family. Sarah's heart creased. But no, she couldn't begrudge others' happiness just because she seemed destined to not have children.

Ange seemed to notice Sarah's discomfort, smiling at her gently. "So you're here for the summer."

"For as much as we can." Again that niggle arose to talk to Dan about Heartsong.

"I hope this means we'll see you two in church again."

"I think so. We'll likely be away some weeks, so don't go planning to use me in the music team any time soon."

Ange laughed. "They're doing much better than when you first came."

"Good." That was the point, wasn't it? To build something that persisted even when she was gone. Her parents' lives as missionaries in Papua New Guinea then as pastors in a church in Sydney had showed that ministry in the kingdom of God could have seasons. Her time with Heartsong, both before the accident and then after, had also showed that laying something down didn't mean it would be forever. People could plan their lives, but God ultimately directed their paths.

"So, how are you doing?" Her aunt's expression held tender concern. "Really?"

Her eyes pricked. God bless Ange for her way of asking that instantly drew Sarah's tears. She'd always had that knack, just like Sarah's mum, of asking in a way that probed below the surface and made the truth—and her tears—leak.

Ange handed her a tissue. "It's sometimes easier to be honest when we don't feel like we have to protect the other person."

Sarah mopped away the latest spill of emotion. "I don't know why this keeps happening. I keep thinking I'm getting better, then something sets me off again."

"Grief isn't something we can package up into a box and say, 'that's done, I've dealt with it'. You know, more than most people do, that grief isn't a linear thing."

So true. Sometimes she still felt a pang of sorrow for Stephen, even though she was married to Dan, and for the most part was blissfully happy. Overcoming grief wasn't necessarily a case of moving on but moving forward, aware that experience had shaped and molded a new reality, as much as one might have once wanted things to stay the same. But stepping forward, trying to trust God with the future, meant one had to keep walking. Staying locked in denial was a prison. She'd been there, done that, got the t-shirt, and couldn't live trapped like that again.

Sarah sipped her tea, and eyed her aunt over the rim. "I know it doesn't it look like it, but I really am doing okay. Most of the time, anyway," she admitted.

"I thought you seemed better."

"I'm trying to remember that I'm loved by God, and staying there. And even though it feels like grief still sneaks up and grabs me sometimes, I feel like I'm doing so much better than when Stephen died." She pressed a finger on a scone crumb, swallowed it. "It's just so hard, knowing that Dan is disappointed, and feeling like I'm the cause of his disappointment."

"You can't blame yourself, Sar."

"I know. And he says that, and I even mostly believe him."

"Mostly?"

Sarah sighed. "He's got to be more disappointed than he lets on."

"But he's also trying to not let you see that."

"Exactly." She sighed. "The doctor said he'd be sending our test results soon, to see if we're chromosome compatible or not."

Her aunt's eyes widened. "I haven't heard of that."

"Because we've had three miscarriages in a row now."

"Three?"

She nodded. See, secrets had a way of coming out. Especially when someone had a sieve for a mouth like she did.

"Oh, Sar. I'm *so* sorry." Ange's eyes sparkled with tears. "That must've been so hard. I didn't know."

Sarah lowered her gaze, studying the William Morris design of her teacup, one of a set of four she'd given Ange for Christmas last year. "Dan didn't want people to know." A burst of additional honesty leaped on board the tell-the-truth train and added, "He accused me of wanting to tell people to get more followers."

Ange gasped.

Oops. She hadn't meant to expose him like that. Even if the memory still stung. "He did apologize though."

"I'm sure he didn't mean it."

Well, Sarah sure hoped he didn't mean it.

Ange sipped her tea, her blue eyes concerned. "We all know grief makes us say things and act in ways that we wouldn't normally."

For sure. Sarah's previous experiences proved she was the

queen of contradictions. The joyous extrovert who had frozen into depression and grief; the worship leader who'd forgotten how to praise. Her heart softened. Dan didn't need her holding this against him. She knew he wasn't that person. He was kind, patient, he loved her. Besides, she'd said she had forgiven him, so that meant not bringing it out for another shake of the dirty laundry again. Besides, forgiveness—hers and God's—meant that laundry was now clean.

"So what else has the doctor said?" Ange asked.

"He mentioned in the latest email the possibility of IVF. But I just don't know."

"IVF works for lots of people."

"Lots of people whose bodies work." Frustration flared. Sarah tried to hide it with a shrug. "The doctors always said after my surgeries in Sydney that there was a strong possibility that the scarring wouldn't allow me to fall pregnant."

"And yet you have."

Three times. "Or carry a baby to full term."

"But God does miracles."

"I know," she whispered.

Ange held her hand. "And we can continue to pray for one."

"I'm praying all the time," she admitted.

Ange squeezed her hand, as a wave of empathy passed between them. See, this was the benefit of family, of being with those who truly understood. Sometimes love could be felt without a word.

A knock came at the front door.

Ange excused herself to answer it, and Sarah relaxed. The view was different here, the beach shared between the two 'cottages' more easily accessed here. Her mind flicked back to when she'd lived here in this house for the six months when she'd first escaped Australia, in a last-ditch effort to find hope after depression followed Stephen's death.

What a special time coming here had been. Escaping the real

world, finding her feet again. Her lips tilted. Much like she and Dan were doing now, resting, allowing God to refresh their hearts, and souls, and minds. Muskoka always seemed to have that soothing effect.

"Um, Sarah?"

At the new voice, she turned in her seat, her breath hitching as she recognized their neighbor from Toronto. Was the woman following her? *Please God, no.*

"It *is* you." Jackie smiled, hoisting her baby higher.

No. She couldn't do this. She might be getting better, but she wasn't completely better yet, and the sight of that baby was like a hot poker in her chest. Being forced to stay and interact would topple her back to heartache.

Sarah pushed back her seat, faked a smile. "Good to see you. Sorry, Ange, I need to go."

"But Sar—"

"I'm sorry, I have a Heartsong thing to do." Any excuse, any excuse to get out of here. Now. She kissed Ange's cheek, heard her, "Sar," but ignored her. Nope. Asking her to be brave right now was a step too far. She headed to the steps and the path that led next door.

Jackie hefted her baby on her hip. "I hope we'll see each other soon."

"Sure," she lied, before waving at a disappointed-looking Ange.

Well, too bad. If Sarah saw Jackie and her too-sweet baby, then she would be heading the other direction.

BY THE TIME Dan had returned with John to his dock he was feeling more relaxed. He always enjoyed time with John. The man possessed the skill of knowing when to speak and when not to. Dan had learned a lot about patience from him over the years, more so than from his own father.

"Well, thanks again for a great afternoon," John said now.

"Any time."

"We'll be praying for you two."

Dan's throat had clamped, forcing him to salute in response, before turning back to the boat and pretend he needed to fix the ties.

God bless John. Dan peered over his shoulder, but John had disappeared along the stone-edged path to the little cottage he and Ange called home. The man might be a pastor, but he was also a saint. He knew when to push and when to leave alone, only asking once how Dan was doing.

Dan had admitted he was doing better than before. "Not as good as Sarah, though."

Which was hard. He was supposed to lead her, but he sometimes felt like she was leading him, showing him how to manage their emotions. Which was a little ironic, considering she was known for her fiery temperament, and he was Mr. Cool, Calm and Collected, but there it was. She seemed to be riding the waves of grief far better than him.

He paused, his ears pricking at the music coming from the house. See? Even now she was playing the piano, last year's Christmas gift that was perhaps as extravagant as Sarah said, considering she wasn't here all that often to justify its expense. And yet it was perfect for a musician who loved to drop whatever she was doing and create music, like she was doing now.

That song. He recognized it now as the one she'd played on their previous stay. He washed off as best he could and ascended the steps leading to the cottage's back deck, keeping his movements quiet to not disturb her.

Then her music stopped, and he heard her voice. "So it obviously needs work, but I thought that might be something to consider for the new Heartsong album."

A new album? Why didn't he know? She usually shared every new piece of Heartsong news with him.

She sighed. "I know. I still need to talk to him about it. I'd obviously *love* to do it, but it's when his season starts, and I don't think he'd be too keen for me to run off for weeks."

Run off? His heartstrings tightened. Was she talking about another tour? The last one she'd been on had seen Heartsong Collective traveling for nearly two months, from Australia to Europe then a bunch of places across the US. Part of him still blamed her exhaustion for why she'd miscarried. How could she be talking about another tour when the doctor had specifically said she needed to take things easy?

He opened the back door into the living room where her piano was, and she jumped. But for once it didn't raise his smile. Her smile soon faded, her gaze questioning, and she spoke to the person on the other end of the line, "I need to go."

Another murmur, then she held the phone at him. "It's Tisha, so say hi."

"Hi." He could picture the bubbly curly blonde who often led the worship songs when Sarah couldn't.

"Hey, Dan." Tisha's Aussie accent was crisper than his wife's. "I hope you'll say yes and let her go."

Let her go? The way she talked it made him sound like some medieval husband locking up his wife. Which he wasn't. But neither was he excited about his wife making plans about a tour and not telling him. Who did that?

He returned the phone to Sarah, who was eyeing him with pressed-together lips. Maybe she sensed his frustration because she soon said goodbye and stood from the piano stool. "So, uh, was fishing good?"

"It was. Until I came home and discovered you've been planning a tour."

Her eyes widened. "Whoa, I haven't planned anything. Like I said, I wanted to talk to you about it."

Oh. His pique decreased. Maybe this was new. And she wasn't pregnant now, so maybe a few weeks traveling in North America wouldn't be so bad. "How long have you known?"

Her cheeks pinked. That was never the sign of innocence. "A few weeks."

"A few weeks?"

She bit her lip.

Her uncharacteristic response only drew his irritation. How could she stay quiet? "What do you think we've been doing here? You've had plenty of time to talk, Sar. Why haven't you said anything?"

"Because there's been a few other important things happening, and I didn't want to upset you."

"Well, not telling me stuff doesn't help."

"Apparently," she snapped. "So I'm sorry."

"Yeah? Well, I'm sorry too."

She stared at him, then her lips twitched, and she rushed at him and hugged him. "I really am," she murmured against his chest. "I was going to tell you, but your contract stuff happened, and then—oh. You'll never guess who else is here in Muskoka."

"Who?"

Her shoulders slumped. "I know this makes me sound like such a terrible person, but when I saw her today, it was all I could do to get away." She sighed. "I think Ange was really disappointed in me."

"Who did you see?"

Her grip tightened around his waist. "Lincoln Cash's wife."

He tensed. Which likely meant Jackie *and* her baby. Great. "Are they following us?" he grumbled.

"That's exactly what I thought."

"Do you think they have contacts in Australia?"

She drew back, her eyes alight. "Oh, are you serious? Can we go? I'd *love* to see Mum and Dad again."

Maybe they could swing a trip. After his camp. Get the

chance to escape from the constant reminders of what couldn't be. "We could think about it."

"Really?" She squeezed him tight again. "Oh, that'd make me so happy. I didn't think it was possible, seeing that's where the tour starts," Sarah babbled.

"Wait." He inched back. "It starts in Australia?"

"Yes."

Oh. That was a very different prospect to a US tour. He clasped her close, holding back the words he knew she wouldn't want him to say.

CHAPTER 9

"Thanks, Suzy."

Sarah collected her tall chai latte from the owner of The Coffee Blend and pushed her sunglasses back on her face as she returned to the street. It wasn't exactly sunglasses weather, but walking incognito around the township of Muskoka Shores demanded it. She sipped her drink, examining the offerings next door at Brandi's Bookstore and Gifts. How long would Dan take? He hadn't wanted to drive into town today, but they'd needed supplies, so he'd said he'd visit the Muskoka Shores grocery store while she got a chai latte. Dan made great coffee, but his preference was always for the straight black stuff, rather than the sweeter side of life.

Still, so far so good. She was glad to be making little forays into the social world again, even if she didn't want anyone to recognize her. And she especially didn't want to see a certain neighbor with a baby who kept popping up most inconveniently.

Maybe Dan had been joking when he'd suggested taking a vacation to Australia. She sure hoped not. Muskoka was nice, but here in town, where he was often recognized by those wanting selfies or to discuss hockey with them, made things trickier, especially as tourist season ramped up. It'd be awesome to continue to live in their bubble for a little longer, to not have to worry about anyone else, to feel like they could just be. And if not here, then Australia was perfect. He wouldn't be recognized there, and she could fly under the radar too. But after his initial comment, she'd kind of got the impression that he wasn't so keen, especially given his expression at finding out where the Heartsong tour would begin.

She peered at the window display offerings at Merrill's Fashions, then decided they weren't exactly going to fit her more vintage vibe, so kept walking to where the grocery store was. The town had a few bulbs out in its street planter boxes, daffodils and tulips adding pops of cheerful color. There were good things in this world, beautiful things that made her pause and smile and feel a sense of joy and wonder. She needed to focus on those moments, rather than—

"Sarah? Is that you?"

She stilled. Seriously? Again? Why did Jackie keep turning up like a bad rash? But Sarah couldn't keep avoiding her. She'd get suspicious, and think Sarah was offended with her. And while she wasn't offended, per se, she was struggling with envy. But running away wouldn't help. So she braced, and turned around. "Hi, Jackie."

Of course Jackie had her baby in a sling. She seemed like a real earth mother type. But the baby made it impossible to ignore, especially with its sweet face staring out, dark eyes taking in all the world.

Her heart squeezed. *Lord, help me get out of here quick.*

Jackie smiled. "I'm so glad to finally catch you."

That made one of them.

The baby at Jackie's chest screwed up his features, and started to protest. Jackie's shoulders slumped.

She recognized that pose. Felt an urge to ask if there was

anything she could do. But she didn't want to. Like, *really* didn't want to. *Lord, You have permission to personally rapture me right now…*

Jackie's phone started to ring, and she hunted through her phone as the baby squawked in protest, her pleading look impossible to ignore.

Fine, God. Have it Your way. "Is there something I can do?" she muttered.

"Would you mind holding Charlie?"

Yes, she minded. One thousand percent she minded. *Lord, I don't want to!* But there was no time to do anything as, with a sigh of relief, Jackie released the baby from the sling and deposited the child in Sarah's hands, and finally answered her call. "Hello, Linc?"

Sarah's arms were stiff, as if they'd forgotten how to hold a child. It wasn't like she hadn't held small children before. She adored her nieces, and had long loved holding them, tickling them, giving them hugs and blurting raspberries against their little necks as they shrieked with laughter. But holding a baby now, knowing she would likely never have her own, only sparked tears and tightened her throat.

Wide brown eyes turned to look at her, the delicious baby smell rising to squeeze her heart.

"Hello," she whispered. A cramp rippled across her insides, as if her womb recognized this was what it had been designed for. She blinked fast. *Lord, this is so hard.*

Around them, the locals and tourists of Muskoka Shores continued, as if oblivious to Sarah's emotional distress. Maybe the baby noticed Sarah's anguish, for his whimpers increased. Or maybe that was simply because Jackie's call had allowed enough time for Charlie to realize that the person holding him was not his mother, and for him to protest anew.

Sarah sucked back emotion and jiggled him. "Hey, it's okay. Mummy is just over there. She can see you."

She veered away, as a sharp pang of grief hit her. His mother could see him, but she'd never see her own child. And while she didn't want to make this about her, she was struggling. But then, right now, Jackie needed her help, and it wasn't her fault that Sarah was finding holding her baby so hard.

Jackie ended her call and put her phone in her bag. "Oh, thank you. That was Lincoln. He only gets a few moments break in his filming, and he always tries to call then. He's supposed to be driving up here tonight, but it looks like he's now delayed."

Sarah pressed her lips together and nodded. She had to exit gracefully, without breaking down.

Jackie held out her hands.

Sarah handed her the child. She needed to get away. Needed to cry. Needed a moment to regain composure and pretend this didn't hurt.

"Thanks again."

"You're welcome." Not really. "I need to go—"

"Oh, before you do, Ange mentioned the other day that you're here for a few months."

God bless her aunt.

"If you are, and you're looking for something to do, then I'm having a little gathering at my house this Friday, and would love for you to come."

No. No, no. She couldn't think of anything worse. "Thanks, but—"

"Before you say no," Jackie smiled, "you'd be very welcome to join us. My friend Serena has been hosting soirees for several years, and it's a great chance to just relax with good company, nice food, cocktails or mocktails, whatever floats your boat. No husbands, no kids, just us."

No kids? That was a plus. She pointed to the baby. "Where —?"

"Oh, Linc will take him and probably hang out with Joel while Serena's free."

"Is this Serena who works at the resort?"

"You know her?"

"She planned our wedding."

Jackie beamed. "Of course, I remember now. Oh, then in that case you *have* to come. And it wouldn't even be that far for you, just a couple of houses down the lane."

Hmm. With no kids and not far away, her defenses were dropping. "Is Ange going?"

Jackie's head tilted. "She hasn't in the past, but there's no reason why we couldn't invite her. These nights really are a lot of fun."

Fun? That was a concept she wasn't too familiar with these days. She and Dan might like the quiet life, but there was such a thing as maybe *too* much quiet, especially when their relationship still didn't feel completely easy as it had before.

"What time?"

"Look, is it forward of me to get your number? Or I can ask Serena to send you a text with the details if you prefer." Charlie started fussing. "I'll do that, as this one doesn't seem to want to hang around. But I really hope you can join us."

"Thanks." Non-committal. No promises. She backed away. Faked a smile. Then turned to see Dan watching her.

THE RELIEF on Sarah's face when she saw him would be comical, if it wasn't so heartbreaking. He knew exactly why she looked that way. He'd no doubt look the same. Watching her hold the baby, his heart had clenched, imagining her as the mother of his own child. Something there was a fair chance would never be.

"I'm sorry for keeping you waiting," she said, climbing into the Jeep.

"Sar." He held out his hand.

She wrapped both her hands around his, her face crumpling. Her breath was shaky.

He wished this vehicle had a bench seat, instead of the gear stick in the way. He leaned across as best he could, and wrapped her in his arms. "Hey. It will get easier."

"Will it?" She sniffled. "Just when I think I'm doing okay, something like this happens and I lose it again."

"You're doing fine."

"I'm not. I feel like such a fake, like I'm struggling to keep my head above water."

Oh, he knew that feeling. Only too well. He kissed her cheek. "I love you."

"I love you too. It's just…" She dragged in a shuddery breath. "I just want a baby."

"I know."

He held her in his arms for a long moment. Then she exhaled and pulled away. "Sorry."

"You've got nothing to apologize for."

"I wish I could do better."

"It's okay to be real."

She smiled as he hoped she would. "Someone sounds like he's listened to a certain podcast."

"Someone might've had that discussion with you before it made it to that particular podcast."

A lengthy sigh escaped her. "Why is it so easy to talk about things but so hard to live it?"

Great question. "Because we're imperfect?"

"So true." She exhaled. Wiped her face. Glanced at him. "Do I look like a mess?"

"You look cute. Like a panda."

"What?" She flipped down the visor mirror. "I don't look like a panda."

"Hey, I said you look cute. Pandas are cute."

She slapped his arm. "I think you owe me a chocolate croissant for that comment."

He smiled. "I think you're right."

Two chocolate croissants later, they were back at the cottage, then, after unloading groceries, they wandered down to the dock, holding hands. It brought back memories of when they first dated, the simple pleasures of enjoying Lake Muskoka and spending time getting to know each other, when they could talk about all kinds of things for hours. Those days might've had their ups and downs, but they seemed a lot less complicated in some ways to now, when there seemed to be an undercurrent of unspoken questions beneath the surface.

"It's such a beautiful day," Sarah murmured.

"Yeah." The lake was still, the reflections of trees on water unimpaired by water craft. It was still too early for the huge influx of summer tourists to be out, which was just how he liked it. One of the appeals of his cottage was the privacy he could get, with the large acreage on one side meaning he rarely saw his neighbors on the south. Beyond John and Ange's cottage on the other side, the road led to Lincoln Cash's extravagant waterside cottage, which was even less 'cottage-like' than Dan's own place, and on its own point on the peninsular. The beach between his and John and Ange's place was only shared between them, which meant this little bay with its own buoy and swimming dock was the perfect nook of serenity, with few summer tourists ever daring to venture in.

He lay back on the boards, enjoying the warmth of the sun heating it, enjoying the way Sarah snuggled into his side.

"This is nice," she murmured.

"Not worried about sunburn?"

A sigh escaped her. "I really don't think it's fair that Australians are so close to the hole in the ozone layer when us

Aussies are not the world's biggest contributor to ozone destruction."

He chuckled. "My environmental activist."

She pinched him. "Don't patronize me."

"I'm not. I'm enjoying you."

"Hmph."

He smiled, wondering how long it would take for her to tell him what had happened before. Honestly, if he didn't know better, he'd start to think Jackie was some kind of stalker, the way she kept showing up.

She sighed again, louder and longer this time, and he bit back a grin. Here it came.

"I don't understand why Jackie would invite me to one of their soirees."

"What soiree?"

"She and Serena have these get-togethers with some of their friends, and Jackie invited me to one this Friday night."

Huh. Good for her. "Well, why wouldn't she invite you? You're amazing, beautiful, and fascinating."

"You're biased."

"I mean it. Lots of people are interested in knowing you. And I've seen some of those comments on your podcasts. Heck, even my friends think you're amazing. I still remember telling my Original Six friends about you and some of them asking if you had a sister."

"Really? Why haven't you told me this before?"

"Because I thought you knew how amazing you were."

"Yeah, right." She scoffed. "I don't feel like that at all."

"Hello, who is the woman with more followers than me on Instagram?"

She snorted. "That's because you don't have an account."

And it would forever stay that way. "Look, people think you're interesting, and want to get to know you more, so it's a good chance for them to do so."

"I don't want to go," she mumbled.

"You don't have to," he assured.

"Hmm."

He bit back a smile. He knew how his wife's mind worked, her need to talk through scenarios and get his perspective, and let things settle before the instant 'no' softened into a 'maybe', before turning into a tentative 'yes'.

The water lapped, lulling him to long blinks that beckoned him to sleep. "When is it?"

"This Friday."

He yawned. "I planned to watch the playoffs with John. Brent Karlsson is in it again, so it should be fun."

"You're ditching me for hockey?"

He would if it meant she got her socializing on again. She needed more friends. Everyone did. "I think you'll enjoy yourself more than you expect."

"I could enjoy you…" she murmured, pressing a kiss to his jaw.

"And you can. Next week, you said. Which is why I'm watching playoffs with John this week."

"Are you saying you want my undivided attention next week?" She trailed a hand down his throat.

He rolled over quickly, startling her to laughter as he kissed her jaw and throat. "I'm saying, that I think you'll have more fun than you think. So trust God that this is part of His plans, okay?"

"Okay," she whispered.

And he cuddled her next to him, and prayed for God to have His way with both of them. With their friends, their family, and their futures.

CHAPTER 10

"I really don't want to do this," Sarah murmured, as Dan pulled up outside the intricately designed heavy iron gates.

"I know." He pressed the buzzer, alerting inside. A humming sound preceded the slow inwards movement of the gate.

"I can't believe how much security he has."

"Hmm. We should probably beef up ours, too," he mused.

"Why? How many death threats have you received lately?"

He glanced at her.

Her breath suspended. "Are you serious? Have people threatened you?"

"No. People say stuff, but they don't mean it." His face held peace, so he meant it. "But Lincoln has *way* more fans than me, and they weren't exactly happy when he married Jackie."

She knew that now. It hadn't taken too much research on the internet to discover that Jackie was not a popular lady in some circles. And now she and Lincoln had a baby, Sarah had new compassion for her. How could people threaten a baby? No wonder the woman seemed keen to connect with someone who might understand some of the pitfalls of fame.

Dan drove up the spot-lit drive, the landscaping on a level far superior to what constituted as landscaping at Dan's, which consisted of mostly trees. The long drive and pines and poplars did a good job of hiding their house from the road, but it was bare bones minimum, the grass consisting more of pine needles. Here, all kinds of flowering bushes and plants were mixed with what looked like palms and ferns. It was eclectic, but it worked.

"I wish Ange was going to be here." She'd asked, and Ange had admitted to a prior event, but had encouraged Sarah to go.

"For I sense that Jackie could do with someone who understands a little about what it's like to have a husband who other women want," Ange had said.

Oh, how well did Sarah understand. She'd seen the women who loitered where hockey players hung out, she'd heard the rumors, and seen the strained relationships affected by gossip and innuendo. Dan had never given her a moment of concern, but other wives she knew weren't so blessed. So that comment of Ange's, along with a little tug in her heart, had drawn her to come. Even if the house looked imposing, and the unfamiliar cars said there would be plenty of unfamiliar faces. At least Serena would be someone she'd recognize.

"You ready?" Dan asked.

"Thank you for driving me," she murmured, as he parked the Jeep, so it'd be easy for her to drive out.

"Hey, someone had to make sure you'd actually get here."

She rolled her eyes. "How do you know I won't just drive out of here?"

He pointed behind her. She peeked over her shoulder. Saw Serena standing on the steps next to Jackie. She heaved out a sigh.

He chuckled. "I love you. Have fun tonight." He passed her the keys, then kissed her.

"You too. I hope Brent wins."

"They're playing Tim Carruthers and TJ Woletsky in New York, so it'll be a good game."

She exited the car, watched Dan wave to the women, then walk down the drive. Maybe it was childish of her to insist he bring her, but she sensed he was glad for her sake. Now if only she could find enough gladness to be glad too.

Still, she was the woman who had once crawled up stairs then stood to lead worship in front of thousands in Manila when she'd been battling the flu. She could fake this moment too.

"Sarah!" Serena hurried down the steps and hugged her. "I'm so glad you came."

"Jackie was pretty insistent," she admitted.

Serena smiled at her friend, standing nearby. "She can sure be that way. You should see her with Lincoln."

Sarah chuckled. "He seems too much of a tough guy to get bossed around too much."

"It's all an act," Serena said in a loud whisper, obviously meaning for Jackie to hear. "Lincoln is a total pushover when it comes to Jackie."

"Are you two finished?" Jackie shook her head, smiling at Sarah. "Welcome. And thank you for coming. I wasn't sure you would."

"I appreciate the invitation."

"I'm sorry Ange couldn't come."

"She explained she had a prior engagement. It's okay."

"Alright, well, come on in. I want to introduce you to everyone. It's a shame your husband couldn't meet the ladies. I think there are a few who'd enjoy meeting him."

"He's watching hockey tonight. With John."

"Oh! Linc said he planned to do the same. I think Joel was going too."

"Great." So there'd be a man club next door to the women's cluckery. Awesome.

Jackie pushed open the heavy front door and Sarah blinked. The white marble entry led to a picture window that showcased Lake Muskoka from a different angle to their own place. "Wow. Great view."

"It's nice, huh? Although I'm sure yours is much the same."

"Ours faces a slightly more southerly aspect."

"Oh, so you get the little island?"

"The one with the Canada flag? Yep. It's so cute, isn't it?"

Jackie's smile held ease. "I love this part of the world."

"It's Muskoka," Serena said. "What's not to love?"

Sarah felt a little shy as Serena and Jackie did the introductions to half a dozen other women. Toni, she recognized, but some of the other faces blurred, and she didn't quite figure out who matched what names. But everyone seemed pleased to see her. Some seemed *really* pleased.

"Oh my gosh, I can't believe I'm actually talking to you." One of the women—Sarah thought her name was Anna—was fanning herself as they ate from the amazing antipasto platters.

Sarah forced a smile as she cut herself a wedge of cheese. "I can't believe I'm here either. In Lincoln Cash's house, no less."

"Right? It was such a surprise when he married Jackie—now that's a story and a half, but you should ask her. But they're happy, and got little Charlie now, so it's all good."

Sarah nodded. "And you? Are you married?"

"Engaged!" Anna waggled a finger with a big rock. "Tom and I are getting married next month."

"Congratulations."

"Thank you. Tom is a local detective, and very, very hot."

Sarah chuckled. "Okay."

"Well, maybe not as hot as your husband, but that would be weird for me to say, so I won't say it."

Another chuckle. Anna was fun.

"Speaking of hot, Sarah, have you got an opinion on what role Lincoln is hottest in?" another woman called.

Jackie groaned. "Rachel."

"Now how many times have we talked about asking questions like this?" Serena said, winking at Sarah.

"At least in front of Jackie." Anna smirked.

"Look, I feel like if an actor is on a TV show or a movie, then he's fair game for us to comment on." Rachel tossed back her hair. "So, what do you think, Sarah? Do you think Lincoln is better in *As The Heart Draws* or that sci fi film with Chlolinda Drewe?"

"Um, I've only watched a few episodes of *As The Heart Draws,* and haven't seen the other," Sarah admitted.

"You're not missing much," Rachel said. "I'm pretty sure she only got that role because her dad was the director, am I right?" She glanced at Jackie, who shrugged.

"I don't know."

Rachel smirked at Jackie then returned her attention to Sarah. "She always does that, says she doesn't know when I bet she knows a lot more than she lets on."

Jackie shook her head.

Rachel continued undaunted. "But as for *As The Heart Draws,* well, you gotta love a nice PG historical TV drama series about Mounties like that, right?"

There were various murmurs of agreement.

"Lincoln used to be the lead in that show before his career took off," she explained to Sarah.

Sarah nodded, and pinched a small bunch of grapes.

"Ooh, speaking of," Rachel continued, "let's have opinions on Harrison Woods in that show. He's the new Mountie hero, but he used to be in *Beach Guard,*" she explained to Sarah.

"I haven't seen that either," Sarah confessed.

"Well, you're *definitely* not missing much with *Beach Guard.* Apart from a couple of scenes when he's riding a horse along the beach with no shirt on, but that's neither here nor there."

Clearly.

"Harrison took Tanner's role, who played the previous Mountie character that Lincoln played, and let's just say that Harrison is *fire*. I'm like, Tanner who?"

The other women laughed, and Sarah joined in. It had been a long time since she'd laughed with other women like this.

The evening continued, with easy conversation and tasty food, and Sarah relaxed some more. These women were fun, their snippets revealing aspects of their lives that helped her piece together where they fit in Muskoka Shores. Most attended John and Angela's church, which was why she'd recognized some, like Serena, Jackie, and Anna, more than others. Others, like Toni and fellow redhead Staci, were newer to town.

Jackie had worked at Golden Elms retirement home, which was how she met Lincoln, who'd been visiting his grandfather. Anna worked as a medical receptionist, with Staci's husband, Dr. James Wells, who was a retired missionary. Staci was a successful author of historical novels, many with a spice rating above what Sarah preferred, but she'd started writing clean and subtly Christian romance in recent years. It was fun joining the dots that showed just how close a small town could be.

But small towns also meant less space to hide, and it was obvious from the conversations that people didn't mind diving into each other's business. Which drew new tension, as she poised for hard questions she didn't want to answer, even as she smiled and pretended she was fine.

"So, can I ask, what's it like—really—to be married to a hockey star?" Staci asked.

"You're not going to put this in one of your books, are you?" Anna asked.

Sarah froze. She wouldn't. Would she?

Staci smiled. "I think Anna has forgotten that I write historicals."

"But that doesn't mean that's all you'll ever write," Anna said. "I don't understand why authors focus on only one genre."

"It's got a lot to do with publishers wanting to satisfy their readership, and not wanting to take risks." Staci shrugged. "But I'm not looking to write Sarah's story, even though I firmly believe everyone has a story. I just don't want Sarah feeling like she's under the microscope here."

"Too late for that." Sarah added a smile to help convince her comment was a joke.

"So, what *is* it like?" Rachel asked.

"It's got some benefits."

"Ooh, like those super cool leather jackets you got to wear for the playoffs a year or so ago."

Oh. "I guess. But I meant more like the fact he gets paid a nice salary, and gets time off for several months a year. And there are some nice opportunities to meet people, and help where we can."

"I think I saw pictures of you at a fundraiser for the Toronto Children's Hospital," Anna said.

Sarah nodded. Back when she'd been pregnant the second time, and dared pray that her unborn child would never have to face some of the incredible challenges these children had faced. That was one prayer that had been answered, she supposed. And one she might have to face if Dr. McKinnon's grim predictions proved right.

"Sarah, are you okay?" Serena asked.

She blinked hard, nodded, and pasted on a smile. "But as good as it is, it's also hard when he's away a lot, or gets injured, or anything he says or does or is thought to have said or done gets gossiped about online."

Jackie pressed her lips together. She'd understand.

"Then there's the tension of how much do you share. Like, I have my own career—"

"I love your music," Rachel said.

"Thank you." That was sweet. "And I guess I didn't come unprepared for what fame could look like. But let's just say there's a world of difference between Christian music fans and some people who watch hockey." Sarah's smile turned wry. "The language used isn't always the same." And had resulted in various troll-like social media users being banned. Which didn't stop them, as they just started new accounts. Then there were others who seemed to enjoy posting comments designed to draw attention to their provocative user pictures. Hmm. Maybe it really was time for her to get a virtual assistant.

"People who love hockey—am I right?" Rachel rolled her eyes.

Sarah stiffened. "It *is* a fun game."

"Oh, I didn't mean to make it sound like that. Sorry. It's just that my husband Damian is *addicted* to the sport. He's probably watching the playoff game now with John, and fan-girling over your husband like you wouldn't believe. He's a big Brent Karlsson fan—and Dan Walton fan, too," she winked, "so he's probably like a little kid in Disneyland right now, sitting there with one of his heroes."

Sarah's lips curved to one side. She wondered how Dan was coping with that. There was a world of difference between being able to watch something for pleasure, and feeling like you were still "on" in front of others and still having to perform. Which was a bit like how she felt now.

"Sarah, I've really loved your music, and I've really enjoyed your podcast too," Jackie said sincerely. "Especially that recent one on thankfulness. It's so true, isn't it? It's easy to only be thankful in the good times, but so hard to remember in the tough times."

There was a chorus of *Amens*, including a loud one from Anna, which drew everyone's attention.

"What?" Anna said. "I'm agreeing like you all were. Sometimes it's hard to practice what you preach. I bet even Sarah would agree."

"It is," Sarah said quietly. "I certainly don't have it all together."

Thankfulness. It brought back memories of something Dan had once said to her, about choosing to be thankful. Even with the recent challenges, there was a choice: look at what she didn't have, or remember what she did, like a wonderful husband, a beautiful life, a dream career, but most importantly, she had God's love. Why was that so easy to forget?

Her eyes pricked with emotion, and she lowered her head to sip her drink.

"I think we should give Sarah a break for a moment," Serena said kindly.

"Amen," Sarah murmured, which drew some smiles.

The conversation soon drifted to other things, giving Sarah a moment to compose herself. She caught Staci's glance and offered a small smile, then cut some of the camembert cheese and placed it on a cracker. Food she wasn't supposed to eat while she was pregnant. It didn't matter now, so she might as well enjoy. Something to be thankful for. *Thanks, God.* She rolled her eyes at herself.

Later, Staci switched seats and murmured, "I didn't mean to put you under the spotlight like that."

"It's okay."

"And just so you know I won't include you in a book."

"I appreciate it. I don't think people would think my story that interesting."

"You're wrong there. A girl who grew up in the remote mountains of a country most people have never heard of, who then marries an NHL star? Yeah, that's interesting."

Sarah shrugged. "It's just my normal."

"But not most people's, hence the interest."

"How did you know that about PNG?"

"You have a Wikipedia page, and a few places where your bio is mentioned. It's not that hard to find."

Huh. Sarah traced the stitching in the white leather couch. "Sometimes it seems like a different life."

Staci nodded. "James, my husband, says the same about his time working in Africa. Maybe you and Dan should come over for dinner sometime. I bet you and James would have a lot in common."

Maybe they would. "Thanks. I'll mention it to Dan."

Staci smiled.

A baby cried.

Sarah stiffened, then noticed Staci had also stilled, her smile fading.

"Are you okay?" she asked Staci.

Staci glanced behind her, then said in a lower voice, "I thought it was safe to come tonight."

"What do you mean?"

"Jackie said she'd leave the baby with Lincoln, but…" Staci bit her lip then looked at Sarah. "You don't have a child, do you? Like a secret baby you're keeping off social media that nobody knows about?"

Her heart panged. "No."

Staci sighed. "This will make me sound like such a bad Christian, but sometimes I can't stand being around women who seem to live in a baby bubble, especially when I," she gulped, "when I have endometriosis and can't fall pregnant."

"I'm so sorry." An overwhelming urge to comfort her saw Sarah hug her, then whisper, "The doctors told me after the car accident when my fiancé died that the surgeries meant that I'd never have children. I've since had three miscarriages, so I know how hard it is to struggle with envy."

Staci clutched her tighter, and they stayed that way for a long moment, until the other room noise ceased, and Sarah realized how it must look for her to be hugging a near stranger like this. She gently pulled away, wiped her eyes. Saw Staci do the same.

"Everything okay over there?" Jackie asked.

"Yep," Staci said, then added in a softer voice to Sarah, "You should talk about that on your podcast."

She should. Why women felt a sense of shame in not fulfilling some people's idea of womanhood was one of those hard things rarely talked about, especially as a Christian. How many people suffered from fertility issues, or suffered the pain of miscarriage in silence?

"I'm still figuring out how to get a godly perspective on this," she admitted. "And how to talk about it when Dan wants to keep things private."

Staci winced. "So that's what you meant before." She nodded. "I get it. I really do. You have to be real, but not too real. Vulnerability is hard, especially in this world of trolls."

"You're preaching to the choir here."

"What are you two talking about?" Anna asked.

"Social media challenges," Sarah said.

"And how she and James have missionary backgrounds, so might need to swap stories one day," Staci added.

"You were a missionary?" Rachel asked.

"A missionary's daughter," Sarah corrected. Then was forced to explain what life was like in the highlands of Papua New Guinea.

"Wow, that sounds almost as rustic as the Lodge."

"The what?" Sarah asked.

"Muskoka Ferns Lodge." Anna shuddered.

"Last year's scandal," Rachel said. "The Lodge was supposed to be a place where high risk elderly people could live out their twilight years in beautiful Muskoka, but it was a scam."

"So awful," Serena murmured.

Anna winced. "I feel so bad. My family knew the people who were ripping everyone off, but nobody knew what they were doing. Until Joel mentioned something to Tom, my fiancé, and got the ball rolling."

"The wrecking ball," Staci murmured.

"Damian, my husband, said it was criminal that such a place existed," Rachel added. "We were all at a fundraising ball last summer when the Craylings got busted."

"Oh, I think I remember something now." Brief glimpses. She'd been caught in the pangs of grief of her second miscarriage to pay too much attention to local Muskoka news. "What happened to all the people who'd been living there?"

"They got shifted to various other homes," Jackie said. "I know Golden Elms took a couple in short-term, but most were moved back to larger facilities in the city."

"It's so sad when they came to Muskoka hoping to escape that," Serena said.

Sarah's heart stirred with compassion. How awful that these poor people were without a home. "I wish there was a way to help them."

"There used to be," Anna said. "My mom was on a charity fundraising committee called the Musko-cheers."

"Cute name."

Anna's nose wrinkled. "She was so embarrassed to be associated with the Craylings that she resigned. In fact, everyone involved in the Musko-cheers was so ashamed that they haven't dared do anything again. And honestly some of the ladies are a little more elderly so I think they won't ever want to put their hand up to do any form of fundraising again."

"That's such a shame," Jackie murmured.

Anna nodded. "Especially when they've done a lot of good with their fundraising over the years." She glanced at Sarah. "Last year's ball was supposed to support the Lodge, but last I heard all the money has been frozen until all the legalities are complete. Which might take years."

"So all those people are still without a proper home?" Sarah asked.

"They've got a more proper home than what they had,"

Rachel said. "Damian said some of them were sleeping in what looked like pig pens."

"That's terrible!" Her heart swelled with indignation. Oh, it'd be good to fix it up and help them in some way.

"Right?" Anna shook her head. "The Lodge is up for sale, but nobody wants to touch it. It used to be an old campground, and while it has a few useable buildings, most of it is unlivable."

"We should pray for a solution," Serena said.

Sarah nodded, catching Jackie's pressed lips and bowed head, before closing her own eyes as Serena prayed aloud.

"Lord, we ask that You be with all those poor people who have been affected by the awful conditions of Muskoka Ferns. Bring righteousness and justice and healing to them, and use us for Your purposes. Amen."

"Amen," Sarah echoed, even as Serena's last five words continued to bounce around her heart *Lord, use me for Your purposes.*

She opened her eyes, glanced around the room, and smiled as peace filled her. She might be friends with a number of the women who were married to Dan's friends in the online Bible study of Original Six players, but being friends with the women here felt like a God-ordained thing too.

CHAPTER 11

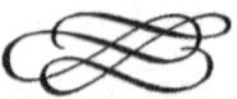

"So you enjoyed going to Staci and James's tonight, then?" Dan glanced over at Sarah as they drove back to the cottage.

"Okay, okay. You were right. Just like you were about me going to Jackie's last week too."

"Mister Right, remember?" he teased, recalling a long-ago conversation.

"Mister Right who is obviously so insecure that he needs to keep pointing it out all the time," she grumbled.

He laughed. "What's got you all riled?"

"Nothing. Sorry."

He arched his brow. "I thought you just said you enjoyed tonight?"

"I did. I don't know if it makes me a bad person to appreciate the fact that others have gone through the emotional wringer, but hearing James's story made me appreciate a few more things."

"I don't know that I'd be so upbeat after having had people shoot at me."

James's honesty had surprised Dan. His willingness to talk

about his mental and emotional breakdown after serving in Africa as a medical missionary had given Dan new respect for the power of honest sharing.

"Do you think he'll ever want to go back?"

"I don't think so." Even though the worlds could hardly contrast more. From poverty to wealth. Fear to relative safety. "Do you think your parents would ever want to go back to PNG?"

"No."

"Would you?" he asked, curious.

She glanced at him, as the lights of various houses washed paleness over her face. "I was just a child when we left, so no, not really. Sometimes it feels like a dream. Like it wasn't really real."

"And now?"

She turned more fully in her seat. Smiled at him. "Well, after last night, I think I'd much rather live in this reality."

"Me too." His heart thudded. Last night had proved a special time for both of them. He picked up her hand and kissed it. "I'd be very happy to revisit that again tonight."

She laughed, and his soul seemed to relax a little more. It had been a long time since he'd heard her laugh the way she had in the last week, ever since she'd returned from Jackie's with a smile, then proceeded to tell him about the funny conversations there.

"Is that a no?" he mock-complained.

"That's a 'we'll see.' It depends on whether your brother has finally decided to appear."

His brother. Sam. He'd been on quite the spiritual journey in recent years, and his on again, off again relationship with a local photographer was currently off. Dan had sent him an invitation to join them in Muskoka, and Sam had said he'd try to show sometime in the next few days, but Dan had come to not trust too much of what his brother said.

"I think we'd be safe."

"You say that, but I can just picture us having fun married times and he knocks on the door, or worse, doesn't knock, and just barges in."

"Sam do that? You're right. He would."

"See? So that kind of kills any amorous mood I might be feeling."

"Amorous mood, huh?"

Her glance at him held fire. "Very amorous."

His breath hitched. He pressed down on the accelerator. Okay, he was getting them home, pronto.

Muskoka was slowly getting them back to where they used to be. At ease with each other, relaxed, comfortable, tease as much as affection signaling their relationship was deep. They'd been friends first, then attraction had set in. He'd fallen first, while Sarah had battled with what a new relationship meant about her feelings for her dead fiancé. But he'd had no doubts about her feelings since. She'd made that very clear on their wedding night. And every other night she could too. And it was only his husbandly duty to reciprocate. Which was what he planned to do as soon as they got home.

MORNING LIGHT STREAMED across the sheets. Last night's muggy temperatures, along with their adventures, meant they were tangled. But then they always were with Sarah. Her sister had warned him before they were married that Sarah liked to burrow into the bedcovers, creating a nest. He glanced across, smiling as she lay there, true to form. One arm under the pillow, the other hand bunching the sheet up to her chin, her eyes buttoned shut in that way he found adorable. "I love you, Sarah."

She smiled, her eyes still closed. "I love you too."

He could stare at her all day. The curve to her cheek that was approaching its normal fullness. The milky white of her shoulder, with its smattering of tiny freckles. She'd always said she found the contrast between their skin tones interesting, and that she'd wished her fair skin didn't burn or show embarrassment so easily. He loved that it made her easy to read.

She was beautiful. And relaxed in their bed like this, after all the weeks of tears and fears, it fueled hope that one day they might find a way forward.

A noise came from outside. He frowned. What—?

He drew on his boxers and went downstairs. The window revealed a sports car out the front. He instantly pivoted, then rushed up the stairs. "Hey, Princess?"

"Mmm?" She stretched, and slowly blinked open her eyes. "Is my handsome husband here to have his way with me again?" She smiled provocatively.

He exhaled. She was tempting. Oh, so tempting. He'd locked the doors, but he didn't trust Sam not to break in. "It's Sam. But I can send him away."

Her eyes widened, all trace of seduction gone. "He's here?"

"I've locked the doors, but—"

"Hey, lovebirds! Let me in!"

Her mouth sagged. Then she pushed him away. "Go! Go fend him off. I'm not dressed."

Dan eyed her appreciatively as she slipped from the bed and dragged on clothes. "I can lock this door, too—"

"Go!"

He laughed, and pulled on shorts and a tee, then descended the stairs, and opened the front door. "Sam?"

"Finally!" Sam clasped him in a bear hug. Pounded him on the back. "Good to see you, bro."

"You too." Even though Sam smelled like a brewery. His red-rimmed eyes looked like he'd slept at one too.

"I wasn't sure you were here. Then I started wondering if maybe you and Sarah were getting your frisky on and couldn't hear me."

Dan's cheeks burned.

Sam laughed. "Ha! So I was right. Where is she?"

"She'll be down soon. She was asleep."

Sam instantly looked contrite. "Oh, I didn't mean to wake her. Mom told me she'd been unwell. How is she?"

"Doing better."

"Good." Sam's head tilted. "But it *is* almost ten."

"Exactly. What are you doing here so early?"

Sam punched him in the arm. "You invited me, remember? So here I am. Hey, any chance for a coffee? The line at Suzy's was insane, which is what I'll be if I don't get caffeinated soon."

"You drive up from the city?"

"Yep."

Dan eyed him. "You okay?"

Sam shrugged. "I don't know."

"What's wrong?"

"Nothing. Hey, here she is." He swept Sarah up in a hug. "How's my favorite sister-in-law?"

She smacked him, laughing. "Shh, you're not supposed to say that out loud."

"Circle of trust here," Sam said, making a looping gesture between the three of them. "And at least Marguerite is nicer than her husband, who always acts like he has a stick up his—"

"Sam, play nice," Sarah interrupted. "Now, how long are you here for?"

"As long as you'll have me."

"What happened to your job?"

Sam winced. "Oh, did the family gossip forget to tell you I got fired from the real estate office?"

"What?"

He shoved his hands in his pockets. "It was a misunderstanding."

Of course it was. Dan folded his arms. It always was with Sam. Since a hip injury derailed his pro hockey aspirations, he'd had a series of jobs that had all ended too soon. He always laid out the other person's faults and waited for someone to bite.

Like Sarah. "What happened?"

Sam went on with some convoluted story, which soon saw Sarah bite her lip and meet Dan's gaze, as if she too recognized what Sam wasn't saying.

"Does that mean you're a free agent?" she asked Sam.

"You could say that."

"Then you're free to go with Dan on his camp this weekend?"

Sam's nose wrinkled. "That's this weekend?"

"Sure is." Dan clapped him on the back. "And you know we always love you being there."

Sam glanced at Sarah. "Are you going?"

She pointed to a fridge magnet which Dan hated but she refused to remove. The vintage looking woman was smiling in bed, with a "I love not camping" banner posted over it.

"Then I'll stay with you."

She smiled sweetly. "No."

"Huh?"

"You need to go camping. With Dan."

"Excuse me?"

"I can smell the alcohol on you, and I don't know what's going down, but I don't want you staying here with me if you think that means you'll just be drinking or whatever."

Go Sarah.

Dan leaned against the kitchen cupboard as his brother whined, "Sarah, I thought you loved me."

"I do." She patted his cheek. "Which is why real love doesn't let someone keep doing the wrong thing."

"It's not wrong to have a drink."

"I know. But if you're drinking so much that it can be smelled the next day, one has to ask why you feel the need to do so."

"I didn't come here for a lecture," he grumbled.

"No, you came here because you know we love you and want the best for you. And this," she gestured to his rumpled appearance, "isn't it."

"Wow." Sam glanced at Dan. "Does she bust your chops like this too?"

"Sometimes."

"Go, have a shower, and we'll make you a nice brekkie."

"Brekkie." Sam rolled his eyes, but a smile played at his mouth. "Will you have avocado toast?"

"Yes, but whether there's any left depends on how long you take."

He chuckled. "I've missed you."

She smiled. "I'm glad you're here."

Sam glanced at Dan. "At least she is."

"Hey, I'm glad you're here too."

"I promise not to get in the way of your married people time."

Sarah pointed to the stairs, her cheeks pink. "Hurry up, else there will be no avo toast for you."

"You're such an Aussie still, with your brekkie and avo."

"Of course I am. Now go."

He saluted her, then murmured, "she's tough," at Dan then disappeared.

"Was I too tough?" she asked, wrapping her arms around his waist.

He kissed her nose. "You were exactly what you needed to be. Like his big sister."

"Hmm." She smiled. "I've never been the big sister, so that was kind of fun." She sobered. "He didn't look good, did he?"

"He's obviously got some stuff going down."

"Good thing we can take him in, and he can go with you on the camp this weekend."

"You think he'll be sober enough by then?"

"I think we won't give him a choice."

He pressed a kiss to her hair. He loved this woman. She was so good for him, and good for his family.

JUST AS SARAH PREDICTED, Sam joined him and Boyd and a few others on the camp. But whether it was the rain, or concern about precisely what influence Sam would have on impressionable teens, or the fact that Dan was just getting old, Dan found his usual enjoyment of camping with the teens wasn't there. It wasn't because of Sarah's absence. As she'd explained after her first camp, she had zero plans to do that ever again. And even the lure of huge stars and marshmallows cooked over an open fire held zero appeal. But even though the past few years he'd managed okay being away from her for a few days, this year felt different.

His body ached, reminding him that he only had a little more hockey in him before he should retire. Or maybe it was missing his wife, with that profound sense of connection they'd started sharing again prior to Sam's arrival. But every time he thought about encouraging Sam to move on, something within him—he thought it might be the Holy Spirit—begged him to refrain.

After packing off the last of the campers he drove home, thankful he'd see Sarah, thankful that there'd be another person to intervene between Boyd's rigidity and Sam's looseness. Boyd was a lot better than a few years ago, but he still held some judgmental attitudes, and hadn't understood why Dan would want to bring Sam along when Sam was hardly living like Jesus. Well, considering Jesus had hung out with sinners, Dan figured Sam was actually not doing too bad a job in some regards, but explaining that to Boyd was a step too far.

Dan turned into his drive, then glanced at Sam, slumped against the passenger door. "Hey, I'm glad you came."

"I don't think Boyd was."

"It doesn't matter now. The guys were glad for someone to bring the fun factor."

"That's me. Bringing the fun factor, even if I don't bring much else."

"Whoa." Dan turned into his drive, then soon parked. "Hey, what's that about?"

Sam shrugged.

"You were pretty quiet during the studies." Dan opened the door. They probably had a few minutes before Boyd joined them. "Are you still going to church?"

Sam looked across at him guiltily. "Did I forget to tell you?"

"Tell me what?"

"I've started attending a Jehovah's Witness group."

"What?" His chest grew tight. "Why?"

Sam shrugged. "You got me sort of interested in God, and these guys who live next door invited me round, got me reading their bible, their magazine. It makes a lot of sense."

No, this didn't. How could his brother, whom he thought was this close to getting saved, suddenly do a backflip and start seeking law? They didn't even believe in Jesus as God's Son, did they?

Sam was looking at him in concern. "You don't seem too happy. What's the problem?"

Dan sighed. *Lord, help me with this.* "Uh, I really want to talk to you about this, but right now I need to check on Sarah. Give me a moment?"

Dan walked off, trying to release the tension, hoping he could talk some sense to his brother. JWs? Unbelievable. *God, what are you doing?*

Again he felt that strange sense, like God was talking to him: **Rest in Me.**

Dan hauled in a breath, tried to be still, but the questions swirling around his heart refused peace. He entered the house. "Sar?"

No sound.

He hurried up the stairs. "Sar bear?" She didn't like that name, did she? "Princess?"

He opened the door, then halted. She was asleep on the bed. "Sar?" He stole over to her. "I'm back." He pressed a kiss to her neck.

She shrieked, jerked, then slammed her head back, catching his nose.

"Ow!" What a welcome.

"Oh my gosh, Dan! What are you doing?"

He rubbed his nose. "I was saying hello to my wife."

She exhaled, her fingers splayed across her chest. "My heart is thumping so fast."

"I startled you. Sorry."

"No, I'm sorry. I don't know what happened. I didn't plan to fall asleep." She yawned.

"Is everything okay?"

"Yes, yes. I just dozed off. Anyway, how are you? How did it go?" She shifted to hug him. "I'm so glad to see you."

The ache in his nose faded as he kissed her properly. Then her response made him realize they were in bed, and were married, and being away at the camp had felt a lot longer than three days, and—

"Ugh! Gross. Shut the door next time," Sam called, before a thud suggested he'd done exactly that.

Sarah looped her hands around Dan's neck. "Do you think he'll stay away long enough?"

"Long enough for what?"

"For a proper hello," she purred.

He kissed her, then scampered off the bed and locked the door. "He will now."

She laughed. "Good."

CHAPTER 12

$\mathcal{D}$inner that night was a funny affair, Dan and Boyd trying to conduct something of a camp debrief, while they all tiptoed around the bombshell that Sam had announced that he was attending a Jehovah's Witness study. Boyd had tried to argue, to no avail. Sarah had murmured to Dan to "just love him," but she wasn't sure if that was enough. He'd been so excited when his little brother had accepted Jesus as his Lord and Savior and started following Him, so to see him veer from the path as he had was concerning.

The way Boyd was carrying on suggested he wouldn't stop. Dog with a bone, was he. But Sam's face suggested he was getting agitated, and that a change of subject was necessary.

"So, Sam, how are things going with Alexa?" she asked.

But judging from the tightness in his face, this line of questioning wasn't much better. "She wanted me to commit, but I wasn't ready, so we're on another break."

"You're nearly thirty, Sam. When are you going to be ready?" Dan asked.

Sam shot him a look. "You didn't even date until my age."

"Because I was waiting for perfection," Dan said, kissing her hand.

"And then when he didn't find it, he settled for me," Sarah joked, which scored a laugh from the others.

"Nobody is perfect, only God," Boyd said.

Sam rolled his eyes as Dan smothered a smile.

Sarah bit back one of her own and nodded. "That's very true. Oh well. It's a good thing God loves us anyway, isn't it?"

Boyd grunted, which she took as an affirmation. "So, what do you think next year's camp will look like?"

"Next year?" Dan groaned. "Come on, Princess. My body is so sore from this year I'm going to need twelve months to forget how much pain I'm in."

Concern panged. "You're that sore?" He certainly hadn't seemed that way when he'd first arrived home.

He sighed, and she suddenly saw new little lines in his face. Had the camp put those there? Or had the trials of the past few years been responsible for this added 'character'?

"You are getting older now," Boyd said. "And I have to agree that it's not quite the same at thirty-five as when we were ten years younger."

"Thirty-five?" Dan protested. "Speak for yourself, man."

"Look, I'm just saying that none of us are getting any younger. And, look, I didn't want to say this now, but I suppose I should, Jo and I are expecting a little bundle of joy this Christmas—"

Her heart cramped.

"—and I don't know if I can commit to doing next year."

"Congratulations," Dan said.

She echoed it, stealing a glance at Dan. He was pale, but seemed determined to not let anything of their frustrations spoil Boyd's moment. So, neither would she.

But as Boyd went on and on about it, it grew harder to pretend not to care. She tried to remind herself to be thankful, that God loved her, which helped somewhat. But still, he kept talking.

She peeked at Dan, saw his arms folded and brow puckered. She half-smiled at him, he half-smiled back, but the pain in his eyes reflected that living in her heart.

Then finally Boyd turned to Dan and said, "So, when are you two going to get on with starting a family?"

Grief slashed her chest, and she pressed her lips together.

Boyd lifted his chin at Sarah. "I suppose you're too busy with all your Heartsong things to want to give that up any time soon."

Oh, if only that were the case. She'd give it up in a heartbeat if she could. She blinked back tears. Saw through blurry eyes that Dan's jaw was clenched, and that Sam kept glancing between them.

She fake-coughed. Stitched a smile to her dial and stood. "Can I get anyone some dessert?"

"I'll help you." Dan got up, and they moved to the kitchen, then wrapped their arms around each other.

She closed her eyes as the heartache from earlier faded in Dan's arms. He might be in pain, but his arms remained strong, his chest was sturdy, his heart was sure. Moments like this felt like they were Team Walton, Dan and Sar against the world. Not that they were against the world, or the world was against them, but just being together, understanding, standing together, was a real blessing.

"You two okay in here?" Sam asked.

"Yep." She let go of Dan, found a smile, and aimed it at his brother. "We'll be out in a moment."

His eyes narrowed slightly, then he nodded, and exited.

"Does he know?" she asked Dan.

"About the miscarriage?"

She nodded.

"I think so. Mom said she'd mention it to him."

They gathered the ice cream and berries and took bowls and spoons out so people could serve themselves. But her steps paused, as the sound of a hushed argument came to their ears.

"—have you thought what it's like for them to hear someone carrying on like that?" Sam swore. "I always knew you were self-absorbed, but man, can't you have a bit of compassion?"

Oh no. She glanced between them, then at Dan.

Boyd's face held shock. "Is what he said true?" he pointed at Sam.

"Depends on what he said." Dan's voice held a growl.

Boyd glanced at Sarah. "Did you have a miscarriage?"

She pressed her lips together. Nodded.

"Oh, man." He looked at Dan. "Why didn't you say anything?"

"Because we didn't want people to know," Dan gritted out.

"But… but I'm your friend." Boyd's face wore hurt. "Jo and I, we love you guys. I can't believe we didn't know."

She ducked her head. Jo was her friend. And hurting others like this was one of the unfortunate consequences of not telling people about their loss.

"I can't believe you didn't tell us," Boyd said again.

"Says the man who didn't tell them his wife was pregnant until now," Sam sniped.

"But—oh." Boyd winced.

"Exactly."

"Oh, man. Dan, Sarah, I'm sorry. I, uh, I feel really bad for going on about it all. If I'd known, I never would have said anything."

"Don't go making this about you again," Sam warned.

"I'm not."

"Can't you see that they're upset and too polite to tell you to stop? Good thing I'm not."

That was for sure. "Sam," she began.

"No, don't tell me to shut up," Sam said, eyes lasered on

Boyd. "Mister Holier-than-thou, Mister I'm-such-a-great-Christian has the insensitivity of a bear. You really need to learn to read the room, buddy."

Boyd's face held chagrin. "I didn't know." He lifted his hands helplessly. "Dan, Sarah, I'm sorry."

Dan shook his head. "I didn't want people to know. I thought it was better to wait, rather than have to deal with all the sympathy if it didn't work out."

Boyd glanced between them. "And how did that work out for you?"

Ouch. A peek at Dan showed clamped lips, like he too was struggling to find words that held an ounce of grace. Sam had his head in his hands, elbows on knees and was shaking his head.

Wonderful. So apparently this was her moment to be the bigger person. "Actually, I don't think there's any right or wrong way," she said. She glanced again at Dan, but his face remained averted. "This was actually our third miscarriage—"

"Third?"

She ignored Sam's gasp, focusing on Boyd. "And it hasn't been easy. So trying to manage our emotions, to not upset others, to support each other, and still trust God through it all, has been incredibly hard. And you know what? We probably could have done things better. But this is us, imperfect us, doing the best we can."

Tears clogged her nose, her throat. She sniffed them back, swallowed. "And I'm sorry if us not telling you makes you feel left out, but like I said, we're imperfect people just trying to figure this out and live in God's love and His promises. And that means it sometimes gets messy along the way."

Dan's jaw tilted, then he swiftly wiped his eyes.

Sam swiped his eyes too, then turned to his brother and hugged him.

Her heart wrenched and she blinked back her own tears,

savoring the moment, as Dan slowly wrapped his brother in a hug. Then Sam pounded him on the back and released him, and hugged Sarah, while Boyd took his own turn at hugging Dan.

"I'm so sorry you've gone through this," Sam murmured.

"It's okay." She rubbed his back. "Like I said, I know that God still loves us, and has good plans for us. We just need to keep trusting Him."

He crouched in a little closer, and just when she thought his hug was going on a little too long, she felt his tears wet her hair.

"What's wrong?" she whispered.

He sniffed.

Oh, she wished Dan could help, but a peek across the table showed he and Boyd were caught in sober conversation. "Sam? You can tell me."

"I wish I could trust Him," he murmured.

Oh, Lord. Touch his heart. "You can."

She pulled back, studying him, this man who might look like Dan, but was a boy still in many ways. "Sam, you know that God loves you. You've felt His love before. Actually, you've *known* God's love before. Because faith isn't about how you're feeling."

His lips pressed together.

Lord, help me say this right. "This past year I've cried so much, I've struggled—I still struggle—with questions, and frustration, and envy, and doubt, but deep down I still know that God loves me. It's like a full stop—oops, another Australianism there—it's like a period at the end of a sentence. God loves me. *God,*" she pointed to the night sky, "loves me. God *loves* me." She clenched her hand over her heart. "God loves *me.*"

How wondrous and impossible and awe-filling and humbling that was. Her eyes filled with tears.

"I know that God loves me. And I know that God loves you, Sam. Period."

He opened his mouth as if to protest, but she shook her head.

"It's not about how good you are, or how much you have it together. Being perfect doesn't impress God because He knows none of us are. All God wants is for us to repent from doing things our own way, and let Jesus be the Lord of our lives and for us to follow Him. He's not asking for much." Her lips tweaked up. "Just your life."

His lips flickered into a smile that quickly faded. "But I walked away."

"So walk back. He's there, waiting, His hand is always stretched out toward you. Just take it."

He shuddered out a breath. "I've really messed up though."

"He still loves you."

"I mean, I've really done some dumb things."

"You don't honestly think that's taken God by surprise, do you? If God loved a man called Paul who was killing Christians, and then used him to write a quarter of the books in the New Testament, don't you think He can love and use you too?"

"Well, I haven't killed anyone."

"That's good. Well done."

He snickered. "You're a smart-alec."

"You're a bigger one."

He laughed.

"You know what we need to do?" She beckoned for Dan to join them. "We need to pray. Right now. And you," she pointed to Sam, "need to repent again and ask God to show you His love and His plans for you. Okay?"

"Okay," he agreed meekly.

"Have I ever mentioned how amazing you are?" Dan murmured to her later that night when they were in bed.

"A few times."

"You're amazing." He kissed her throat. "I can't believe that one little talk with you and bang, Sam is ready to recommit his life."

"Come on." She pulled away. "He'd just spent the last three days with his big brother and Boyd and hearing all this stuff about how great God is. God was prepping the soil. I was just there at the end."

He sighed. "I thank God for you."

"And I thank God for you."

He kissed her thoroughly. Then groaned, wincing as he eased back.

Concern roiled within. She stroked his cheek. "Are you okay?"

"Man, I know that I sound like an old man when I complain, but my body really feels so much more sore this time round."

"Maybe you do need to do the camp differently. Especially if Boyd is not around."

Dan exhaled, and rolled away, popping his neck and shoulders before settling on the pillow. "I just hate to give it up. It's been such a blessing and touched so many lives."

"Boyd mentioned that Travis was a junior leader this year."

"Yeah. He and Georgia are still going strong." He sighed. "That's why I don't feel like it's something I should just stop. But my body says I can't keep doing this anymore."

She turned to face him, head propped on her hand. "Are you saying you want to try glamping with them instead?"

He rolled his eyes. "I'm not a glamper."

She snickered. "Could've fooled me. I've seen that you don't mind a bit of luxury when you can get it."

"That's only because my wife refuses to tent again."

"It's sleeping bags and air mattresses I have a problem with," she corrected.

"They don't all have mice."

"Once was enough. I now have trust issues. And I'm okay with that."

He laughed. Then sighed. "I wish I knew what to do."

"Hey, God knows what to do."

"Then I wish He'd tell me. I felt like a liar today telling them that we'd be back next year when every molecule in my body was protesting the idea."

Hmm. "Lord," she prayed aloud. "What is Your solution?"

She closed her eyes, and silence filled the room. Dan was quiet, too. Then a conversation trickled back to awareness. Her breathing hitched.

"What is it, Sar?"

Lord? "Probably nothing."

"But possibly something?"

"Possibly." She told him about the conversation that she'd heard at Jackie's about the former campsite, and how it had housed poor elderly people who had been scammed. "I remember thinking at the time how awful it was for them, and that it'd be awesome to somehow fix the place up and see it get used for housing again. But maybe it'd be better for your camp."

"There's plenty of camps up this way."

"Yes, but most of those are the glamorous types, with all the facilities and things. Not the tents and *Survivor*-like type you're so fond of."

"But that's the thing. I don't think I can do *Survivor*-style anymore."

"But maybe you could tweak it so it's better sleeping accommodation, with the option of tents for those who want it, and still do your rustic stuff."

"Maybe."

He was silent for a long moment. Why was she saying all this? She'd be more than happy to keep Dan to herself. But he was right. Seeing how people like Travis and Georgia had grown so much in God since she and Dan had encountered them at their first camp all those years ago, well, it'd be cruel to stop it. Cruel to stop the chance for someone to find hope in God, like Sam had rediscovered tonight.

Then he heaved out another sigh. "Sar, I like your enthusiasm, but how do we even know it's suitable?"

"Someone—Anna, I think—said it was once used as a campground. So I guess it wouldn't be too hard to return it to that again."

"If it's available."

"I got the impression from what the others were saying that apparently the locals aren't fans because of what's happened before. So you might be able to find an estate agent who'd be very happy to negotiate the price with you."

"Where is it?"

A few moments later they were peering at some images of the old Muskoka Ferns site on his phone. The mix of rugged terrain, lake frontage, and assortment of buildings certainly didn't scream luxury. Certainly didn't scream appropriate accommodation for the vulnerable in any way, shape or form. But as Dan flicked through the pictures, she sensed his interest. Certain pictures showed scenes that didn't look too dissimilar to the campsite Dan used that she recalled from her trip before.

She pointed to one picture of a white, weathered tree lying on a sandy shore. "Look, it even has similar trees like I remember."

"I remember that too." He smiled at her, then returned to frowning at the pictures, then put his phone away.

"Hmm."

"What are you thinking?" she murmured in the darkness.

"I can't believe we're even talking about this."

"Hey, you wanted a solution. We prayed, and God reminded me of this. It may come to nothing, or may just be something that opens your eyes to thinking about the camp in a different way."

"You've always been able to help me see things in a different way. That's one of the things I love about you." He nuzzled her neck, and soon all thoughts of camps or anything else fled, except for how good it was to be back in Dan's arms, kissing him, feeling the deepest sense of connection, until they were both exhausted and slept.

Later, she woke, the soft snuffles of Dan's snores bringing a smile to her lips. Poor man was exhausted. And considering all the hits he took on the ice, he did deserve a good sleep. Both now, and for any future camp experience.

She lay there, thinking over their earlier conversation. Was the use of the old Muskoka Ferns property a God-given answer to Dan's dilemma? Maybe.

Lord, if it's Your will, make it plain, and make a way.

Then another thought hit. If Dan was somehow able to use the site, then what would that mean for all those poor people who had been kicked out? Was there a God solution to both dilemmas? Her heart thumped, suggesting there quite possibly was more than just one use for a site once known for corruption. But then, God was a Redeemer, and liked to use broken things for His purposes, after all.

CHAPTER 13

*D*an paused, the sounds of the piano trickling outside to where he was cleaning his fishing gear. Sarah's song was sounding a lot more polished now, which meant it was probably time to talk about the possibility of a Heartsong tour again. Not that he wanted her to leave him for weeks again. But she had to follow God's call on her life, just as he needed to as well.

Which was what? Hockey? He still needed his agent to call and confirm if a new deal had been offered. But even so, he didn't want to do this forever. But then what would he do? Study? Run a campsite? He scoffed at himself. He wasn't such a people-person that he'd be great at that. Sarah was definitely the friendlier of the two of them. And while she might thrive on doing something like that, he could see that slowly killing him. Which left what? *Lord?*

He grimaced. So many things to talk about, not least of which was the ramifications of not telling their friends about their troubles getting pregnant. Boyd wasn't the only one who'd be upset. His friends in the online Bible study group, men he regarded as brothers who played in other Original Six teams, he needed to share this with them too. Most of them might have families now, but he could count on them to pray, that they'd care, they'd be sensitive.

Poor Boyd. He probably hadn't meant to sledgehammer his way through the conversation. But that was the price of not telling people. People then couldn't know what topics of conversation could hurt. And the fact that something so life-changing, so huge, remained off-limits, or was taboo—he'd never heard the topic of miscarriage come up in one of Pastor Josiah Abraham's Bible talks—meant it continued to hurt more people than those directly affected. Which was perhaps what Sarah had been trying to explain when she'd suggested talking about it on her podcast.

"Dude."

He glanced up. Sam stood, dressed and ready for his important interview today. "Well, look who's trying to make a good impression."

Sam looked shamefaced. "A man's gotta try, right?"

"Absolutely he does. Especially when he's in the wrong."

Sam winced. "I was just figuring myself out."

"And you're all figured out now?"

His brother shrugged. "I'm more figured, but whether she thinks I'm figured out enough remains to be seen."

That it did. Alexa Reddick was Dan and Sarah's wedding photographer, who Sam had bumped into at a Muskoka Shores pumpkin festival a few years ago. She'd ended up coming to a Christmas meal at his parents', then going to the Philippines with Sam to take photos for Mission Possible for Future Generations, before her burgeoning career had taken her overseas. A Google stalk had revealed she was back in town for the Canada Day celebrations, which meant Sam might have a chance to finally make amends.

"I'm praying for you," Dan offered.

"Thanks. I have a feeling I'll need it."

"Don't we all?"

And that was the truth. In not telling people, people had been deprived of the chance to pray, and to trust God for something beyond themselves.

Sarah's music started again, which tugged Dan's attention again. They really needed to talk. He nodded to his brother. "Well, hope it all goes well."

"Thanks."

Dan finished cleaning up, then walked up the steps to the back deck where the piano music had stopped, and Sarah was now talking on the phone. He paused at the open door.

It might be a public holiday here, but it wasn't everywhere in the world, and her juggle with time zones, not just with family but with the other Heartsong Collective songwriters and collaborators, meant constant awareness of hours in various places.

She nodded, her head away from him. "I know, but I'll talk with him today. I was waiting on a doctor's report, and it's just arrived, so I will talk to him."

Hurt creased his heart. She'd gotten the doctor's report? Why hadn't she told him? Hadn't they agreed to be open and honest about things? Unless she thought the news too devastating to admit to. Her voice sounded a little tense but not too upset, so maybe it was good news.

Hope flickered, a fickle flame. *Please, Lord.* He stepped inside. Sarah looked around, her face brightening. That was something. She wouldn't look like that if she was trying to hide something.

"Mm hm. I need to go. I'll be in contact soon. Thanks, bye." Sarah put her phone down on top of the piano and moved to hug him. He wrapped his arms around her, and they held each other.

He rested his cheek against her hair. "You got the doctor's report?"

She nodded. "It just came in."

"On a public holiday?"

"I think it was sent yesterday, but automated delivery meant it was delayed until now."

"What did it say?"

She pulled back. "I haven't read it. I was waiting for you to return so we could find out together." Her lips twisted wryly. "I might have courage sometimes, but I'm not brave enough for that just yet."

"It might be good news."

"I hope so."

"So do I." He kissed her cheek, then held her a long moment. How would they cope if it wasn't? Probably as they did already. Not very well, imperfectly, as she'd said to Boyd the other day, but trying to trust God.

He exhaled. "We should probably go check, right?"

She nodded. "At least that way we'll know instead of having this question mark hang over us."

"Rip off the band-aid?"

"Then we know what we're dealing with."

"Right."

They moved to the sofa, and he tucked her in his arms as she opened the email app on her phone. "You ready for this?"

Nope. "Sure." *Please Lord.* "Whatever the result, I love you."

She pressed a quick kiss to his lips. "I love you too. And God loves us as well."

He did. Dan needed to remember that.

He watched over her shoulder as she scrolled to her emails and opened the one from Dr. McKinnon. Held his breath as she tapped on the screen and enlarged the font so he could read the words more easily.

The words that said, according to the blood tests, their chromosomes compatibility was very low, and their chances of having a live birth, let alone a healthy baby, was negligible, not a viable option. That any child that might survive would likely have—"brain damage."

Sarah gasped, and he felt himself stiffen. Then his arm clutched her strongly. And she burrowed into his chest.

"I love you, Princess." He stroked her hair as she sobbed next to his heart. His battered, near-broken heart. His own tears escaped, and he thumbed them away. She didn't need to see his tears. He had to be strong, even as his doubts assailed. How could God do this to them? Why could other people fall pregnant and then abort their child, while they desperately wanted one and couldn't? Well, according to this report, they could fall pregnant, but the likelihood of reaching full term was incredibly low.

He might love this woman, they might be a perfect match in so many ways, but it seemed they were incompatible in one of the most fundamental ways, and couldn't have a child together.

Her tears eased, and she hiccupped and then lay her cheek on his chest. He shifted, and they lay on the sofa, her in his arms, as the news sank in.

He wouldn't be a dad. Wouldn't get the chance to make up for the past. And that was something he'd thought he'd dealt with, but life had a way of prodding to see if that wound was truly healed. And God might be Jehovah Rapha, the Lord who healed, but healing wasn't always an easy or quick thing. This would take time to process, time to recover from.

"I love you," he whispered.

She nodded, kissed his hand. "I love you too."

"I'm sorry this isn't what you wanted to hear."

"It's not what either of us wanted."

"But God is still good, right?"

Her voice came as a whisper. "Right."

"And God can still do miracles."

"He can."

It was funny. His heart was bowed, battered, and bruised, yet he sensed these words needed to be said, that their ears, the very atmosphere in this room, needed to be filled with words of faith. "And God still loves us, still has good plans for us."

"Amen."

Amen. He placed a hand over her abdomen. "Lord, heal us."

"Amen."

Rest in me, echoed across his soul. And they slept.

WHEN HE WOKE, it was to empty arms and the sound of a kettle switching off. "Sar?"

"I'm in the kitchen."

He padded out, found her staring out the window, hands clasped around a mug of tea. "How long have you been up?"

"Long enough to realize it's still a beautiful day."

It was. Muskoka shone in all of God's beauty. "Did you want to go into town? See anyone?"

"No."

Silly question. "Did Jackie or Staci or anyone have plans?"

"They mentioned something about watching the fireworks tonight, but," she faced him. "I think I'd rather stay here."

"Did you want to invite John and Ange over?"

"No." Her head tilted. "And I think I'd like to tell Sam not to come over either."

His heart lifted. "And why might that be?"

"Because I might want to spend some quality time with my husband."

"I like how this is going."

"I thought you might."

"You want to create our own fireworks?"

"Yes." She placed her mug down then slid her hands around his neck. "We might not have received the result we wanted, but that doesn't mean we can't still enjoy trying."

"I like the idea of trying."

Some of the light faded from her features, as her gaze turned pensive. "Even if it means we have another miscarriage?"

"Even if it means that."

"Even if we had a child who might have 'limited health outcomes'?" she quoted the report.

"Even that." He pecked her cheeks. "God is still able to do exceedingly abundantly above all we can ask or imagine, right?"

"Right."

"So the doctor's report is just that. A report on what he sees now. Not on what God might be able to do in the future."

"Mm, I like that way of thinking."

"And if it means I get to enjoy you, then I'm totally okay with that too."

She chuckled. "I thought you might be."

A NIGHT of fireworks was followed by more heavy conversations. Dan sensed that with one of the biggest questions over their lives now having been addressed—at least by human standards—that they now shared a sense of resignation, and that leaving things up to God and His plans and timing would have to do. Which meant other aspects of their lives could now move forward and be tackled too.

"I think we need to tell people," he said.

She glanced up at him over the breakfast table. He'd heard Sam come in after midnight, so he hoped that meant things had resolved with Alexa, but he'd be really happy if his little bro didn't make an appearance just yet.

Sarah's eyebrows arched. "Tell them about the miscarriage?"

He nodded. "I felt convicted by what Boyd said. Boyd's reaction made me realize how much others will feel hurt if they don't know. So, I want to tell the guys in the online Bible group."

She nodded. "Okay."

"And if you have anyone you want to tell, then do it soon, before this spills out another way." Like the media.

She bit her lip.

He knew what she hesitated to say. "And yeah, then when everyone knows who needs to know, then I think it's probably a good thing to share on your podcast."

"Really?"

He nodded. "Really. It's the only way to own our story without it being shaped by other people's agendas, so yeah. And like you said before, if it helps others feel a little less alone, then maybe this is what God wants us to do."

"Oh, Dan, thank you." Her hands crossed her heart. "Would you want to come on it with me?"

He'd refused until now. Exposing his private life for others to feast on wasn't his scene. But there wasn't much more personal than exposing infertility issues, was there? "Maybe."

She smiled, then got up from the table and hugged him, her arms around his shoulders as he sat. "I love you."

"I love you too."

Sam entered, but Sarah didn't move. "Am I interrupting?"

"All the time," Dan joked.

"Hey, I left you two to it yesterday. Did you do anything after I left?"

Plenty of things. But he wasn't about to describe that to his brother.

"We caught some fireworks," Sarah said, finally unwrapping Dan from her hug, before shooting him a sexy wink.

Dan stifled a grin. "The more important question is how did things go with Alexa?"

Sam lit up. "She was actually glad to see me. Can you believe it?"

"Well, of *course* she was. You're a catch," Sarah said.

"See? Favorite sister-in-law status right there."

She laughed. And it was like yesterday had put a period on

their grief. Yes, there was sadness, but if God didn't have a baby in their future, then He had to have something better.

"So what are you doing today?"

"It's supposed to be a warm one. I wondered about fishing. You know, with my favorite brother. If my favorite sister-in-law could cope."

"She'd cope if she could come too."

"You want to go fishing?" Dan asked. A Muskoka miracle, right there.

"Not to actually fish," she said. "But if there's swimming involved, and it's such a hot day, why not?"

"Okay then." Huh. This was more like the excitable Sarah he knew.

"I'll pack some lunch, so if there's anything you especially want to have, then sing out."

Sam glanced at Dan. "She's such a musician, huh?"

"You know it."

"Oh! Speaking of," she glanced at Dan, "I meant to talk to you about the Heartsong tour." Her nose wrinkled. "It's in mid-October, so just after the regular season starts, and will run for four weeks. Maybe six if tickets sell."

Six weeks? He hid his disappointment with a dip of his chin. "It starts in Sydney?"

She nodded. "Then goes to Auckland, Manila, then we fly to Durban—"

"Where?" Sam asked.

"South Africa. Then we'd go to London, Paris, then we're doing the North American east coast, the Midwest, then west coast."

"It sounds intense."

She nodded and pushed back her shoulders. "But we've done it in the past, so it's do-able again."

And if there was no pregnancy that could be affected by all

the stress of travel and late nights, then it wouldn't matter. "You really want to do this?"

"If you get signed again, then yes."

"*If?*" Sam scoffed. "Everyone knows he's the best part of that team. You just need to figure out if you want one year or more."

"I don't think this body of mine can take more than one."

"Then that's your answer." Sam rubbed his hands together. "The real question is what will you do next?"

"Why are you looking like that?"

"Because it's exciting. Like, a new stage of life for you. So what do you want to do with the rest of your life?"

Excellent question.

"I mean, you'll probably have bundles of joys popping out of your ears—"

Sarah laughed, then quickly sobered. She glanced at Dan.

Okay. The next moment of transparency was here. "Actually, we just got a doctor's report that suggested that is unlikely."

Sam blinked. "What?"

Dan held Sarah's hand as he explained, to Sam's disbelief.

"No way. I can't believe that." He frowned. "And I can't believe you're both so calm about this."

"We weren't yesterday," Dan admitted.

Sam nodded. "So that explains the text to stay away."

Sarah's hand squeezed Dan's. "It took a bit to come to terms with, but," she glanced at Dan, "we're not choosing to believe it, are we?"

He kissed her hand. "Nope. God can still do miracles."

"One hundred percent," Sam said, even as his brow wrinkled.

The room grew silent, as Sam continued to frown at Sarah. Sarah glanced between him and Dan. She lifted her brows, and Dan shrugged. Nope, he didn't know what was going on with his little bro, either.

Sam finally blew out a breath. "Huh."

"What?" Dan asked.

Sam peered at them. "Nothing."

"That's not nothing," Sarah countered. "What? Why are you looking at me like that?"

"It's just a weird thought I had."

"Hey, you know us. We're okay with weird."

"I've been used to weird thoughts from you all my life," Dan teased.

Sarah snickered as Sam—fortunately—broke into a smile. He looked at Sarah again. "Look, you can say no, because I sure as heck want to, but I just felt this weird feeling to pray for you."

Emotion clamped Dan's throat. Was that his *brother* saying that?

Sarah seemed similarly touched as she sniffled. "Why would I say no to that? Go on then. Pray."

He looked awkward. "But I felt like I should put my hand on you."

"Then do so."

Sam winced. "Like, on your stomach."

"Well, that *is* weird, and I'm guessing you haven't thought to do that before, so that might just be from God."

Sam glanced at Dan, as if asking for his permission. Dan nodded. So Sam tentatively placed a hand on Sarah's abdomen. Dan covered his hand, then Sarah placed hers on top of his, as Sam then cleared his throat.

"Hey God, we know You can do anything, like change a life, or even raise the dead to life. So we ask that You prove the doctors wrong and bring new life. Like Jesus did. In Jesus' name. Amen."

"Amen," Sarah echoed.

Amen, Dan agreed, but couldn't speak, his throat was too tight.

Sarah exhaled, wiped away tears, then hugged Sam. "Thank you. You know, you might just be my favorite brother-in-law too."

Sam chuckled. "What about your sister's husband?"

"Oh, that's right. Okay. He's my favorite Australian brother-in-law, and you're my favorite Canadian one."

"I can live with that."

"Thank you." She squeezed him again. "I don't know if you felt it too, but I felt a weird heat when you prayed."

"Huh. I thought that was just me."

"I think that might just be God," she said.

"Wow." Sam shivered, as if he felt the same tingles as Dan did. Then he blew out a breath. "Okay, then. Who's going fishing?"

He exited, and Sarah turned to Dan. "I wonder if your brother has a healing ministry?"

Only God knew. He nodded to her phone. "You better make that call to Heartsong and confirm, before the doctor finds out his test results were wrong."

She grinned. "You man of faith, you."

He pushed back his shoulders. A man of faith. That had a better sound to it, something he could live up to, rather than letting circumstances dictate a smaller life. And if God could turn around his brother in such a short amount of time, then who knew what else He could do? "Amen."

CHAPTER 14

For a redhead with freckle-prone fair skin, spending time on a boat in the sun was not Sarah's usual way to spend a summer's day. But there was a world of difference between the bite of the sun here in Muskoka and the burn she'd experienced at home. And being out on the water, even with all the other pleasure craft enjoying the lake, was relaxing. Being with Dan and Sam was comfortable too. Sam was as relaxed and easygoing as Dan, and it was fun listening to them talk and tease. It was good for Dan to just relax.

She placed a hand on her bare stomach, where Sam had prayed before. She was glad she'd been wearing her t-shirt before. How amazing to think he'd thought to do that. And the heat that had flowed… She hadn't been joking. Maybe he really did have a healing ministry. She glanced at her white stomach, criss-crossed with silvery scars, legacy of the accident that had stolen Stephen's life on that New Year's Eve five and half years ago.

Life. So uncertain. Not guaranteed. But still God-ordained. She pressed a hand to her abdomen. "Life."

She wasn't a 'name it and claim it' Christian, but still, faith was found in those words. Jesus didn't focus on the problem. He asked the question: do you want to be healed? So, "Yes, I want to be healed. I want—no, I *receive* Your life."

Her fingers tingled again, her skin burning as it had before, but not from the sun. God was able to do miracles. He'd done it in Muskoka before.

A reel of other miracles scrolled through her mind. Finding hope. Emotional healing. Dan. Returning to songwriting. Rejoining Heartsong. All had come about from her time here.

Her heart swelled, as a new kind of confidence dared her to have courage once again. Because looking at God's faithfulness and what He'd done in the past built confidence for the future.

And not just for a baby, but that Dan's career, hers—Tisha was so excited when she'd confirmed she'd do the tour—and even Dan's camp, might be trusted to God's capable hands and get sorted. It was like that old, tired saying that still held truth: *let go and let God.*

She snickered, remembering a similar situation several years ago. Would she ever learn?

"What's so funny, Princess?" Dan shifted closer to where she lay, legs stretched out on the padded bench seat, trying to get what meagre tan her skin allowed.

"Oh, I'm just enjoying the day."

"You? Enjoying fishing? Amazing."

"Don't tell anyone."

"Too late," Sam called. "I heard."

"He's got big ears." Dan grinned.

"But a good heart."

"I heard that too. Love you, Sar!"

"Love you too, Sam." She traced a hand down Dan's bare chest. "And I love you most of all."

He leaned down, bracing his arms either side and kissed her.

And kept kissing her, more deeply still, as his fingers moved to her bikini strap. And she was suddenly very aware that as much as she loved Sam, she'd really prefer him to be elsewhere.

"Looks like that's my cue." Sam's call was quickly followed by a splash.

She sat up. "Where?" A squint in the distance revealed he was swimming to the floating platform.

"Don't think about him right now," Dan murmured, his lips at her throat. "I'd much rather you think about me."

"Except if you keep doing that"—she gasped as his mouth found her ear lobe—"and he returns then you'll be thinking about him too."

"You're worth the risk."

She laughed, and indulged him for a while, as he moved to kiss her stomach's scars, just as he had when he'd seen them for the first time on their wedding night. Then, when his caresses grew a little too much for her to feel comfortable in public, pushed him away. Her eyelids were heavy, as was his breathing. "I think we should return to the cottage soon."

"And kick my brother out. He does have his own home to return to."

And she kissed him again, her smile a promise for the future.

The weeks passed with a wedding—Anna's, which Sarah attended but not Dan, to not overshadow the bride—then a quick trip to celebrate their third wedding anniversary in a revisit of their honeymoon on Prince Edward Island, this time without her family joining them partway through. Then it was back to relaxing in Muskoka as some more of those ambiguous questions over their lives were gradually sorted. Dan told his online Bible study friends about their news, and on that same day got his contract for another year, with the option to discuss another year after that. His agent assured that the handy eye-popping sum being offered for Dan to play would've been less if he'd signed for two years straight up.

She glanced across the living room at where Dan was flicking through his phone, probably reading another fishing article online. She didn't dare say it aloud, but she liked the idea of Dan finishing hockey. There was so much potential for injury. Several of the other guys in the Original Six Bible study were also eyeing retirement. Some, like Brent Karlsson, seemed fit and able to play forever, but the toll of injuries, and concussions, and the challenges of careers and raising a family, meant retirement wasn't too far from other people's minds.

The sending of flowers, well wishes and "praying for yous" that came through the members of Dan's Bible study group and their wives—good women, like Bree Vaughan, and fellow Aussie Holly Karlsson—buoyed Sarah's hopes, especially when her cycle started again. Part of her was tempted to think that strange moment of Sam's prayer hadn't worked, while another part refused to believe that. She had definitely sensed something in that moment, that hadn't been faked. And even the very fact that *Sam* of all people was the one who would offer to do something so out of his comfort zone suggested God was in it.

So if God was in it then, then God was in it now. And even though plans were now underway for her to join the Heartsong tour in October, she still felt this sense of expectancy, like hope. She felt a bit like the swimming platform that floated in Lake Muskoka, tethered to God's depths while the waves of life rocked her, but she remained buoyed by others' prayers. Just because their prayers were unanswered at the moment didn't mean they would stay that way.

Which led her to another realization. Dan had said he was happy for her to share their news on the podcast, but there was a world of difference between sharing when they were in the midst of not seeing an answer, as opposed to sharing when she was pregnant. So it only made sense to share sooner rather than later.

She sat up from her slouch on the sofa opposite him, and moved to join him on his couch. "Hey Dan, do you remember saying yes to me sharing on the podcast?"

He winced. "Yes."

"Judging from that face, you're *super* keen for me to do it. I don't have to though."

"I think we both know you do."

She nodded. "Did you want to talk about it with me?"

"Does it make me lose good husband points if I say no?"

"You're got so many points you can afford to lose a few."

He laughed. "Wow."

"Just keeping it real."

"You're a card."

"You're a dish."

He kissed her nose. "I love you."

"I love you too."

It was that love which brought her back to the city to her mini-studio to finally record this podcast. Dan had to sign his contract and do a photo opp then some other team things, but he'd agreed to speak with her briefly on the show.

He dropped her off at the apartment, and she nodded to Davis, the concierge.

"Mrs. Walton, welcome back."

"It's good to see you, Davis," she said. "How is Doreen?"

"She's not loving this weather, but apart from that can't complain. How was Muskoka?"

She sighed. "So beautiful. We're only here for a short visit then we'll return."

"No trip to Australia this year?"

She smiled. "I'm going in October, for another tour. I can't wait!"

His eyes brightened. "Will you be playing here?"

"Not this time, but if you want, I can reserve a ticket for you and Doreen in New York."

"New York." Davis smacked his lips. "Tell me the date and I'll mark my diary."

She did, and he did, and she put a note in her phone to organize two tickets for them, then rode the elevator up to their floor.

A few moments later, she was in their apartment's foyer, looking at the wedding photograph taken by Alexa, which portrayed Dan looking intently into her eyes as he kissed her hand. Such a romantic goose-bump inducing photo.

She blew a kiss at the photograph of Dan, switched on the kettle for that very necessary cup of hot tea, then moved to the second bedroom where her mini studio was set up.

Hmm. Maybe once Dan finished hockey they could move to a place with more room in the suburbs. While it was just the two of them it made sense to live near his training facility, but Sam was right. The end of Dan's playing career actually meant the start of new adventures. Like where they lived. Would they even have to live in Ontario? Maybe they could live in Australia! She wondered what he'd think about that. But it would be nice to be nearer her family, to see more of her parents, Bek, Joe and the girls. To feel *warm* and not have to endure another Canadian winter. Snow was pretty, but it was cold.

She opened some windows, allowing for some of the musty air to move around. Imagine living somewhere with fresh air, not city-scented. Muskoka was good for that, too.

"Thank You God for Muskoka." They'd return soon, then Dan had a skills camp, and they'd make the most of summer before he'd need to return for skills training, and she'd need to prep for her Heartsong tour.

She exhaled, sat at her desk, and switched on the computer. Deleted a bunch of emails her phone hadn't synced and dealt with already. It was nice to feel like she could take control of her life in some ways, and not be at the mercy of everyone who wanted or said they needed her. Then she paused, eyeing an email she hadn't seen before.

She opened it. Then read it, her mouth sagging as an offer for a different kind of album was put to her. Really? They thought she could write and record a secular album of love songs? Hmm.

"Lord?"

Her eyes closed, and she propped her head in her hands as she let her mind wander, remembering the many actions of a man who was faithful, kind and patient—hallmarks of real love —that begged her to describe him, their journey, what love looked like. It wasn't the first time she had toyed with writing about love in a more secular way, but she'd never had a request for an album of such songs. It wasn't a Heartsong Collective album, that was for sure.

"Lord, what do You think?"

She stilled her mind, stilled her soul, listening to what God might say, but didn't sense a *no*. She could see how an album like this could reach people who weren't Christians, so maybe that was a reason to consider this. And God knew that Dan was worth it...

The temptation to dwell on this tugged at her, but Dan was supposed to return in several hours, and she still had to pray, and go over her podcast's script and notes, and check the recording timing would work considering there was so much to say. This album offer was something to think about another day.

She spent the next hour praying, revising her program notes, tweaking things, asking God for direction on what was best to say and what was less valuable. Then, as the time of Dan's arrival drew near, she set up her script, and cued her computer, and microphone.

When the door rattled, she jumped up to answer it. "Look! It's my favorite hockey player in all the world!"

He grinned, accepting her hug. "Hey, Princess."

"How did it go?"

"Great. Everyone's very happy so it should be good."

"I bet they were happy to sign you up now so they can build their team around you."

"I don't know how much building they can do when I'm only here for another year, but I'll take it."

She kissed him. "Want a cup of tea?"

"You and your cups of tea," he said affectionately.

"Hey, tea is good for you, and doesn't raise the heartrate like coffee does, just remember that."

He smiled. "So, how has the podcast prep gone?"

"Good." She'd save the news about the album offer for another day. Or maybe not at all. If she did do the album, it could be an awesome surprise for him. *If* she did it at all.

"Have you got notes on what you want me to say?"

"Oh! Um, I hadn't really thought about what or how much I want you to say. I figured it would probably be good for you to be there as I talk, and if there's anything you want to add or change, we can edit it straight away. Is that okay?"

He sighed. "Yep."

"It won't take long."

"I hope not. I've got other things I want to do with you instead."

"You always do." Especially now she'd stopped bleeding again. "First things first. Let's pray, then let's talk."

. . .

IT PROVED to be a very different podcast to the last. But the concept of thankfulness, in the midst of uncertainty, was a message that everyone needed reminding of. How could people truly claim faith if their faith was only based on things going well?

"But I've come to realize that real faith is only truly earned when we're in the gritty moments of life, when things look destined to fail, and there's no hope in sight. That's what walking by faith and not sight is about." How she hoped and prayed that her words would bring courage and not despair.

She glanced at Dan, whose lips tweaked up, his arms crossed over his chest.

"Which leads me to something that's pretty personal." She swallowed. "Most of you would be aware that I've been married to my personal Mr. Darcy for the past three years. But what you may not know is that in the last two years we've had three miscarriages. And we've just received news that the doctors believe that we can never carry a child to full term."

She swallowed. Peeked at Dan. His lips were flat. But she'd discussed the content of this with him, and he'd agreed she could be honest. This was their chance to tell their story and own it in a way that they'd prayed would be framed in faith and hope.

"And I'm not saying this to get your sympathy. I'm saying that I know what it's like to have to trust God when it seems impossible. I know what it's like to hope against all odds, only to see things fail. And I also know that underneath all of that, I still have this sense of peace, that I have this strong assurance that God loves me, that I'm still held in the palm of His hand."

Tears pricked and she swallowed to clear the emotion. "And I want to encourage you today, that whatever hard thing it is that you're facing, that God is there in the midst of it with you. God still loves you. He still has good plans for you. You can trust Him."

She sniffed. Glanced up, saw Dan's dark eyes intent on her. He mouthed a, "Love you."

She smiled at him, then leaned closer to the microphone. "I wrote a song a while ago that many of you have said that you enjoyed. It ends with the chorus about how 'we can trust Him with it all, yeah!'" She sang those last few words. Caught Dan's smile. Sipped her water.

"I recently wrote another one, and I sang it in this very room on the morning of my latest miscarriage. It's a real faith statement. I felt like as I was writing and singing and declaring these truths that I was pushing back the darkness that threatened to overwhelm me."

She sipped her water, again, clearing the lump within. "And today, I want to encourage you to do the same. Speak God's promises over your life. Speak out His truth, don't let the darkness win. The Bible says that the devil is a liar, and he seeks to steal, kill and destroy. So don't let him win. Don't let him lie to you and say that God doesn't love you. Don't let him steal your peace or your joy. Don't let him destroy your life by giving into the darkness. Instead, stand on God's promises and declare *them* out loud. Things like God loves me, God has good plans for me, God is with me through it all."

She glanced at her notes and continued. "I don't know about you, but sometimes when I speak things out loud, it's like my heart and my soul hear it more. That's why worship is so powerful. That's why it's important to gather together with other believers, so we get out of our own negative headspace and can be in a place where we are encouraged."

Dan nodded and gave her a thumbs up.

"And so today, I don't know where you're at, but I really felt like I wanted those of you who are like me, like Dan, facing disappointment, facing what looks impossible, to remember that our God is the God who does impossible things. The King of kings and Lord of lords, the God who can do exceedingly abundantly above all we can ask or imagine. And even if He doesn't answer our prayer the way we hope He will, it doesn't mean that God is finished with us yet."

She swallowed, the moment feeling weighty. "We know that in Romans chapter eight it talks about God working for the good of those who love Him and are called according to His purposes. Which means for believers, that God is working in us now. For our good. And sometimes that doesn't feel good. But I think we need to switch our focus from what we think good is —easy, comfortable, happy, rich—to what God thinks is good. Which is there in the very next verse. That is, that we may be conformed to the likeness of His Son. So the things we face are to help us grow to become more like Jesus. It doesn't mean it's easy, but it does mean we can trust Him with it all. And it means we can always trust Him because we know He loves us. Amen."

"Amen," Dan echoed aloud.

She laughed. "And that was Dan Amening in the background. Dan, have you got anything you'd like to say?"

He shrugged, then leaned forward, and she swung the microphone to face him. "I think you said it all, Sar."

She shook her head. "Come on. There's something."

He rolled his eyes then inched closer. "It's okay to not have all the answers. It's okay to not feel okay. But if you don't feel okay, then keeping that to yourself and not talking to anyone can cause your heart and mind to spiral into dark places. I didn't want people to know about these challenges we've been facing for a long time. I don't know why. I guess I felt ashamed, or inadequate, or people would judge me. But I've learned that holding things in like that doesn't help. We all need light to shine into those places, and talking about things, being reminded of God's truth, is a way of breaking the darkness over our lives. That's proved true for me, and for Sarah, and I believe it will prove true for you too." He pushed the microphone arm, so it was her turn again.

"Thanks, Dan." Her heart was so soft toward him. What a good man he was. "I'm going to finish a little differently today and pray. Lord, thank you for Your love for us. Thank You that even in the hardest moments of our lives, You were there. You are *here*."

Sarah paused, her spine tingling. "Help us to be still, to know that You are God. You are the creator, the giver of life, the Alpha, and the Omega, the beginning, and the end. You oversee the universe, and You see our hearts and our lives. Thank You for Your miraculous interventions. Thank You for breaking chains, thank You for bringing hope in dark places, thank You for Your love and the fact that nothing can separate us from Your love. Lord, we choose to follow You. Amen."

"Amen," Dan echoed.

She smiled at him. "Friends, I know that was a heavier topic today, but thank you for listening. If you want to leave a comment, feel free and I hope we can encourage each other in the things of God. And if nothing else, I hope, no matter where you stand with God, that you can repeat this with me: *God* loves me, God *loves* me, God loves *me*. My prayer—and Dan's too—is that you would truly know that for yourself. This is Sarah Walton, and you've been listening to *Time Out with Sarah*."

She pressed the cued outro music, then ended the recording. Sank into her seat. And let Dan wrap her in his arms.

"You did great," he murmured.

"I hope it touches people's hearts."

"It will. We prayed it would, right?"

She nodded. *Lord, be glorified, and have Your way.* "Thank you for speaking. What you shared was perfect."

"I learned from the pro."

"Jesus?"

He chuckled. "And you."

"Ha." She yawned. "I'm exhausted."

"Sounds like you need a sleep."

"A sleep," she warned. "Nothing else."

"Nothing else." Yet, his eyes seemed to dance, as he leaned forward and swept her into another kiss.

She closed her eyes and tugged him closer. Okay, maybe sleep was something to reconsider.

CHAPTER 15

The sunset dipped into Lake Muskoka, drawing a sigh from their host, Lincoln Cash. "I don't think that view ever gets old."

"God's country," Dan agreed.

Linc—he'd asked them to call him that—peered at Dan. "How long did you say you've been coming here?"

"For twenty-something years."

"I don't blame you." Linc yawned. "Sorry, it's been a big few weeks."

Dan glanced across the table to where Sarah was smothering a yawn too. She smiled at him, then glanced apologetically at Jackie. "I agree."

"Well, with the way that last podcast of yours went viral, I don't blame you for feeling tired," Jackie said. "How many comments did you get?"

Sarah's smile held shyness. "Over a thousand."

"And counting," Dan added. "And she's replied to them all."

"No wonder you're tired," Linc said, to her nod.

Sarah's exhaustion had set in almost as soon as they returned from Toronto a week ago. She kept telling him not to be concerned, but if she was this tired before the tour, how on earth was she going to cope when it actually started? Whenever he tried to say that she dismissed it, claiming it was simply because she felt so relaxed that she was enjoying feeling tired, rather than feeling exhausted like she normally did. Which didn't quite make sense to him. Her claims of regular exhaustion worried him, but she wouldn't listen to his pleas to rethink the tour, or take time out from socializing.

Which was why they were here, with Jackie looking a little bit guilty. Dan suspected he knew why.

"And uh, yes, about that podcast." Jackie glanced at Sarah. "I listened to it, then made Linc listen to it too. It was such a powerful testimony."

"Really powerful," Linc nodded.

"And I wanted to thank you for being courageous enough to be real and raw and still testify of God's goodness and grace in the midst of pain and disappointment." Jackie's eyes sparkled with tears. "And I'm sorry. I realize now how hard things must've been for you, when we"—she winced—"well, you know, had little Charlie. Anyway, we—I—wanted you to know I never meant to cause you further pain. Especially when it's been such a hard road for you. Anyway, I'm sorry."

Sarah shook her head. "You can't be responsible for how others may be feeling. Especially when you didn't even know the situation."

Jackie bit her lip. "It's a tricky balance, isn't it, trying to figure out what should be shared before somebody else feels like they need to share it on your behalf."

Sarah glanced at Dan. "That's why we didn't say anything to anyone for a long time. It's hard enough to find the words, especially when you're going through grief yourself, let alone figure out how to share things with others. But then not saying anything also has consequences. Like this." She gestured between herself and Jackie, then shrugged. "I don't know if everyone needs to share like we did, but I have to admit that having now said it, I do feel a lot lighter."

"I do too," Dan admitted. His friends and teammates had been so supportive. It wasn't just him and Sarah as part of Team Walton anymore. Now his whole team were on his side, their partners supporting Sarah, just as his Bible study buddies and their wives checked in with them often. Knowing this was just part of his life instead of something that he thought he needed to hide, made him feel more comfortable. He didn't have to apologize for turning down birthday invitations for one-year-olds who wouldn't remember his presence. On the days when they weren't doing as okay, it was easier to simply decline, and he trusted that their real friends would understand.

His parents had—as expected—been shocked that Sarah would dare to confess something so private in such a public manner. Her parents had—as expected—understood.

"When you have a public ministry," James had said, "then you can't hide things, because secrets always have a way of coming out. And because you've been open about this, it means you can be open about the other times when things aren't so easy. People won't see you as super Christians, but real people who don't always have it all together, and the fact you have to depend on God encourages others to do so, too."

"It's hard to live in the spotlight, but still keep things real," Linc mused now.

Dan glanced at him. The movie star possessed more fans than his whole team had combined. "I can't imagine how you try and balance that."

Linc shrugged. "That's why I have an agent and a publicist. They screen most of that for me, and Jackie screens the rest." He smiled at his wife, who smiled back.

"I've been wondering if I should get somebody to work as my VA," Sarah said. "I just can't keep up with all the comments, not when I'm trying to focus on my music."

"And her husband," Dan added, winking at her.

She blushed, and Linc laughed. "Yeah. I'm all for people who can do some of that heavy lifting, especially if it means my wife can pay attention to her husband."

Jackie rolled her eyes. "He's so needy."

"Men." Sarah snickered.

"Look, we can't help it if we're merely men," Linc said. "That's why God knew we needed amazing women like you in our lives."

"He's slick," Sarah said to Jackie.

"I sometimes wonder if he quotes lines from his movies at me."

"Babe, no. Everything I say to you I mean. And I genuinely mean that."

Dan chuckled. "I sometimes used to wonder when I heard Sarah sing if I was the one she was describing as amazing and strong. Then I realized she was singing to God."

Linc laughed. "Yeah, that's a little hard to live up to."

Sarah glanced at him. "Are you saying you want me to write you a love song?"

"At the risk of sounding as needy as Linc there, I'm just gonna say that other music stars have done that, even worship leaders. So if you feel the need to write a song about me, then I'm okay with that."

"I'll keep it in mind."

Sarah's smile tweaked higher, holding peace. It was good to see.

The evening had been good, the company relaxed. Lincoln had a small window of time away from his filming schedule in the city, which allowed for this brief catch up before Dan's training ramped up before preseason. He had a few more charity events to attend, and his and Sarah's schedules were looking busier next month. But not as busy as when Sarah would fly to Sydney to begin her tour.

She'd mentioned earlier that she'd need to leave a few more days earlier than anticipated for rehearsals. "I don't know why I didn't think of it before, but apparently they actually want me there to help manage the stagecraft."

"Are you sure you'll be okay to do so?"

"I'll be staying with Mum and Dad, so it'll be fine."

He knew Lindy and James were vigilant about their daughter's health, but it wasn't the same as Dan himself being there, keeping an eye on her to make sure she didn't push herself too much.

"I'm really glad that you could both come over because there's something that we've been thinking about." Jackie glanced at Lincoln who dipped his chin.

"See, when we had that soirée here a few weeks ago," she looked at Sarah, "I remember we were talking about the Muskoka Ferns Lodge—"

Dan stilled.

"—and Anna's family friends who need to sell it. And, correct me if I'm wrong, but Sarah, I just felt like you had this sense that something needed to be done about it."

Whoa. That was a conversation that had slipped to the back-burner of his mind. Dan peeked at Sarah who nodded. "I did. And Dan and I have talked about it, but haven't really investigated anything."

"Do you mind if I ask what you've talked about?"

Sarah glanced at him and gestured for him to speak.

He shifted in his seat. "I've been running a Christian wilderness camp for city teenagers for nearly ten years now. I love it, but my body says I can't keep doing it the same way, so when Sarah mentioned that the lodge used to be a campsite I was interested. But I haven't chased it up at all."

Jackie nodded. "See, when Anna mentioned that it was for sale, I immediately thought of all those poor people who had been trucked back to the city, unable to live there anymore."

"I thought that too," Sarah admitted.

"And I wondered if there was something we could do about it—"

"*We* meaning me and Jackie," Lincoln clarified.

"—to fix it up for those people to live there again," Jackie finished.

Oh. A ping of disappointment suggested he'd let the idea of having a camp there burrow deeper than he'd realized. "Well, like I said, it was just a thought. I can probably keep going with what I was doing." A peek at Sarah's creased brow suggested she didn't agree. Okay, then.

"But here's the thing," Jackie continued. "From all that we've been able to discover, and a quick visit out there last week, the place is so dire that it will require years of work to bring it up to any kind of government code. But we wanted to secure the land. Golden Elms, where Lincoln's grandfather is, is a fantastic facility for the elderly, but not specifically designed for people with some of the special needs who were basically incarcerated at the Lodge."

Jackie glanced at Lincoln, who took the lead. "So, Dan, we wanted to know if you were potentially interested in joining with us to secure the land and invest in a new venture to construct a facility that is designed for people with special needs."

"Wow." That was something he'd never considered before in his life. "Um, I need to think—and pray—about it."

"The property is large enough for you to still hold camps, and feel as wildernessy as you like," Jackie said. "And because it will likely take a number of years to get all the proper permissions before building can even commence, it will be good to see the land being used and not see what infrastructure remains just rotting away."

The idea had merit. A glance at Sarah's wide eyes and smile suggested she was a fan. *Lord?* "Are you saying that the camp would have to stop after it becomes a special needs facility?"

"I don't see why it would," Lincoln said. "The property is over a hundred acres, not all of which is suitable for residential purposes, so it's definitely a big enough location."

"And you want us involved—why?"

Lincoln shrugged. "You've been known to have a connection here in Muskoka for years. You've even had your house featured on MTV."

Oh, that. Back when he'd been young and proud of his new contract with Toronto and just bought his cottage in Muskoka, and doing what he could to keep the team's PR team happy.

"Your connection here is entirely different to someone others see as a 'blow in,' as I think I heard myself described recently." Linc grimaced. "Someone with no roots, just money, who wants to try and change things."

"But Jackie, you've lived here for years, haven't you?" Dan asked. He thought that had been mentioned before.

"But I'm not the one with the high profile." Her voice held wryness.

"Oh, I seem to recall something about a Muskoka chair." A moment when she'd gone viral for fending off Toni's ex by wielding a heavy wooden chair.

"Please." She shook her head. "That wasn't even fifteen minutes of fame. Maybe ten."

Dan smiled. "I think it was enough that people would know who you are."

"But I'll always be known as Lincoln's wife, not in my own sense. And while I'm okay with that, it does mean that people will look at him and disregard my connection because they're so focused on Linc."

Huh. He'd never really realized just how much of a woman's identity could be lost because of her more famous husband.

Gratitude struck him that Sarah's career meant she had already established her own identity separate to him.

Linc sat back in his chair. "So that's why we wondered if perhaps you would be interested in partnering with us in this project."

"Are you saying you'd want me to be the spokesperson?"

"To be the name attached to it," Linc said. "We'd be the charitable organization in the background who puts up the funds."

"How much are we talking?"

Lincoln named a figure which was about twice Dan's annual salary.

Whoa. "Sorry. That's way too much for me." Which was a shame, as he'd started to feel interested—

"No, that's the total. You'd only need to put in twenty percent."

Huh.

"Oh my gosh."

He glanced at Sarah. Her green eyes had gotten even wider. "What is it, hon?"

"I, um, you won't believe this, but I had wondered about something like this. Back when we first talked about it."

"You did?"

She winced. "There was a lot else going on, which is why I didn't say anything. But yes, I had wondered whether a site could incorporate a camping side of things as well as what was needed for a special needs' residence. I agree with Jackie. It just seems so wrong for these poor innocent people to have been ripped off like that."

Dan nodded, turned to Jackie. "You said you've seen the site?"

Jackie looked abashed. "We might've ventured there without telling anyone. It's not like it's public knowledge that it's up for sale yet. But from what Anna was saying it sounds like it will go on the market soon, and then it will likely be a free for all among developers who'll just want to develop the land and sell off hundreds of housing sites. Can you imagine how that would change the local communities, including Muskoka Shores?"

His nose wrinkled. "Everybody might like to own a piece of heaven, but it doesn't mean they should."

"Which is why someone who's known to have invested years into loving Muskoka would make a great ambassador."

"I need to give this a lot of thought."

"And a lot of prayer, too," Linc said. "But we wanted to talk to you first. There are others who might be willing to come on board."

"Like Toni," Jackie said. "She loves Muskoka too."

Sarah nodded. "Her paintings are awesome."

"And a great advertisement for keeping things natural and protected from over-development," Jackie said. "And her husband Matt is involved in property investment, and knows a few things about how to take on projects of this size."

Sarah's head tilted. "What was that fundraising group Anna said her mother was involved in? The Musko-cheers or something?"

Jackie smiled. "Are you thinking what I'm thinking?"

"If it's that we might need to see if they would like some younger members, then yes I am."

How quickly the world could pivot. One minute, feeling like he was facing a fog and at a loss as to what his future held. The next, pieces of the puzzle falling into place like they'd been dropped from heaven. Which was true. And should be expected. For if people prayed for God to open the doors, then they should expect some of those doors to open eventually.

Between this proposal from Linc and Jackie, and contacting his old university and learning he could do some courses part time, he felt like they were taking positive steps forward. Even if

Sarah still seemed to be battling exhaustion, that had him second-guessing whether he should go to Peterborough for a hockey skills camp with lots of young teens.

"Sar? Are you sure you're okay? Do I need to stay?"

"I'm fine. Just tired."

"Then can you please visit the doctor to get your iron levels checked?"

"My iron levels?"

"Look, I remember Bree Vaughan had problems with her iron, so you need to be careful."

"I'm fine," she insisted. "I've just been doing lots of prep for the tour." She held up a hand. "Please don't say anything. I'll be fine. I can't wait to see my family in eight weeks."

Eight weeks. They had a lot to deal with in eight weeks. His preseason training had ramped up, as had her conversations with Jackie and Serena about forming a committee of potential Young Musko-cheers, as they called themselves, that they hoped would include Toni, Anna, and Staci. Then Sarah was prepping for her tour, and he had to organize something special for her birthday. Her birthday? What would she like?

He knew it was a super lame husband question to ask, but he didn't like to get it wrong. "Hey Sar Bear, what do you want for your birthday?"

She eyed him, her lips pulling to one side.

He exhaled. That was a given. "Apart from that."

Her lips lifted. "I don't know. How about a new fishing rod?"

"Done."

"Don't you dare!"

"Hey, I aim to please."

"I don't think that's all you should be aiming for."

He smiled. "I just know that you'll want to do something special, and I'll be away for a few days in Peterborough for the hockey camp, so it'll be nice to reconnect with you in a good way. Unless of course, you've changed your mind, and you'd like to come."

"As tempting as it sounds to hang out with hundreds of kids, my days of teaching are done. I'm very happy for you to go do you, and I'll be ready for a nice reunion on your return."

"You'll stay here?"

"I don't want to go back to the city a second sooner than I have to. I love Muskoka."

"That's my girl." He kissed her cheek. "I'll see you when I return."

"AND NOW, I'd like to call the meeting of the Young Musko-cheers to order." Serena banged the gavel, and smiled at the women surrounding her dining table.

Sarah sat there along with Jackie, the newly-married Anna, Toni, Staci, and a few others. The speed at which they'd managed to pull this together was astonishing, except maybe not, considering these women were used to gathering for their soirees.

Serena explained some of the goals of their time together, then handed the floor to Anna, who gave a little of the history of the fundraising committee. Her mother had been one of the key fundraisers of the original Musko-cheers, until the Crayling's Muskoka Ferns Lodge fiasco had shattered all motivation.

Yet the need for charity fundraising remained, as Anna explained. "Because there are all kinds of deserving people and organizations out there. But I hope we'll be more committed to focusing on what will raise the most money for the needy, rather than what will prove to be most fun for us."

"We can still keep the fun in fundraising though, right?" Rachel asked.

"For sure." Anna smiled. "Just not at the expense of the deserving."

"Such as those poor residents who got caught in that scam." Jackie glanced around the room. "And I have to say, I think this is a solid group of women who can help with this task."

Sarah nodded. Many of the women—Serena, Jackie, Anna, Rachel—had lived in Muskoka for decades, and had long-standing connections to the church or local businesses. Some of the women, like Toni, had shown their love for Muskoka through their work. Others, such as Staci and herself, had strong fan-bases. Everyone here brought their own unique skills and talents to the table, united by a heart for God that resulted in a heart of compassion for others. And, apparently, a heart for fun.

As the meeting progressed, she thanked God that He'd brought her into their midst. Obviously, God knew what He was doing, weaving lives together, bringing people to this exact place for this exact time. Almost like He knew His plans needed them here for this right now.

And if He knew that the timing had to be just right for this to happen, then that meant His timing had to be just right for all good things to happen.

She relaxed. God could be trusted to have the right timing with everything.

Sarah groaned, rolled out of bed, and staggered to the bathroom. She deposited her stomach's contents in the toilet, as had often happened since that dinner at Jackie and Lincoln's. She hoped she'd be better before the Heartsong tour kicked off. Tisha and the others were getting so excited, so glad she could join them again. And it felt good that with all the other uncertainties in life, she could plan something. She'd been a part of

Heartsong tours for years, and fans were always asking when she'd next perform.

Announcing her involvement with the tour on her last podcast had seen a flurry of excited fans, many of whom told her they'd buy tickets to see her. And while she wasn't going to get carried away, it felt good to feel the love. Especially in moments like now when she felt so gross.

After wiping her mouth and brushing her teeth she made her way out to the living room. Magazines and newspapers lay scattered on the floor from where she'd left them for the past three days. She blinked. Dan's house had *never* looked so messy. A sigh escaped. He'd been so patient with her these past few weeks, caring for her amid her exhaustion, doing what he could when possible, and warning her not to overdo things. And she hadn't. All she'd done was prep for the Heartsong tour, reply to excited fans, and attend Serena's Musko-cheers meeting yesterday. That hadn't pushed her energy levels too much, even though she'd needed a nap afterwards. But with Dan coming home tonight, she should make an effort for him now.

After making his favorite cookies—white chocolate and macadamia—another wave of fatigue hit her, forcing her to grip the side of the kitchen counter. Ugh. This was getting ridiculous.

Her phone rang. She peered through half-closed eyes at the screen. Rebekah. She put it on speaker mode. "Hey, sis."

"Sar! How are you doing?"

She wandered into the living room and flopped onto the lounge. "Busy." She told her about the Musko-cheers and the plans for the Sydney trip. "I can't wait."

"It'll be awesome to see you," her sister said. "It's just a shame Dan can't come."

Sarah closed her eyes. "He'll be starting his season then."

"I'm sorry we couldn't get over there this year. But the kids

got the flu, and we figured you didn't need that on top of everything else that was going down."

"There's been a lot going down." She told Bek about the
album offer, something she still hadn't responded to, but now
she thought about it, it could actually be the answer to the question Dan had posed a few weeks ago. "I do have a bunch of
songs that could suit, but I just don't know."

"Why wouldn't you?" her sister asked. "People know that you
love God, and they know you are married. Surely you can do
both kinds of music still."

"But what if people think I've crossed over to the dark side?"

"Then they're judgmental. You can sing songs about love and
relationships that don't have to just be about God."

"So you think it's a good idea?"

"I think if you turned it down, you'd regret it."

Sarah nodded. The project would keep her busy, especially
after the Heartsong tour. Hmm. Maybe she could even use some
of the income to support the Musko-cheer project. People
might be more inclined to want to support it if there was a good
cause attached to it. Something to think about, anyway. She
yawned, as another wave of tiredness washed over her. "I just
don't want to overcommit myself."

"Sar, you'll manage."

"It's just I feel so tired all the time."

"Still?"

"Yeah. I honestly think I must've picked up a virus somehow.
It's been like this for weeks. Yesterday morning I nearly threw
up when I visited Ange's and smelled the coffee."

Rebekah was silent for a long moment. "Sar, have you
thought about what you've just said?"

"What?"

"The symptoms you've described?"

"Symptoms?" What on earth was she talking about?

"Sar, how long since your last period?"

"I was bleeding just last week."

"Oh. I thought—"

"No." Her heart cramped. "My periods have never been regular since the accident, but even I know you can't bleed and then be pregnant when you haven't, ah, had the opportunity to."

And she'd really thought she might. Sam's prayer, and that heat that suggested healing, along with something stubborn within still insisted that she could be. One day. But obviously not right now.

"You know we're all praying for you."

"Thank you," she whispered. "I wish I could give you good news, but it's just tiredness."

"Well, you take care of yourself, okay?"

"Yes, Bek." She yawned. "I better go make somebody's dinner."

"Happy reunion-ing."

Hmph. The way she was feeling, Dan would be happier without her.

CHAPTER 16

The scent of sizzling garlic wafted through the cottage. "Hey, hon. Something smells good."

Sarah wasn't in the kitchen, yet the pan was still spitting. He turned off the stove. "Sar?"

He went upstairs. Nope. No sign of her. Then he heard the downstairs toilet flush. He hurried down the stairs as she opened the door. "Hey, are you okay?"

She wrinkled her nose. "I feel gross. Happy that you're back, though."

"Hey, come here."

She backed away. "Don't kiss me. I just threw up."

Okay, then. A hug would have to do. He took his time with that, then murmured, "Is this a new bra?"

"Why?"

"Because you're feeling a little fuller than normal."

She looked at her chest. "I feel more sore." She winced.

"Are you okay? Do you need to lie down?"

"I'm so sorry. I just feel so tired, and I had a big headache today, so I didn't clean up like I'd planned, and—"

"Hey, it's okay. Go sit down, put your feet up. I've got this."

"Thank you." She nuzzled his jaw with her cheek, then staggered to the sofa.

He rushed to grasp her arm, steady her feet. "Whoa."

She sank onto the sofa. "Sorry. I feel so gross."

"Close your eyes. It's all good."

She obeyed, and he found a blanket and laid it over her. Poor thing. She didn't seem good at all.

He looked at the meal she'd started cooking, and salvaged what he could. By the time it was cooked, she still hadn't stirred. Hmm. This definitely wasn't the welcome home he'd envisaged.

He went over and gently shook her awake. "Hey, Princess, how's your headache?"

She wrinkled her nose. "It's mostly gone."

"Are you ready to eat?"

She yawned. Then covered her mouth and winced again. "I'm so sorry. I'm not hungry at all."

"Want to keep me company while I eat then?"

"Sure."

He helped her up, and she clung to him, arms around his waist.

"I'm sorry for being such a wussy little dandelion."

He laughed. "You can be my wussy little dandelion any time you like."

She sank into the kitchen stool, while he plated his meal. "So how was the skills camp?"

"Good." He told her about the defensive skills he'd taught alongside Brendan and Marc.

He moved to the dining table, prayed, then ate. He felt bad to be the only one eating, but she still looked too pale. "Are you sure you're okay? Have you seen a doctor?"

"I don't think there's any point. They'll just tell me to sleep better." She brightened marginally. "Which I probably will now, now that you're home."

"You don't mind me snoring?"

"You don't snore too bad. It's when you steal the blankets that I have a problem."

"Excuse me, Ms. Blanket Thief? That's you projecting, that's what that is."

"Ugh." She covered her mouth. Winced. "Projectile vomiting. Excuse me."

He watched her exit, frowning. Maybe he should call Dr. James and see if he made house visits. She seemed a lot worse than when he'd left four days ago.

He tapped on the toilet door. "Sarah? Are you okay in there?"

"I'll be out in a few."

Hmm. That wasn't convincing.

He got his phone, found James's number, and dialed. "James? It's Dan Walton. Hey, sorry to bother you, but I was wondering, do you do house calls at all?"

"What's happened?"

"It's Sarah. She's been exhausted for weeks, and I'm getting concerned, especially now she's vomiting."

"Ah. Okay. Well, there have been some cases of the flu around here lately."

That must be what it is.

"Unless you think she might be pregnant."

His heart thudded. "What? No. She was bleeding last week."

James paused. "Are you using contraception?"

"What?"

"Is she pregnant?"

"Wouldn't she know?"

"Get her to take a test. Then you'll know."

"'Kay. Thanks." He ended the call. Felt like a fool, even as a tiny hope started dancing in his soul.

He knocked on the door again. "Sar? Have you got a minute?"

She flushed the toilet, and opened the door, her eyes blotchy, as if she'd been crying.

He moved to hold her.

"Don't touch me. I was sick again."

"I don't care." He held her. "I love you."

She clung more firmly. "I'm so glad you're home."

He led her to the sofa and helped her sit again. "Sar, how long have you been feeling like this?"

She pressed a hand to her forehead. "Since we had dinner at Jackie and Lincoln's."

He nodded. He didn't want to freak her out, he had to stay calm. But now he thought about it, these symptoms weren't that dissimilar to what she'd experienced in the past. "How did the fundraising meeting go?"

"It was good." She glanced up at him, her face pale. "I think getting involved is a good thing."

"Me too. I'm glad you went." He gently cupped her cheek in his hand. "Especially when you haven't felt well."

She nodded. "It's the right thing to do."

"Speaking of right things, it's not right that you're feeling so unwell. We should take you to the doctor's."

"I hate going to the doctor."

"I know." After her car accident injuries meant she'd spent months in hospital, she avoided medical appointments like the plague. Hmm. Clearly, he had to find another way to broach this. "It's just, well, I was wondering, seeing you've been feeling off-color, do you think there is any chance you might be, uh, expecting?"

She squinted up at him, clearly confused. "Expecting? Expecting what?"

He smothered a smile. He had to make this plain. "Do you have a pregnancy test somewhere around here?"

Her eyes widened. "What?"

He grabbed his car keys. There had to be a pharmacist still open at this hour. "I'll be back in—"

"Wait. There might be one upstairs. Why?"

He looked at her.

"Oh, Dan. No." She shook her head. "I was bleeding last week, Dan. Remember? I even had cramps too, and I—"

"Sar, sit down, and relax. I'll go see if there's one upstairs."

"But—oh." She slumped back onto the sofa.

Whoa. That wasn't supposed to happen. "Sarah?"

She opened her eyes. "I'm so tired."

"Do I need to take you to the hospital?"

"What?"

As he'd hoped, the threat woke her up. She didn't like hospitals, after her months of enforced stay after the accident. Call him cruel for suggesting it, but it worked.

"Wait here." Like she was going anywhere.

He hurried upstairs to their bathroom and soon found the packaged kit. Then returned downstairs. Handed it to her. "Can you take this test?"

"Why? So you can be disappointed again?"

"Please?"

She sighed, he helped her up and she moved back into the toilet. Closed the door. And he prayed.

The sound of flushing and rinsed hands preceded her return, a little stick in front of her.

"How long do we need?"

"Two minutes."

She placed the test on the plastic packaging, and he set the timer. They held each other, not looking at it. He didn't want her spirits crushed again.

He so needed to man up right now and be the husband she could lean on, no matter what happened to that little white stick.

"Hey, Sar, it's gonna be alright. I love you."

"I love you too." He gazed into her green eyes steadily, watching as the worry and fear faded and a measure of peace filled them instead.

"Whatever happens. God is with us, He'll help us, we can trust Him."

She exhaled, nodded, and their torturous wait continued.

Lord, please...

The phone alarm beeped, and they studied each other. "Ready?"

She shook her head.

He smiled, swiped her hair behind her ear. "God's got this, no matter what it is."

"But it won't be, because I was bleeding last week."

"Let's see what the test says."

She drew in a shaky-sounding breath. Nodded.

And they turned back to the stick.

SARAH HELD a special secret inside her. No-one, apart from Daniel and Dr. McKinnon knew. That first test in Muskoka had seen Dan rush out to buy another two, and they all said the same thing. She was pregnant. With none of the tests holding the wavery pink lines of the previous three times. They'd returned to Toronto and made an appointment with Dr. McKinnon as soon as possible. The bleeding she'd thought was her period he'd put down to implantation bleeding. And while he'd said her blood test result indicated her hCG level was healthy, it wasn't until last week's ultrasound had showed a little heartbeat that she'd dared believe this could actually be real.

Still, Dr. McKinnon's cautions about their history, and the likelihood of spontaneous miscarriage given their supposed incompatibility, or health issues should she carry their baby to full term, threaded fear into what otherwise would have been pure joy.

Because they'd been here before. And while they knew God was good, there was always the chance that—miracle though this may be—that God's timing would see heartbreak much like before. Faith was a hard place to live in. And so once again, the hard challenges of faith meant they hadn't told anyone yet, despite their recent attempts to be open.

"You almost ready, Sar?"

"Yes." She pinned her hair behind her ears, her movements flattening her dress across a stomach that revealed no telltale sign of a bump. That was no surprise. She'd been sick most days, so she'd been losing weight, even if her chest was fuller than usual. That was a good sign she supposed. Something must be working okay.

Dan entered the bathroom, his eyes widening at the dress. "Is this new?"

"It's another vintage piece." Also known as second-hand designer. The world didn't need to drown in more cheap cast-away clothes. She'd bought it when she'd been less busty.

"Well, I like."

He drew close, as if he wanted to kiss her, but she inched away. "You'll have to wait."

"Okay." He grinned. "You look great."

"Thanks."

It was nice to have this feeling of accord. He hadn't liked it yesterday when she'd said she still wanted to go on the Heart-song tour. "But this is our child's health you plan to risk."

"I don't *plan* to risk anything," she'd snapped. Man, hormones that exacerbated her tendency to fly off the handle were the pits.

"I just want you to be careful, Sar," he'd said, caressing her stomach. "I love you, and I love this child, and I don't want anything to happen to either of you."

"I don't want that either." And she'd kissed him in a way that soon ended that argument. Or at least put it on pause.

She was trying to enter into Dan's excitement, to paste a smile over the fears. God was good. She knew that. God loved her. Yes, Amen. But still… still… *Oh, Lord, could we please have a better outcome this time round?*

"Hey, Princess, are you ready for your birthday surprise?"

She nodded, pushed aside the worries, focused on the now. "Sure am."

He pulled out a tiny, gift-wrapped box. "Ta da!"

"That doesn't look much like a fishing rod."

He smirked. "I was saving that for after dinner."

She laughed, and read the birthday card, then unwrapped the present. "Oh!"

Beautiful earrings sparkled in the apartment's dim light, a perfect match for her Christmas pendant and engagement ring. "Thank you. They're so beautiful."

"You're so beautiful."

She kissed him, his passion quickly igniting hers, until she was forced to push him away. "We can't."

"We can. You're the birthday girl. The party can't start until you're there."

She smiled, but shook her head. "I think I'll wait for that part of my present until later."

"Your wish is my command." He held out his arm. "Now, are you ready?"

"Can I guess where we're going?" she asked, as they descended in the elevator.

"Probably not."

She snickered. "You're so mean."

"Even if we both know I'm so right. You haven't been able to guess right once in all the times I've been taking you out for your birthday dinner."

"But that can change," she insisted. "Is it Feretti's?"

"Nope."

"360?"

"Guess again."

"McDonald's?"

He shot her a look.

"Oh well, looks like I can't guess. I suppose that means you're Mr. Right again."

He placed a hand carefully around her waist, his caress of her stomach nearly imperceptible as they walked to his car. "You know it."

He *was* Mr. Right, and she was so blessed in so many ways. And about to celebrate her birthday with friends and Dan's family when she'd already been given the greatest gift of all.

"Did you have a nice time?" her mother asked on the video call the next day.

"It was great." Sarah glanced at Dan. "Somebody here booked a private dining room at this amazing French restaurant, and we had so much fun."

Some of Dan's teammates had joined Sam, and Helen, and Andrew. Some of her new Muskoka friends had come too. Jackie and Linc, Staci and James, Toni and Matt. It had been nice to chat with them and discuss Musko-cheers progress among other things. The only thing that would've made it perfect was seeing her family. She would've *loved* to have them there, this ache at missing them growing each day. Still, that was part of the purpose of this birthday call.

"Are you feeling better now?" Bek asked, from her square of video.

"So much better." She gripped Dan's hand, and he squeezed gently. It was time to tell her parents and sister. "I went to the doctors again recently, and they told me what the problem is."

"And...?" Her mother leaned in toward the screen.

"And it seems I'm going to need a few more months until I'm sort of back to normal."

"What do you mean?"

Sarah smiled as her dad on the computer screen leaned in

now too. "It seems the condition I have will take about nine months to fully develop."

She watched her parents gradually comprehend what she was saying. How she wished she could be telling them this in person. Emotion hovered. She batted it away. She was way too prone to tears these days.

"Sarah, you don't mean…?"

Hope shone on their faces, and she was so glad she could confirm the good news. "Dan and I are having a baby in April."

"Oh, sweetie, that's so exciting! Congratulations, Dan."

"Thanks, Lindy." Dan leaned into the shot, broad grin permanently attached these days.

"Congratulations to both of you! We know this means so much."

"Congrats, you two! Sarah, I wondered if you were, when you complained about being so tired and sick all the time," Bek crowed.

"I didn't think it was possible, what with the cramping and blood and stuff." She snuck a peek at her dad. He looked a little gobsmacked. Oh well. "Sorry, Dad. Just keeping it real."

Just not so real that they needed to know about the doctor's cautions about their child's potential to be born with health issues. Saying it aloud seemed to add weight to that diagnosis. And she didn't want to do that and spoil her celebratory birthday video call.

"So what does this mean for your trip to Australia?" Bek asked, oh-so-practical as ever.

Ah. Great question. Sarah felt the tension emanate from Dan. "The doctor said I'd be over the worst of the sickness soon," she said carefully.

"But you need to take care, sweetheart. Especially when you've been so tired."

"See?" Dan murmured. "Even your own mother agrees."

She kept her gaze on the computer. "I'm not going against medical advice."

Yeah, from the looks of her family, nobody was buying what she was trying to sell.

"I'm not," she insisted. "Dr. McKinnon said I'd be fine by then."

"But it's only a few weeks away," her mother protested.

"Exactly. So it's too late to cancel now."

"Sarah…"

Irritation spiked, and she turned to Dan. "Do you know how hard it's been to not see my family this year? *So* hard. And now I finally get the chance to see them and you don't want me to."

"Sar, this isn't the time," he said in a low voice.

"No, it's exactly the right time. They're my family. They want to see me." She sniffed. "And I want to see them. I *need* to see them, Dan."

"They could fly here—"

"No! Why does it always have to be they come here? What if I want to be there? What if I don't want to feel cold for once, and want to actually see the Pacific Ocean, and smell gum trees, and hear accents that sound like mine? I *want* to be there." She wiped away stupid tears. Oh, these hormones were making her so emotional.

"We all understand that," her mother soothed. "It's just we're concerned about your health, and the health of the baby."

"I'm *fine*."

"You're not fine," Dan said gently. "You're exhausted."

"How are you going to cope with all the traveling that the tour involves?" Bek asked.

Another excellent question. Touring was demanding at the best of times. But stubbornness refused to give in. Not yet, anyway.

"Princess," her father said, "We just want you to be okay and give your baby the best chance possible."

"I know," she said. "And like I said, if the doctor is happy, then I don't see why I can't." And part of her also felt a little fatalistic, especially after the last few times. Chances were that she'd have another miscarriage and *que sera sera*, whatever will be would be. "God has got this sorted, whatever happens."

Silence followed that, then Dan sighed. "I'm sorry. I need to go soon. We'll have to continue to talk about this later."

She faked a smile as her family quickly agreed, then turned to him as soon as the screen went black. "Why did you have to do that? I hate when we argue, especially in front of my family."

"Sar, I'm concerned about you. I understand you want to see your family, but it's a long way to travel when you don't feel well."

"I know, but I'd sleep on the plane—"

His look of skepticism took the puff out of that.

"Okay, I'd sleep as much as I could on the plane, then when I arrived, I'd be staying with them."

"For a few days until the tour begins. Then what? Long bus trips, late nights, more plane rides. You're already exhausted and you haven't even left. I'm worried about what this would mean for the baby."

Guilt stabbed. She'd once thought she could give up Heartsong in a heartbeat, but now, the thought of losing a certainty for something that still remained a little nebulous seemed like an overreaction. But saying that felt impossible, especially when she knew Dan's comments came from a place of love and concern. She couldn't admit that she couldn't get too attached to this baby. Not again. Not if it wouldn't even be born.

"Dr. McKinnon said I was fine to travel."

"Yeah, I don't think he realized you meant a trip around the world." Dan hauled in a deep breath, exhaled, calmed. "Look, I know you want to go, and it's not good for you to get agitated. Can we please just talk to him and explain the situation fully, and make a decision based on what he has to say?"

What choice did she have to say but, "Fine"?

She averted her gaze, shifted away.

But Dan-the-persistent moved back into her personal space. "Why do you want to do this so much, anyway? It's not like you haven't toured lots of times before."

Tears trickled from her eyes. "I miss them." Missed her Heartsong friends, missed feeling strong and capable and like she had purpose, missed her family most of all.

"I know, honey."

She let him wrap an arm around her shoulder. "And they're my *family*, Dan."

His face sobered. "I thought I was your family now."

Her heart hitched.

"Me, and this little one." He pointed to her stomach.

Her bottom lip quivered, and she covered her face. "I'm sorry."

Oh, she was an awful wife. She knew Dan wanted a baby more than anything. And yes, she wanted this child too. She *did*. Yet fear had crept in so insidiously, sucking away joy, even as she prayed, and praised, and tried to cling to hope. Dr. McKinnon might mean well, but the constant tests and cautions was having the opposite effect, spiraling her anxiety into levels even she could feel was unnatural.

She wiped away more stubborn tears. "Everything feels so out of control," she finally managed. "I just wanted to feel like I could plan something and see it through. There's just been so much disappointment lately."

"I know, Princess."

"I don't know if I can take much more. And," she swallowed, but honesty meant she had to be truthful, "and part of me is even questioning whether this will even come true. How do we know it won't end the same way as the others all did?"

"Oh, Sar." He smiled softly. "How do we know it won't be different this time around?"

Her tears expanded into sobs, and he enveloped her in a hug. Trying to walk by faith wasn't easy.

And as he held her, and murmured of God's faithfulness and love, Sarah wondered again at the wisdom of waiting to tell Dan's parents, especially after this fail of an encounter with her family. Sure it was only two weeks away, but doing the whole Thanksgiving announcement thing had the potential to backfire.

CHAPTER 17

"Y ou want to do what?"

Dan watched Sarah's face tighten as Dr. McKinnon explained a myriad of reasons why she should give up the Heartsong tour, that traveling to Australia and then going on tour was a risk she shouldn't undertake.

"You're a high-risk patient, Sarah. And your baby will likely already have sizeable health issues and doesn't need any other factors contributing to that."

"See?" Dan murmured.

Sarah's glare at him could shoot satellites from space.

"I know this isn't what you want to hear, Sarah," Dr. McKinnon continued. "But you need to be careful. You can't afford to let your blood pressure get high. Oh, and I want to schedule more tests."

"What for this time?"

"We just want to rule out other complications."

Other complications? Dan ignored the trickle of fear and glanced at Sarah, wanting—needing to hold her hand. But she'd folded her arms and pressed her lips together, her frustration plain.

Which left Dan to ask the question. "What other complications?"

Dr. McKinnon explained, throwing terms at them, most of which he didn't recognize, but some that he did. Like spina bifida. Down's syndrome.

Sarah's sharp intake of breath echoed the fear loitering in his chest, and try as Dr. McKinnon might, his remaining words didn't help.

"So I'd like you to schedule an appointment for another ultrasound in three weeks."

Three weeks? When he was due to go on a road trip, so Sarah would be forced to do this alone. Unless he found a support person for her. His heart softened. No wonder she wanted her mum. Maybe he could ask his mom.

He glanced at her, caught her wipe a tear from her eye, then realized: three weeks was when she was scheduled to go on the Heartsong tour. Sympathy panged. Poor thing.

He nudged her hand, but she moved it away. His heart panged. Ever since that phone call with her family he'd known she was finding the idea of withdrawing from the tour difficult, but surely she should be excited that they were having a baby?

"Any other questions?"

Sarah jerked her head no, forcing Dan to thank him for his time as he escorted her outside the office.

Dan sighed. "Well, that's that, then." He glanced at her. "Want to get lunch?"

She inched her arm away from where he tried to hold her. "I need the bathroom."

"Okay."

He nodded to some other partners waiting outside the clinic's toilets, then realized, as recognition stole across their faces, that probably wasn't wise. So he ducked his head, pretending to check his phone, and prayed Sarah wouldn't take too long.

That hadn't gone well. And he could tell from Sarah's icy

demeanor, lunch with him would likely be the last thing she wanted.

She returned sooner than he thought, and he escorted her to the front where he paid, and she scheduled the next appointment. Then he walked with her to the car.

"Sar, come on. You can't blame me for the doctor saying no."

"Oh, you'd be surprised," she muttered.

No, he wouldn't. Sarah had her good qualities, but her ability to hold onto a grudge wasn't one of them. Still, he had to try to be the peacemaker here. "Want to go have lunch now?"

"No." She clicked in her seatbelt. "I want to go home and figure out how I'm going to explain to everyone that I'm not going on the tour I said I'd be going on just a month ago."

"Why would you have to explain too much? People cancel tours all the time."

"But Heartsong won't be cancelling the tour. It'll still happen, just without me."

He exited the parking garage and joined the traffic. "I'm sorry you're disappointed."

"Don't patronize me." She folded her arms. "Honestly, sometimes you treat me like I'm five years old."

Maybe if she acted a little less emotionally then he wouldn't. Which meant he had to be the calm one now. "Just tell them you have health issues."

She huffed.

"It's true."

"I have people who have *bought tickets* because I said I was going on this tour."

"Are you seriously more concerned about the tour than you are about your own child?"

"We don't even know if there will be a child, do we?"

This again. He drove into the street their apartment was on. He so didn't want to continue their argument upstairs. "Look, can we talk about this rationally?"

"Excuse me? I'm being rational. This," she pointed to her face, "is me being disappointed. I'm allowed to be disappointed, aren't I? Or is that not what a perfect Christian does?"

A dozen things wanted to erupt from his lips. He bit them back, settling for, "Sarah, I'm concerned about you. I don't understand why you're so frustrated."

"Because I'm more than just a baby incubator, Dan. And now this thing I really wanted to do is suddenly forbidden and I'm upset, okay? Or am I not allowed to be upset as well? Let's add that to the things I'm now not allowed to do. No getting upset," she ticked off her fingers, "no eating soft cheese, no seeing my family, no going on tour."

Man. Arguing with her was like reasoning with a tree. "You have to let the tour go. We agreed, remember?"

"I don't think we agreed. I think you told me this was what we'd do, and now you're just expecting me to be the little submissive wife, just like Marguerite. Well, I'm not like her."

That was for sure. "Sarah, come on, please—"

"I don't want to give up the tour."

"I know that," he said, through gritted teeth.

"And now I have to explain to Tisha and the others, people who have put in all this work—just like me!—and then tell all my fans that I won't be there after all."

Irritation pricked. "Do you even hear yourself?"

"But *I'm* whom they want to see!" she yelled.

"Stop yelling, Sarah. It's not good for the baby."

Her fingers clenched.

"You need to get over yourself," he continued. "All this talk about your fans missing you, that's just pride talking."

She gasped. And yeah, he hadn't meant it quite that way.

"Sometimes I don't like you very much," she muttered in a voice he guessed he was meant to hear.

The feeling was mutual, but saying so would only inflame matters.

The diamonds on her engagement ring caught the light. He remembered the night he'd given her that ring, on a beautiful evening in Sydney, with the lights of the Harbour Bridge and Opera House glimmering on the water. Back when they were so much in love and things like living miles apart and a childless future hadn't seemed so unbearable.

Now, they might share a bed, but she might as well be in Sydney for all the connection they had, and it felt like this miraculous answer to prayer was being battered at every turn. Why did everything have to go wrong? How had they grown so far apart? "Sarah, I love you."

She huffed again, shook her head.

"What? What do you want me to say? Sure, go on your tour, get exhausted, and let's have another miscarriage like last year."

Her mouth dropped. "Are you seriously blaming me for that?"

He winced. No.

"Don't you remember what the doctor said? We have chromosomal incompatibility, Dan. So we're not one of those couples who get the dream pregnancy. Or any kind of pregnancy that lasts long enough to have a child, it seems."

"That's not true." It couldn't be true. "Please don't say that anymore."

She muttered things he couldn't quite catch, but it sounded like she was reeling off a list of yet more things she couldn't do.

He needed to rein in his temper, get this back into level ground. He hated arguing with her. She was too good at making him feel bad. "I didn't mean to say that before, Sar."

Her eyes sparkled with angry tears. "Oh no, it's good to see you being honest for once, instead of pretending everything will be fine when clearly it's not."

Oh, he was glad they were in the car and couldn't be heard by anyone else. What happened to Team Walton? *Lord*, his heart ached, *please heal us.* "I don't understand why you're resisting this, Sar. Surely you want this baby to be healthy."

"Didn't you hear the man just now? He clearly doesn't expect this child to be healthy. I don't think he even expects this baby to live."

Her words slashed at his heart, voicing his own silent fears. But faith couldn't let those words stand, even if his heart wavered sometimes. "This baby will live."

"Will it?"

It had to. "In Jesus's name."

Her face crumpled. "I hate going there each time and only hearing what is wrong."

He did, too. "So what are you saying? You want to find another obstetrician?"

"I don't know what I want, except to find some hope, instead of feeling like I'm living in a world of 'no, no, no' all the time."

A faint verse rang softly in the back of his mind, something about God being the God of Yes and Amen. But he didn't know where that was, so said nothing. Nothing, except, "I love you, Sarah."

She covered her face in her hands. "I love you too. I just wish this wasn't so hard."

That was a definite yes and amen.

"And so," Sarah sniffled, "I'm really sorry, but it turns out that I won't be able to join the Heartsong Collective tour after all."

Sarah wiped away stupid tears, and finished reading her script. "I'm really sorry for letting people down, but thanks to medical advice, I need to stay put for the moment. But I hope to see you sometime soon." Although how she would ever manage that she had no idea. "Anyway, on that sober note, thanks for listening to *Time Out with Sarah*. We can trust Him with it all, yeah?"

She played the outro music, wincing. She hadn't meant to finish that last word with an upward inflection, like a question. Even if it did feel true.

She sagged into her seat. Plopped her head in her hands. Trusting God in the unknown seemed so much harder this time around. Yes, she'd seen His faithfulness in the past. Yes, she'd witnessed His miracles. She placed a hand on her belly. This life was a miracle. She *knew* that. But God had let her down before. And if the doctor was right, then the latest round of testing would reveal a problem.

Oh, *why* did Dan have to be away on a road trip? He'd suggested his mother accompany Sarah to the clinic, but she'd rather not have that woman's negativity compound her own. Telling Dan's family about the pregnancy at Thanksgiving had not met with the joy they'd hoped, apart from with Sam. God bless Sam. And God needed to bless Helen and Andrew, because Sarah was finding it hard to. Their congratulations had been muted at best, almost like they were thinking, 'what's the point?' as if they expected news of another miscarriage in a few weeks.

No, she needed Dan's faith, because hers felt so weak. "And who else have I got right now, Lord?"

Other names, faces, floated to mind, then were instantly dismissed. Ange? Lived too far away. She could ask Jackie or Toni she supposed. But the fact those women had children while she had none meant they wouldn't understand. So no. Not an option. Not a viable option.

She cringed. Ugh. Now Dr. McKinnon's clinical speak was infecting her brain!

She closed her eyes, willing the tears to stay away. She'd looked up the test Dr. McKinnon had recommended, and realized one of the risk factors for that kind of intrusive test was miscarriage. How could he recommend a test like that? Was this test even necessary? Did it even matter if the baby had major health issues? They'd still want the child, regardless. *If* the baby survived long enough to be born.

If. Always if.

THE SOUND of the front door opening made her switch off the light, and pretend to be asleep.

"Sar?"

No. The heart was a messy place, and she couldn't play nice with him. She was too tired from the past three weeks of playing nice with everyone else that she had nothing left for her husband. Her husband, the traitor, who had insisted on her cancelling her tour, then gone off on his own road trip not five days later.

Her husband, the impossibly patient, who like the doctor, didn't seem to understand that she was good for more than just being a baby incubator. She wanted to argue with Dr. McKinnon, but he was always warning her about high blood pressure, so she liked to save that for when she and Dan were in the car.

She huddled in the bed, tugging the blankets up to her ears so she didn't have to see or hear him. Why couldn't Dan understand her perspective? She'd never once canceled on a tour. Not once. So when she'd tearfully announced it on her podcast, her fans had been devastated. *Dev-a-sta-ted.* She felt like such a fraud. People had bought tickets to see her, and now they wouldn't. Tisha and the rest of the crew had been upset, forcing her to explain more of the reason why. They'd understood, then offered congratulations, and agreed to keep her reason for not touring limited to 'health issues.'

Not that Dan appreciated the sacrifice she was making. Sometimes she wanted to scream at him, their arguments such that she hoped none of the neighbors could hear. But how could they not, stuck in this stupid too-small apartment? But any time she raised her voice he simply repeated the line: "Stop yelling, Sarah. It's not good for the baby."

Sometimes she wanted to hurl more than just words at him, but he turned and walked away. Why couldn't the man fight for once? She was tired of being the only one who did.

No tour. No career. No travel. No family. Dan had said he'd pay for her family to come visit for Christmas, but it felt too much like a handout, something designed to shut her up, that she'd snapped and said she'd rather wait until April when the baby would be born. *If* the baby was born. She placed a hand on her stomach. There were still no guarantees.

Dr. McKinnon had been cautious in Sarah's last visit, noting the baby's heartbeat was weaker than he liked, advising that she attend another scan as soon as possible to investigate the issue. "We want to rule out things like congenital hearts defects, hydrocephalus, water on the brain, or other birth defects."

Birth defects?

She placed a hand on her stomach, prayed for the tiny one inside. Surely God wouldn't let them get this far to have something like birth defects? And yet, plenty of people had children born with medical issues. There were no guarantees. Just like Dr. McKinnon had cautioned that there were no guarantees that she would make full term.

And it was that fear that lurked in the background, refusing to let her fall in love with this child. She couldn't have her heart ripped away. Not again. Even if this was the furthest she'd been able to carry a child.

These emotions were like a rollercoaster she couldn't get off. Up one minute, down the next, never anything calm and in the middle. She'd always struggled with moderating her emotions, of letting the Holy Spirit calm her, and lately, it felt like these extremes were growing into normality.

Which wasn't fair to Dan. Which made it a hard habit to change. Why did she have to be the one who changed, anyway?

Oh, that's right. Because she was the one who always had to give up everything – her life, her career, her family, her country—to support his dreams.

The bedroom door opened. "Sar?" he whispered. "Are you awake?"

An opportunity lay in the air. She let it float to the floor. Feigned a snore.

He sighed, and closed the door.

CHAPTER 18

The sonographer frowned, peering at the screen.

Sarah's heart clenched. "Is something wrong?"

"Excuse me for a moment. I need to get my supervisor in."

Sarah glanced at Ange, who reached out a hand. Sarah clutched it.

"It's okay," Ange soothed. "Whatever is happening, God is still here with us."

Sarah nodded, as a savage longing rose for her husband to be here too. Oh, she *wished* she was a better wife. Wished she hadn't let offense creep in and crowbar them apart. Suddenly all her petty behavior was held up to the light. Her heart might be caked with anger and frustration, yet this man, *this* man, kept loving her through her imperfections. Dan's love was like a beam of warmth that tugged her from this prison of disappointments and scars. She didn't deserve him. Her eyes welled.

A moment later, their sonographer returned along with another man. They murmured to each other, then asked Ange to leave. "We need to speak to Mrs. Walton alone."

"What?" This wasn't good news. "What's wrong?"

"I'll be right outside, praying," Ange assured.

Lord God. Help. Sarah nodded, her fingers clasping her belly.

The older man sighed. "I'm sorry, Mrs. Walton, but there seems to be some irregularities with what we're seeing on the scan."

"What do you mean?"

He cleared his throat. "The scans suggest that there is a problem with the ventricle of the left chamber, which hasn't developed properly."

Her own heart stabbed. *Lord?*

"And—"

There was more?

"—there is some issue with the spinal cord, which suggests…"

He went on to use words like spina bifida and hydro-cephalus, just like Dr. McKinnon had warned. *No, no, no,* her heart screamed.

"…why we want to send you to the city's children's hospital pediatric unit where their specialized equipment will give a clearer indication."

They had to have this wrong. Had to.

"And we want you to schedule it soon. Like tomorrow."

"Tomorrow?" she repeated, mind awhirl.

"Then you will know what your best option is."

Her heart wrenched. Surely, they didn't mean to imply—?

"It's probably best you have your husband with you."

"He… he's away."

"He should probably return for this."

Her hands were shaking, her legs like jelly, when Ange finally was re-admitted, and they exited. "Sar?"

Sarah managed to share the most pertinent truths, which saw Ange clasp her in a hug.

"Don't fear the worst. We trust God, remember?"

"They want me to go tomorrow."

"So soon?"

"They said…" She gulped. "They said it's better to know the result sooner, as it gives more options."

Ange gasped. "Oh, Sar."

"Dan…"

"I'll call him now." Ange dug out her phone.

S HE WAS A GHOST. The sense of unreality that had set in yesterday had tripled when they saw the specialist, a head professor of prenatal and pediatric medicine, who had called Dr. McKinnon in. If it wasn't for Dan's warm hand grounding her, she might fly away, never to return, as the professor's shocking words revolved around her brain.

The left side of the heart wasn't growing. There were definite signs of spinal issues. Hydrocephalus. One of these neural tube defects might indicate a virus, but the fact the 'fetus' had all three simultaneously suggested a genetic issue, and therefore the 'fetus' was unlikely to survive. "Just as I expected," Dr. McKinnon said. "If it survives, it's a matter of hours, not days."

Delivered in an unemotional manner with no empathy. No sympathy. No sense that their worlds were falling apart.

"You've only got two weeks, then it's a different matter."

Dan cleared his throat. "Two weeks?"

"To terminate the pregnancy," Dr. McKinnon replied, as if it was obvious that was what should be done. "After twenty weeks it becomes more complicated, and there are government forms and death certificates and the like."

Dan's grip tightened. "Are you saying that you expect our baby to die?"

"The fetus," Dr. McKinnon said, as if correcting them, "is not viable, nor compatible with a healthy life outcome. So yes."

"No," Sarah murmured. "No, I don't believe it."

"I know this is a shock, even though I've tried to prepare you for this. We've talked about chromosome incompatibility many times before."

Oh, they certainly had.

"I can see you two need a minute." The professor stood.

At least someone had eyes in their head.

"I'll be back in a moment, and we can discuss when to schedule the appointment."

"For the abortion?" Sarah whispered.

"For the termination, yes."

Sarah could barely breathe. She turned to Dan who wore his own look of shock. "Dan." Her voice, her heart, was broken.

Then she collapsed in his arms.

NEVER HAD he ever been so glad to see John and Ange. As soon as they entered the apartment John stood and opened his arms. They huddled together, hugging, crying. But this time Dan didn't feel the need to hold back his tears like he had in the specialist's office, trying to keep it together while his wife fell apart. He had no strength, barely any words, except for a stubborn sense that the doctors were wrong, and that their child who had lived this long could be born. Which meant they'd refused the termination, much to Dr. McKinnon's obvious dismay.

"You're setting yourself up for a very long and difficult journey, with likely heartbreak," he'd warned.

Difficult was something they were used to. Heartbreak was nothing new.

John took his time hugging Dan, and it was like in that moment that the man's strength imparted Dan with more strength, too. "God's got you in the palm of His hand," John murmured. "This hasn't taken Him by surprise."

Rest in Me.

Dan's throat clamped. *Help me trust You, Father.*

"Dr. McKinnon always warned us, but we… we didn't believe him," Sarah murmured. "But we couldn't agree to terminating."

"It doesn't matter what health challenges our baby has, we're going to trust God through it all." Dan glanced at Sarah's red-rimmed eyes, knowing his words held a challenge similar to a song she'd once written. It was one thing to sing it when things were going well, another when their world had imploded.

Sarah nodded, reached for his hand, and in that moment, they were Team Walton again. Standing against the naysayers. Standing for what God could do.

"Our God can do anything," Ange said, her voice thick with tears. "You wrote that Sarah, and it's true. So stand firm on the truth of God."

"I feel like we need to pray," John said. "I know this feels devastating right now, but this is our God who can do the impossible, can make the lame walk, the dead come back to life. He is here with us now, here in the midst of this storm. We can trust Him." John moved Dan's hand to Sarah's stomach. "God gives the barren woman children, like Hannah, like Sarah. This is who our God is. Strong, Almighty, which means *all* mighty, and nothing is impossible for Him."

"Amen," Ange and Dan echoed.

John continued to pray, and some of the anguish faded, Dan's emotions easing back from the sharp pointy edges of pain. As they each took turns in praying, a sense of peace stole into the room. God *was* here, His presence tangible.

By the time John finished, Dan was wilting, and Sarah was clearly exhausted.

"You two need to rest," Ange said kindly. "John and I are staying with his parents here in the city. We can stay here if you like, but understand if you want time to yourself."

They needed time to themselves. Dan glanced at Sarah. "I'm so tired, I can't even think."

Ange hugged her, glanced at Dan, must've caught his wish to be alone with Sarah as she then nodded. "You both need some sleep. There's a casserole in the fridge."

Sarah groaned. "Mum, Dad—"

"I can contact them if you like," Ange offered.

"Please."

John gripped Dan's shoulder. "I know you have praying friends. Ask them to pray."

"Yeah." He would. But first he and Sarah needed time to process.

"If it's alright with you, I'll ask our friends at Muskoka Shores to pray, too."

"Thank you," Sarah said.

Two more strong hugs later, and they were alone again. But not quite alone. For as John and Ange had reminded them, God was there in the midst. They could—would—trust Him. And rest in Him.

PRAYER REQUESTS WERE SENT around the world. Responses quickly flooded in, with everyone from Tisha and the Heart-song crew to Dan's online Bible study teammates expressing love, support, prayers, offers of help, and whatever they could do.

Sarah's parents had offered to fly over immediately. She'd told them no. Not until the next scan's results anyway.

They were due to have another scan in two weeks, then four weeks after that.

"Long enough for God to do a miracle, anyway," Jackie said.

In addition to the prayers came a few more startling words too.

Some fans of Sarah's sent messages saying they'd seen visions of Dan and Sarah's daughter getting married.

During one video call, Bek said she'd had a dream where God took their baby's heart and closed His hand around it, then when He opened His hand, the baby's heart was healed.

Others, like Ange, shared Bible verses, like the words given to Moses, who commanded the Israelites trapped between the Egyptians and the Red Sea to fear not, but stand still and see the salvation of the Lord. "For the Lord shall fight for you, and you shall hold your peace."

And this verse, as much as the others, provided a shield of comfort, of supernatural peace, as their friends and faith-filled family members stood with them, holding up their hands like Aaron and Hur held up Moses's weary arms, while the battle raged in front of them.

Peace that reminded them that God was here. And whatever the next scan said, God could be trusted with it all.

A SLIGHT JOLT WOKE SARAH. What? The morning's sounds crept to her ears. She rolled to the side, saw Dan with his eyes closed. Poor man was exhausted.

The fluttering feeling came again. She inhaled sharply.

"Sar?" he murmured sleepily.

"I just felt a funny sensation."

"A good one or a bad one?" He blinked, squinting at her. "Do we need to go to the doctor?"

"No." She grasped his hand, placed it on her stomach, as another tiny kick came. "Feel that? That's your little son or daughter wanting to say hello."

"Wow." His face softened. "Hello little one." He spent the next half hour touching and talking to her tummy while hoping for more kicks. "Thank you, God, for this precious life. Please protect this little one, and my beautiful wife. Amen."

"Amen," Sarah whispered.

"Hмм."

Sarah gripped Dan's hand. She'd been here before. The fetal sonographer's frown wasn't encouraging. Today's fetal echocardiogram was to check on the heart issue, whether it was growing or—*No, God, I'm going to trust You.*

He peered at the screen, glanced at them, then murmured about getting his supervisor.

"It's okay," Dan murmured.

She nodded. A supernatural peace flooded her soul, like someone somewhere had just prayed for her.

The sonographer returned, accompanied by a gray-permed woman, who greeted them then looked at the screen. They conferred with each other, then looked at the previous results.

"What's happened?" Sarah asked.

"This echo seems to be suggesting there's no issue."

"What do you mean?"

"Well, this previous scan suggested there was a problem in the valves on the left side of the heart, but today's scan shows no sign of that."

Sarah's heart thudded. "What are you saying?"

"I don't understand this."

Sarah squeezed Dan's hand, as hope flickered.

But when they returned to Dr. McKinnon he wasn't encouraged. "It's likely there was a problem with their machine," he scoffed. "I want you to schedule another appointment."

She clamped her lips. She didn't want to.

"I know you might like to think going against medical advice is nice for your 'beliefs', but you need to prepare yourself. The chances of a live birth are next to nil."

Why did that man's words poison her seedling faith?

"I can't stand that man," she muttered when they exited the room.

"You want a second opinion?"

"Yes please."

"Okay. Wait here."

"Dan?" She watched as he marched back in, and from the closed door heard raised voices then silence. Two minutes later, Dan reappeared, an envelope in his hand.

"That was fast."

"We got our referral." He held the envelope higher.

"You mean we don't need to see him again?"

"Let's hope not." Dan's lips tweaked. "And after that encounter, I don't think he wants to see us again either."

"Oh, thank you." She squeezed him—hugs were getting more squashy now—as thankfulness bloomed for this man who fought for her, for them, for their child.

How did other people manage when they didn't have the finances to fight for a second opinion, and took whatever the medical professional said as gospel?

"God help all expectant parents."

CHAPTER 19

*D*an slapped the puck to Toronto's Matt Reynolds, watching as the star forward neatly scooped it before sending it into the net to score. The siren blared and he high-fived his teammates and skated back to the bench, glancing up to where Sarah would normally be sitting with the other wives and girlfriends. But she'd hardly come at all this year, what with their fight following Dr. McKinnon's virtual banning of her involvement with the tour, then feeling too tired after all the scans. He was glad their days of fighting were done. It was easy to see how the strain of these situations caused couples to buckle under the pressure.

He sucked down an energy drink, glad that his shift had ended, that he'd get a break to sit and pretend to watch the play while his thoughts trudged back to his absent wife. *Lord, be with her.*

"Dan?"

A nudge from Brendan drew his attention behind to an assistant coach beckoning him urgently. He followed him down the passage away from the stadium's roar. The coach's grizzled face frowned, his forehead wrinkling. The hairs on Dan's neck prickled.

"I'm sorry, but there's been an accident, Dan."

His chest clenched. "Who? What?" It couldn't be Sarah. She was at home with Ange. Wasn't she?

Compassion washed across the coach's face. "It's Sarah. She was in a car accident."

Oh Lord, please help. He rushed to take off his gloves and helmet and handed them to the equipment guy, and followed him to the locker room to remove his skates and gear, and find his street clothes.

"Sarah's aunt rang. She's at the hospital, wants you to come in now."

"What about the…?" *Baby.* He could barely bring himself to say it. This couldn't be happening. Not again.

"I'm sorry. I don't know anything more."

Dan swallowed, his heart hammering as he finally tugged on his trousers and grabbed his jacket, wallet, and keys.

"Mick will drive you. I've given him directions. Dan, we'll all be thinking of you, and praying for the best."

Oh Lord.

Trust Me.

The drive was silent. Young Mick, the second equipment guy, was desperate to stay on the slippery road, but the snow from yesterday still lay thickly, making handling difficult. Dan was grateful for the silence, sending texts asking for prayer to the Bible study guys, to James and Lindy. He didn't want to scare Sarah's parents, but they'd need some warning.

Mick finally pulled into the emergency entryway, Dan thanked him and raced inside like a wild man. Only to be stopped by John McPherson just inside the foyer near the information desk.

"Where is she? What's happening?"

"Dan, they're okay. Calm down, they're going to be okay."

"What happened? I need to see Sar. Where is she?"

"Walk with me." John led him to a nearby elevator, pressing the buttons, explaining briefly what had happened. When they finally got to the maternity section it was to find Ange, a big white bandage on her head and with her arm strapped, obviously anxiously awaiting their arrival.

She gave Dan a swift, awkward hug. "Dan, she's just being monitored. She's right this way."

She led him to a private room, the dimness revealing a curtained bed, at the foot of which stood a blonde nurse holding a chart.

She glanced at him, then said softly, "You're the father?"

He nodded. "What's going on?"

"Sarah's going to be fine."

"And… and the baby?"

"The baby should be fine too. The shock triggered some early contractions, but the doctor has given her something that's stopped them. We're just monitoring the heartbeat now."

Contractions? He moved closer to the bed, dimly aware of the faint beeps coming from the machine next to the bed. Sarah's hair was strewn across the pillow, the only bright thing in this pale, too cool room of gray. She was asleep, and a cut on her forehead had been patched up with white puffy bandage. He sat down in the chair next to her, holding her too-still hand. At least it was warm.

He caressed her fingers, wishing that he could infuse some of his life and strength into her. "What happened?"

Ange placed a hand on his shoulder. "Sarah was driving me after a meeting with Dr. Feldman."

"Who?"

"Your new obstetrician."

"Our what?"

Ange's brow creased. "She said it was new, but I didn't realize…"

Neither had he. Wow. Okay.

"I'm sorry, Dan." Her gaze was troubled. "I thought you knew."

"She—we," he corrected, "found the previous one pretty negative."

She bit her lip. "A second opinion is always worthwhile."

He nodded. "So, what happened?"

"We'd just come back from the appointment—Dr. Feldman seems lovely, by the way—and Sarah was driving me back to John's parents' place. We were slowing down for an intersection when a pick-up slammed into us at the rear."

His chest squeezed, his grip tightening on Sarah's hand.

"We got knocked about a bit, but fortunately the airbags deployed, though Sarah hit her head and got knocked unconscious. The paramedics were great, and she got here amazingly quick."

Well, that was something. But, "She had contractions?"

Her grip on his shoulder firmed. "They were able to stop them, so she's fine."

Wetness filled his eyes. He blinked it back. "We should call her parents."

"I'll do that now," Ange said.

"Tell them to book the first flight they can. Bek too, if she wants. I'll cover it."

She squeezed his shoulder again, and he vaguely heard John murmur that he'd pray, and that the doctor was here.

"Mr. Walton?"

Dan looked up to see the doctor approach, a light of recognition in his eyes. No, now was not the time to talk hockey.

"Mr. Walton, your wife should be fine. We've run scans, and it looks like your baby is okay. The baby is well protected in the big cushion of the uterus, so it's very unlikely that there's been any trauma."

Dan took a deep breath, fighting the tears that begged for release. "I… I can't lose…"

The doctor looked at him with compassion. "We'll be taking another ultrasound soon. You can be assured that there has been no bleeding or any other signs of fetal distress."

"But what about the contractions?"

"That's something that can happen with a great shock. They've stopped now, and we'll be monitoring her overnight, especially given her history."

Her history. Their history. Woven with pain, and rawness, and grace, and hope. God had been there in their past. And God would be there in their future. And God was here right now, His presence unseen yet as tangible as the love that swelled his soul. For despite everything, he loved this woman. He kissed her hand. He couldn't lose her. *Couldn't.*

WHITE WALLS. That horrible antiseptic smell. Flowers. No. All of this was wrong. She thought she'd left that bad dream behind years ago. Why was she still here?

Slowly the blur of images sharpened, and she finally caught the tangled dark head of Dan resting against the mattress of her bed, holding her left hand in both of his. What was he doing here?

She licked dry, chapped lips. She was so thirsty. What was that beeping noise? Why was she here? What was that thing around her stomach? As the panicky questions increased, swirling around her brain like a merry-go-round, so did the stupid beeping machine's pulse and volume.

No. This wasn't right, she wanted to get out of here.

Dan stirred, sleepily looking up at her. "You're awake! Thank God."

A blonde nurse appeared, talking at her like she was a

schoolgirl, before murmuring something to Dan who nodded, glancing at her as he rubbed his hand over his face then through his hair. Didn't they know she knew all about hospitals? That they were places where dreams died? She had to get out of here. Agitation rose.

She shuffled on the bed. "What...?" Her voice was raspy. She could barely talk. Someone get her a drink.

"Shh, Princess, it's all okay."

Nope. Nothing was okay if she was lying strapped down in a hospital bed.

"Sarah." The nurse spoke firmly to her. "You're in the hospital. There was a car accident yesterday. You're okay, and so is your baby."

Baby?

Oh! She shifted, desperate to reposition the strap so she could feel her stomach. But when she felt her stomach there was no reassuring kick. *Oh, Lord!*

The nurse patted her hand away, rearranging the equipment once more to her satisfaction. "Sarah, the monitor tells us your baby's heartbeat is fine. Hear the sound like a galloping horse?"

Under the steadying beep of her own heart beat Sarah could hear a faster sound.

"That tells us that the baby's heart valves are opening and closing as they should."

Thank You, Lord.

Dan's face loomed over her. "Here you go, Princess." He gave her a bottle of water with a straw.

"Thanks," she managed to croak out, before blessed coolness slipped down her throat.

Dan's face relaxed in relief. "Oh Sar, you had us so worried." He pressed a kiss to her hand. "I love you so much. I can't lose you."

The emotion in his voice and on his face stirred deep inside her heart, welling moisture in her eyes.

"Hey, Princess, don't cry. You're okay, the baby's okay."

She placed a hand on her stomach, and he gently laid his over the top. She threaded her fingers through his.

"We're not okay."

His brow creased, and she had to make him understand.

"You and me. I've been so frustrated about things and taken it out on you. I'm sorry."

"Hey, it's alright," he soothed. "Everything will be alright. We'll be okay. I know things have been disappointing for you. I understand that."

Tears trickled onto her pillow. She sniffed them back. "I hate that I've been crying so much."

He thumbed away her tears. "I don't mind your tears."

"You'll be a good dad," she murmured.

"And you'll be a good mum."

She smiled at how he said it, like she did. Then her emotions wobbled. "If we get that far."

"However far we get, I'm glad I'm doing it with you."

Oh, why did the man have to be so nice to her? Her tears swelled into sobs, and the monitor started to beep at a higher pitch, which brought the nurse rushing in.

"Mr. Walton? Sarah? Is everything okay in here?"

"It is now." Sarah sniffled, nodding. "He's so good to me," she wailed.

"Okay then." The nurse shot a smile at Dan then exited, closing the door behind them.

Sarah gripped his hand. "Can you hold me?"

"I don't know if I can with all those wires." He gestured to her stomach.

"Get on the bed then."

"Are you sure?"

"Please?"

He took off his shoes and gingerly climbed on, spooning her, his front to her back, as he laid his arm across her belly. "I love you," he whispered.

She gripped his hand, needing his strength, needing his warmth. She drew his hand to her chest, right next to her heart. "I love you too."

CHAPTER 20

Two days of personal leave allowed for time to return to their apartment, where time to reconnect could occur. Sarah had explained about wishing to see Dr. Feldman and apologised about keeping him in the dark. Dan had met Dr. Feldman yesterday when she'd dropped by Sarah's room, and was impressed by her optimism, and that Sarah seemed far more relaxed and willing to listen to her advice. It gave him more confidence knowing that he had another lengthy road trip coming up, and he was relieved when he received a call saying the most important part of his plans was ready.

"Okay, hon. I've got a surprise for you."

"Another one?" Sarah gestured to the bouquets decorating their living room. "I don't think we have room for any more."

"It's not flowers. Come here." He drew Sarah to the apartment's hallway. "Now close your eyes."

She obeyed.

"Now, I want you to hold your hands out."

She did, squinting a little.

"No peeking."

She laughed, and squeezed her eyes shut.

"That's better. Now, on the count of three, you can open your eyes."

He opened the front door, and pointed to Sarah.

"What's going on?" Sarah asked.

"Keep them closed until I get to three." Dan counted, "One… two… three."

She opened her eyes. Gasped. "Mum?" She threw her hands over her mouth. "Bek?"

"Surprise!" they chorused.

Dan looked on in satisfaction as Sarah hugged the two women she loved most in the world. He might've gotten a few things wrong over the past few months, but this, this had right written all over it. Their huddle of love contained as much laughter as it did tears, and he realized afresh how much she'd missed her family.

"It's so good to see you," Sarah wailed.

He smiled at his wife's emotion. He hoped her emotional outbursts would be limited to ones more like this, and no more of those angry frustrated ones like before.

"Your father wanted to come," Lindy said to her daughter, "but he had a cold, and knew he could be here later when the baby comes."

"Okay." Sarah sniffed.

"I told Joe I had to see you, and wasn't taking no for an answer."

He bit back a smile. He'd often thought Bek was as strong-minded as her sister.

"And now I'm here." Bek shot a smile his direction. "Thanks to Dan."

"Thanks to Dan," Lindy said, gazing at him fondly.

Sarah finally released them then moved to him. "Oh, Dan." Sarah hugged him. "Thank you so much."

"You're welcome, Princess," he murmured.

"How did you manage this?"

"You needed them, so we made it happen, didn't we Lindy?"

His mother-in-law nodded and gave him a hug too. "Thank you." Her eyes, so like Sarah's, shimmered with unshed tears. "It's so wonderful to see her. And to see you both doing so much better than before."

He dipped his chin. There was still a way to go, but he felt that too, that they were finally on the right path.

"Oh, there's way too many tears today. Honestly, what is it with you all?" Bek teased. "Now, let me say hello to my niece or nephew." She bent down and murmured a hello to Sarah's stomach, then her mother took a turn too.

Bek ran a hand over Sarah's bump. "You're so beautiful."

"No, I'm not. I'm so fat."

"You're not fat. There's barely a bump, is there?"

"I've been throwing up so much."

"But the baby's weight is okay?"

"The doctor is happy enough," Dan said.

He glanced at Sarah, caught her wince. Knew she felt bad for going behind his back about switching doctors. He'd forgiven her, but needed to make it plain. With all the emotions flying around these days, things needed to be made very plain.

"We have a new obstetrician," he explained. "Dr. Feldman. She seems a lot more positive than the last one."

"Oh, I must say I'm relieved to hear that," Lindy said.

Relief pinged. So Sarah hadn't talked it over with her family instead of him.

"That other one seemed to be sending you off for tests all the time," Lindy continued. "I don't think people realize just how stressful this can be. Especially considering, well, what's happened in the past."

All that had happened in the past. Sarah's accident. His pre-Christian history, where he'd got a woman pregnant then selfishly prayed for the baby to die. Which it had. He knew now that God had forgiven him, knew this was why Sarah had warned him away, considering her own medical challenges regarding fertility, thanks to the accident which had scarred her reproductive organs. All of that coupled with the toll of three miscarriages, it was no wonder that Sarah had struggled.

The mood had sobered, and he knew it needed to be salvaged. He gestured for them to sit in the living room. "Now who's ready for a cup of tea?"

"Oh my gosh. It's so cold outside, and I thought you'd never offer," Bek teased.

Three hot tea orders later, he moved to the kitchen.

"I'll help," Sarah said.

"No, you sit down, spend time with your family."

She shook her head, retrieved the special cups that got used rarely. "Mum is in the bathroom, and Bek just said you've arranged for them to stay here while you have your road trip."

"Stay here or in Muskoka. Whichever you prefer."

Her lips twisted, which made her answer plain. "Did you arrange that for me?"

"Of course I did."

She slid her arms around his waist, her bump protruding into him. "I can't tell you how grateful I am," she murmured against the scar on his jaw. "You're so good to me."

"Because I love you."

"I love you too." She tugged his head down and pressed her lips to his. There was healing in that kiss, hope too, and soon heat. She pulled away with a quiet gasp. "Are they staying here tonight?"

"Not tonight. Not until I go away."

She smiled at him. "So maybe tonight I can show you how grateful I am?"

"If you're up for it."

"Hey, are you two okay in there?" Bek called.

"Very okay." Sarah's smile held joy, and a promise.

"Amen," he agreed.

He and Sarah made a round of hot teas. It was good to be stealing kisses, working in partnership with her, feeling like Team Walton again. They might each have had their moments of stumbling over the years, but just like Ecclesiastes said, "Two are better than one" because when one fell, the other could pick him up. And with God at the center of their lives and marriage, "a cord of three strands is not quickly broken."

And later, as they drank tea, and ate the Tim Tams Bek had brought, and Sarah settled on the couch, laughing like the woman he remembered, he knew that whatever still faced them, God would help them find the love and light again.

SNOW FELL outside the big picture window at Muskoka. The fire crackled, sending welcome heat, especially for the two non-acclimatized Aussies whose shivers had necessitated buying appropriate winter clothes the day after they arrived.

Sarah settled onto the leather sofa in the Muskoka cottage. After Dan had left for his latest road trip, she'd lasted two days in the city. Two days taking Mum and Bek to visit shops and museums like the Bata Shoe Museum, before the call of Muskoka drew her to drive them here in Dan's sturdy Jeep. Muskoka always brought a sense of peace.

"This is the life," Bek declared, glancing over with a smile from where she was lying on the sofa, magazine in hand, hot chocolate in easy reach.

"I'm glad you approve."

Her sister snorted. "How can I not? I'm here, my kids are being looked after by my husband, while I get to meet famous actors and authors and pretend to look after my little sister. It's been tough, but I'm managing."

"Looks like it." Sarah smiled.

Oh, this was so good. Time here with her mum, and sister,

and aunt, was like what she imagined an extended girls' weekend must be. They'd met up with Jackie and Lincoln, Staci and James, and some of the other Musko-cheers, for a pot-luck meal where her mum and sister got the chance to learn more about these women.

Mum had gravitated to James once she'd learned about his missionary work, and they'd swapped stories while Bek found herself giggling with Anna and Rachel. And the time with these women, their hands of friendship extended so freely, reminded her that there were many blessings to be found, even in the midst of challenges.

"So, how are you really doing, Sarah?" her mother asked now.

"I'm doing a lot better."

"You seem so much better than your birthday."

That total cringe of a birthday Zoom call, with her embarrassing argument with Dan. "It took time to get my head around a few things."

"You are okay about missing the Heartsong tour?"

She nodded. "I know now it was the right call to make." Ugh. How could she have thought to lead people in worship around the world when she couldn't even do it at home?

"You know Dan was just concerned about you."

"I know."

God bless her husband. *Lord, thank You for Your mercy and grace.*

"So things are better between you two now?"

"Yes." She sighed. "I don't know why I always tend to fly off the handle like that."

"Um, I think it has something to do with hair color," Bek said, waving her ponytail at Sarah.

Her smile twisted. "I don't know how much longer that excuse is going to wash with Dan." Or if it ever had.

Her mother laughed. "It'll be good to have him back."

She nodded. "I'm glad he got the chance to go to the west coast to see some of his friends."

"And how about you?" her mother asked. "Have you been keeping in touch with any of your friends?"

"Well, you met most of them the other night." When she'd hosted her own version of a soiree.

"They're the ones involved in the Musko-cheers thing?"

Sarah glanced at Bek.

"Hey, I might be your sister, but I still follow you on Instagram."

"That's right. I forgot I mentioned about the fundraising for the Muskoka facility on there a while ago." She plucked a grape and unpeeled it, then popped it in her mouth.

"That's kind of gross," Bek said, wrinkling her nose.

"It's also fun." Oh, the things that she enjoyed now, now she wasn't on the frantic mouse-wheel of life.

The Heartsong tour season was done. She realized that now. She could maybe write more music, or possibly join a couple of nearby North American city concerts, but the frantic pace of what she used to be able to do she didn't want to anymore. Which made the album offer all the more interesting.

She'd replied, but all the baby drama had meant she hadn't responded to their contract. She grasped her phone, opened up her email, and studied it. Then prayed, felt a yes, and signed.

"Whatcha doing?" Bek asked.

Sarah told her, swearing them to secrecy. "I know you want me to be open with Dan, but I'd like this to be a surprise."

"I think he'll get a real kick out of it."

"Such a romantic gesture." Mum sighed. "So, did I hear something about Dan thinking of retiring?"

Sarah explained a little more, which was why the campground and special needs facility could make a lot of sense. "This could be a good thing to do."

"A good thing or a God thing?"

"We've been praying about it, and both of us think it's a God thing."

"It really sounds like you've been bonding well with these women."

Sarah nodded. "It's funny that although we live in the same apartment in the city, I only got to know Jackie more while in Muskoka." How ironic that it was here, and not there. Except not so ironic, when she had only wanted to avoid her before. "Jackie and Toni, who also lives in Toronto, both pop in occasionally. They've both been great in sharing a bit about what to expect when you're expecting." She groaned. "There's just so much, isn't there?"

Bek shot her a sympathetic smile. "It might be an answer to your prayers, but it doesn't mean it's easy."

That was for sure. "I really thought that by four months I'd be over vomiting by now."

Just like last time her body had reacted strongly to the little creature it was growing, and instead of putting on weight, she'd been losing it. Ginger helped, and the rest. Dr. Feldman was really happy with their progress, apart from slightly elevated blood pressure, which saw encouragement—not warnings— about the need to relax, to try and get her blood pressure down.

What a difference Dr. Feldman's outlook had. She might have similar suggestions to Dr. McKinnon, but she framed it in a way that Sarah wanted to try, rather than resist. When Sarah had first talked to Jackie about her desire for a different obstetrician, she'd put her in touch with the Christian woman who city friends had recommended to her. And yes, she knew going behind Dan's back about that hadn't been good, but he'd agreed after their meeting that Dr. Feldman's supportive nature was refreshing.

"From what I've seen with all your notes, it appears that there's definite improvement in the heart."

"Dr. McKinnon thought it was an error."

"Well, my opinion is that it's an improvement."

Oh, thank You God. "But what about the amniocentesis that Dr. McKinnon recommended? Doesn't that have a risk of miscarriage?"

"Mm." Dr. Feldman had tilted her head. "I think I'd prefer to wait a few more weeks and use an ultrasound. But really, the best diagnosis happens at birth or shortly after. So in order to keep your mind at ease, I'd be recommending that."

"Thank you."

Dr. Feldman had smiled. "So, I'd advise for you to make the most of this time as much as possible, because this is the last time you'll be able to put your feet up for a while. At least for eighteen years." She'd winked. "So my prescription for the Mummy-to-be is to relax."

Mummy. Her heart tickled with excitement.

She placed a hand over her abdomen, felt a flutter in response, and she got her mum and sister to feel the baby.

"Oh, he or she feels like a strong one."

"You're not going to find out the sex?"

"No. It doesn't matter. The main thing is that's it's healthy."

"What's the doctor saying?"

She told them of Dr. Feldman's opinions, then confessed some of what Dr. McKinnon had said, earning gasps in return. "Oh, Sarah. No wonder you were so stressed."

"He kept going on about birth defects, thanks to our chromosome incompatibility." She groaned. "I know I'm supposed to be a woman of faith, but it was like his words slid in and even though I'm feeling a lot better, sometimes I still can't help but feel afraid."

"Every child is a precious gift," her mother said.

"That's what we believe, but he wasn't even confident that we'd make it to a point of viability."

"Point of viability." Bek made a face. "That's an awful phrase when you consider we're talking about a child."

"I know." Sarah winced. "And I know I should've told Dan about this new doctor, but I couldn't face another round of Dr. McKinnon, especially by myself."

"It sounds like God has led you to the better doctor, even if the way you went about it wasn't perhaps as it should be." Mum squeezed her hand. "Just keep talking to Dan, Sarah. You know that closing things off isn't good for you."

She touched her belly. Or good for the baby.

"Well, how about we pray?" Mum said.

She nodded, closed her eyes, and her sister and mother held her hands and prayed. Prayed for wisdom for the doctors, wisdom for Sarah and Dan to go forward, blessing on their marriage, protection on Sarah's health, and for the baby. And their prayers of faith surrounded her, feeding faith, like a shield. And she relaxed and remembered her God was able to do anything, He could be trusted, and she could trust Him with it all.

"In the mighty name of Jesus, Amen."

"Amen and Amen." She sighed. "Thank you."

"And thank *you*," Bek said. "I certainly didn't expect my time here to mostly consist of lying around catching up on my fill of entertainment gossip and luxury living."

"I'm sorry it's been a trial."

"I'm prepared to forgive you."

"That's my girls," Mum said, which drew their laughter.

Peace settled across her soul, just like it did each time she visited Muskoka.

This break away, organized by Dan, had proved the perfect respite after several tumultuous months. And time with her family had filled her heart's cup to the brim. So much that she almost felt like she could face Christmas with Dan's family again.

CHAPTER 21

December passed in more games, two short road trips, and more appointments accompanying Sarah. The more he got to see Sarah with Dr. Feldman, the more he thanked God for this woman who seemed to connect with Sarah on a way that had only drawn resistance with Dr. McKinnon. It helped too that the next scan confirmed the previous one, and showed a significant improvement in the left side of the baby's heart.

Or maybe that was simply the fact that Sarah seemed so much more relaxed than before. His prayers, and those of her parents and sister, were answered, as Sarah was slowly returning to writing music, a special project, she'd shrugged, but not for Heartsong. But the fact her music seemed to have helped renew her love of God—and her love of him—helped Dan also settle into finding hope among the uncertainties.

For uncertainties remained. They'd agreed to have an ultrasound that Dr. Feldman had suggested, but not demanded, and one of the scans had drawn her concern.

"What is it?" he'd asked, as Sarah clutched his hand.

"I just will keep an eye on the spine and brain. It's likely nothing to be worried about."

"Dr. McKinnon once said our chromosome incompatibility might lead to water on the brain."

Dr. Feldman's brow furrowed. "Chromosome incompatibility sounds worse than what it is," Dr. Feldman said. "A man and a woman cannot be genetically incompatible so that it's impossible for them to have children together, but not with another partner."

Bands across his chest eased. He'd once thought that.

"Is that what you were told?"

"Words to that effect," he'd admitted.

"But Dr. McKinnon did say something about hereditary recessive disorders," Sarah said.

He gripped her hand. He would not let her spiral again into doubts.

"That can be a factor, in a very small amount of cases, but from what I've seen of your blood tests, and from the ultrasound scans, I don't see you belonging in that category."

"Then why the concern now?"

"Some doctors," she'd eyed them over her glasses, "have an abundance of caution, and, may encourage testing to ensure the healthiest possible outcome for a child."

Sarah's clasp tightened. "You mean they encourage parents to test and determine whether a fetus is viable."

She cleared her throat. "I do not like to use the term fetus with prospective parents, but yes. More common in IVF, but it can happen with natural pregnancies too."

"Survival of the fittest."

Dr. Feldman winced. "I don't like to say that."

In other words, yes.

"Which is why I'm advising you two, who are committed to raising this child no matter what, to put that from your mind. As a fellow believer, I love to encourage my Christian patients to keep trusting God, no matter what. He is the divine Healer, and in cases like this, there are miracles that can occur in the womb, but also through surgical intervention upon delivery. Which is why," she eyed them sternly, but with a twinkle in her eye, "I want you to take time to relax this Christmas and holiday season, and don't give fear an inch to dwell. Okay?"

"Yes, ma'am," Dan said.

"Amen," agreed Sarah.

THEIR INTERPRETATION of their "doctor's advice" meant they had an excuse to get out of unwanted holiday obligations. Not that he wanted to get out of spending Christmas with his family, difficult as they could sometimes be. At least this year was better than the last, when it had been a case of striving to overcome his envy at Luke and Marguerite's children, while wondering why he still had none. This time, their hope for April, along with Sam's recommitment and new job—and bringing Alexa to join the festivities again—made it a lot more enjoyable.

Sarah seemed to think so too, her conversation with Alexa about her recent travels adding zest to the usual family intoning of finance-based conversations, Sarah's hand on his thigh under the table reminding him they needn't stay late. Dinner, presents, dessert, then they'd need to go home to "rest."

He caught Sam's smirk across the table. "What?"

Sam shrugged. "I was just thinking it's nice to see you two looking relaxed."

"And here I was thinking how cute you two look together," Sarah said. "Alexa is a catch, huh?"

"I thought you said I was a catch," Sam mock-complained.

"I did. And you were."

Dan chuckled at his little brother's look.

"But now I know Alexa loved her time in Australia, well, she's an even bigger catch." She winked at Alexa.

"I'm sure I'd love my time in Australia too," Sam insisted.

"I know you would. Don't worry, I still think you're a pretty good catch. Especially with your new job. Cheers!" She lifted her glass of lemonade and there was a clink of glasses.

"Thanks, Sar bear," Sam said, using Dan's nickname for her.

Her nose wrinkled. "Speaking of catches, it looks like Alexa has caught you."

Those privy to the exchange laughed, except for Sam, who shifted in his seat to face Alexa more directly. "Except I haven't officially caught you, have I?"

"Officially?" she murmured, wide-eyed.

"Well, there's nothing like a gift at Christmas, and so I wondered if you'd like this."

He put a ring-shaped box in front of her as the rest of the table held their breath.

"Sam," Alexa whispered, looking up, then glancing around at everyone, her cheeks pinking.

"Open it."

Sarah put her head on Dan's shoulder, both hands around one of his, as they watched. He would never have expected his little bro to be so bold. At the family Christmas table, no less.

Alexa's fingers were shaking as she opened the box. Then laughed.

Laughed?

Then she held up a Fruit Loop.

"What the?" someone muttered.

Then Sam slid from his chair and captured her hands in his. "I know this is probably not what you expected when I asked you here today, but if you're willing to be caught by a Fruit Loop, then I'd be honored to love you for the rest of my days."

"Sam," she murmured. Then she kissed him. "Yes."

"Ohh." Sarah clapped her hands, almost vibrating in excitement. "That was just the most beautiful thing ever." She sighed, as the happy couple kissed, oblivious to everyone's congratulations, including Mom and Dad's shock.

"More beautiful than a proposal in Sydney?" Dan murmured in Sarah's ear.

"Okay, second most beautiful."

"Good answer."

She rolled her eyes. "Always so insecure."

He wasn't, but was reminded later that complacency had a soft underbelly that could be prodded. Such as when he caught Sarah watching Luc and Marguerite's children be the center of attention. His mom seemed determined to shift the focus from Sam's surprise proposal to a blue-haired photographer, and place it squarely on her grandchildren, almost forgetting she had another on the way. While Adam and Lucy were cute at almost four and two years old, they were a reminder that if their baby had lived, they too would be sharing in the joy of watching a little person's excitement at their first Christmas. A couple of times he caught Sarah looking at Adam and Lucy with a pensive expression on her face. He recognized the longing. He went up to her, wrapped his arms around her. "You okay, Princess?"

She twisted in his arms, turning around to kiss him, before leaning back in the circle of his embrace. "I'm fine. I just can't help wishing…"

"I know."

He placed a hand on her stomach, on the little one who still lived there. "This time next year, Princess."

She tilted her head up, smiled at him, her green eyes holding stars. "Amen."

～

SOMETIMES WHEN SHE first stirred in the morning, in that place between sleep and wakefulness, she forgot all the drama that swirled around her. Forgot the pressures, the numerous medical appointments, the worries. It was just her, and God, and peace.

Then she woke fully, and the pressures crowded in, and she was forced to fight to stand still, to know that God was in control. To rest in the knowledge of His faithfulness and grace.

Often an encouraging text message would come in, from her parents or Bek, or her friends like Jackie, or Serena, Bree, or Holly. Words to lift her soul just when she needed it, as if God had prompted people to do so right then. Other times she'd feel a sudden calm, like somebody else had just prayed for her.

Sometimes, if Dan wasn't there, she'd even sing aloud, declaring to the atmosphere and her heart that Jesus was in control, and that God loved her. *Your love is beautiful. Your love so undeserved. Your love stretches out forever to me.* As she sang, it was like her worries rolled off her back and were placed at God's feet.

There was a lot to be thankful for. *Thank You God for Your mercies. Thank You God for Dan. Thank You for my family. Thank You God for friends. Thank You for this child. Thank You for the last scans showing improvement.* So much to be thankful for. So much.

Such as this new year being quieter than the last. Last year had been filled with busyness: attending games and team functions, Heartsong, her podcasts, travel, and Zoom meetings and catch ups. This year, however, while she still attended the occasional game of Dan's, she was more selective about which ones. Such as games when she might talk and encourage a wife or girlfriend of one of Dan's teammates. Or see one of his Original Six friends, or their wives. Heartsong was shelved, as far as her involvement was concerned anyway. The podcast was too. Her energy levels varied, but when she had energy, she wanted to spend it on writing the love songs for the album she'd agreed to do. Not that she'd told Dan yet.

When he was training or playing away games proved the best time to fine-tune them. She had to send a sample to the record label in a few weeks, and had decided to give Dan a special birthday surprise, not dissimilar to something else she'd once done. He might be the better of the two of them at surprising with a special dinner location, but she suspected he valued her efforts just as much, if not more, judging from the worn-out CD she'd once made him that she'd discovered in a drawer.

She hoped he liked this birthday surprise.

Dan spent his birthday in Dallas. The lengthy road trip had taken in games in Florida and Texas over the past few days, so he was itching to get home. At least their early hours flight after the game meant they'd get a much needed couple of days rest before the next game.

He made his weary way to his apartment and unlocked the door, noting the darkened room, before noticing some balloons and a little handmade sign with "Happy Birthday Daniel!" inscribed on it. He gently placed the keys on the side entry table, then slowly, quietly made his way to bed.

Sarah's sleeping form stirred. "Hey there, you. Happy birthday."

He shifted closer to her, wrapping an arm around her satin clad middle, before kissing her on the cheek. "Thanks."

"Good result tonight," she mumbled, eyes closed.

Yeah, it had been, as they'd won, and he'd finally scored a goal, the first one since preseason. That was a nice monkey to have off his back. "Good result today."

Today's scan had showed signs that the hydrocephalus markers were improving, so Sarah had reported.

"It's so good to have you home," she murmured.

"It's good to be home."

She opened her sleepy eyes then, moving so she could place her arms around him. "Back where you belong."

Exactly.

THE NEXT DAY, a day off, meant he could celebrate his birthday in a more relaxed manner than yesterday. Which meant sleeping in, spending 'quality time' with his wife, then sleeping some more, then eating a very late brunch.

The plan was to have dinner with his folks and Sam and Alexa and maybe talk wedding things, or so Sarah had said.

But right now she was eyeing him with that expression that said she was up to something. "Why do I get the impression you're planning something?"

She instantly tried to blank her face, scraping her hands down her cheeks as if that could help. It couldn't. He could still read her like a book.

"I might just have a birthday present for you."

He caressed her middle. "This is the best present a man could have."

"Well, I hope you might like this one too." She held out her hand.

"Fine. Where are we going?"

A few minutes later he was seated in her studio, while she sat at the keyboard. "Am I getting a private concert?"

She pouted. "You're not supposed to guess."

He stifled a chuckle. "Sorry. I meant, are you demonstrating how to put together a baby cot?"

Her nose wrinkled. "I don't really want to do that just yet."

He glanced around the room. Did it need painting? "We probably do need to think about doing that soon, though."

"The baby is not supposed to come for three more months," she protested.

He loved that they were now talking *when*, not *if*. "Three months will fly by. What else do we need?"

She gave him a list of baby essentials, including strollers and car seats and all manner of things.

A tiny baby needed that much? Huh. "I'm sure we'll be given some. I know my parents want to buy a baby car seat."

"They do?"

"Mom mentioned it last week."

"I didn't know."

Oh. "Maybe that was supposed to be a surprise."

"I can act surprised."

So could he. "So." He rubbed his hands together. "When does the cot putting-together begin?"

"Well, I know this will shock you, but I wasn't actually going to do that."

"No way. You weren't?" He glanced around, frowned. Was this space going to be big enough for her studio, and that much baby paraphernalia? Especially if this baby had some special needs?

"What are you thinking?" she asked.

"Look, don't get excited, but if—when—I retire, where would you like to raise our family?"

"Our *family*?" She smiled. "You sound like you're planning more than one."

"I'd have a whole hockey team if I could, but I'm not the one who has to carry them for nine months."

She grimaced. "Men have no idea how lucky they are."

Oh, he had some idea. "So, where would you want to live if you could live anywhere at all?"

"You mean that wasn't a rhetorical question?" She peered at him. "If not, then really, do you have to ask?"

That meant Sydney, then. Just the thought of moving countries and all that would entail was liable to melt his brain.

Although, come to think of it, that's exactly what she'd done…
But there was time to think about that.

"Hey maybe once the baby is born, and as soon as you're well enough, we'll go visit."

"Really? You'd be willing to travel for all those hours with a screaming newborn?"

He smiled. "*Our* screaming newborn."

"Ours." Her face held awe. "Do you wonder if it's a boy or a girl?"

"All the time," he said promptly.

She laughed. "Then why don't you want to know?"

"Because there are so few surprises in life, I feel like this should be one of them."

"I don't care what sex it is," she said softly.

"Neither do I," he said, wrapping his arms around her waist. "Can you believe it's only three months away?"

"No. Considering all we've gone through it sometimes still seems unreal."

He kissed her nose. "So, back to that question before. Depending on what I end up doing, we don't have to stay in this apartment."

"We don't? Oh Dan, I'd *love* to live somewhere else. Can you imagine how squashy this will be once the baby arrives? And how on earth will we lug up strollers and baby stuff? Jackie's told me she's often gotten down to the car and strapped little Charlie in, then remembered she's left something up here, and had to unstrap him and come all this way again, then do it all over." She gestured to the room. "This space has been perfect when it's been just us, but add one more—especially one who'll have so much stuff—then how on earth are we going to fit that in?"

"So that's a yes, then."

She got up from the seat and flew at him. "That's a total yes. Yes, and *please*."

His laughter was stolen by her kiss, and it took some time before they finally returned to the purpose of their visit here.

She finger-combed her hair. "Sorry for distracting you, birthday boy."

"Hey, this birthday *man*," he emphasized, "is happy to be distracted like that any time you like."

She smirked at him, then gestured for him to resume his seat. "Okay, I'm giving you a preview of a new song."

His chest warmed. He could count on one hand the number of times Sarah had done that. "Is this for a new album?"

She bit her lip and nodded.

"You haven't mentioned a new album. Is this for Heartsong?"

She shook her head. "I think that season is done."

"Whoa. Really?"

"The touring part, and maybe the recording too. Tisha has said she still wants me to write, but I feel like my time doing the other things is done."

Wow. His heart was soft. "That's a big call."

"It feels like it."

"Heartsong has been a big part of your life for a long time."

She sniffled. "I know."

"Hey." He opened his arms, and she crawled onto his lap. She fit a bit less easily these days. "It's okay to cry."

"I'm not crying because I'm sad. Just…feeling emotional because it's the end of an era, I guess."

"God has new adventures up ahead." He placed a hand on her belly.

She tucked her face next to his jaw. "And not just with a baby."

That's right. "Your new album. Can I hear something from it?"

"Okay." She kissed his scar then slowly extricated herself from his arms and the chair, and moved to the keyboard and piano stool. "But this is the first time I've played it for anyone, so you need to tell me if it's too cheesy."

As if it would be. And as if he would. "It'll be perfect."

She rolled her eyes, but then smiled and ran her fingers over the keys, and began to sing.

By the time she finished he was wiping away tears. Who cared if he was now thirty-four? She'd written that song for *him*. Described *him*. To a tee.

"You okay there, tough guy?"

He blew out a breath. "I didn't think pregnancy hormones were catching."

Her smile turned tender. "So it's not bad, then?"

"It's beautiful. You should sing it at Sam and Alexa's wedding."

"Hmm. Good idea."

"Seriously, Princess. I don't think anyone has ever made me feel quite so honored before."

Her face lit, like she had another secret she couldn't spill. But he'd let her keep that one. This gift she'd given him was the best gift of all.

CHAPTER 22

"You're looking really well, Sarah," Dr. Feldman said in their next appointment.

"Did you say swell? Because swollen is how I'm feeling."

"What do you mean?"

Sarah waggled her fingers. "I can't wear my rings anymore." It had taken ages to get her engagement ring off, even with all the lubricants they could find.

"Let me see your ankles."

Sarah stuck out her jean-clad leg, tugging at the hem.

Dr. Feldman frowned, the first time she'd ever seen a frown from her, and Sarah knew a fissure of fear.

"What is it?"

Dr. Feldman's face blanked. "I know we've still got four or five weeks to go, but I'd like you to do another blood fasting test."

"Why?"

"It might be nothing, but it's best to rule out risk factors associated with gestational diabetes. Your last result was a little high, remember?"

"Right," she lied. She didn't remember. The last few weeks had rushed by in a blur. Between finishing and submitting the songs for Dan's album, to a Valentines' date he managed to fit in around his games, Musko-cheer meetings, Boyd's son's christening, Sam's wedding plans, and planning for the baby's arrival, she barely remembered her results.

"Can you do that tomorrow?"

"Tomorrow?"

"If you do it tomorrow, we can schedule an appointment the following day, as soon as the results come in. Can Dan come in too?"

"He's playing in New York at the moment."

"Ah."

"Why? What's wrong?"

"Nothing is wrong, you're perfectly fine. I don't want you to stress, remember?"

"It's hard not to stress when you're saying things like this."

"Like I said, it's probably nothing, but best to rule out anything that might make delivering a challenge because your baby is too big. Speaking of, have you started those pre-natal classes?"

"Yes. Dan *loved* it." Watching his face had been fun. Nice to see the men who'd attended finally starting to understand what giving birth meant.

Dr. Feldman smiled. "Many of the women say the same." She printed off a form. "Take this downstairs and make your appointment so the lab can test you first thing tomorrow."

"Okay." Sarah stood, a little unsteady. "Are you sure there's nothing for me to worry about? You've always been open and honest with me."

"There's nothing to worry about, Sarah. *If* you get that urine test sample done tomorrow."

. . .

After arranging the appointment, she returned home in time for another virtual Musko-cheers meeting. But this one saw Jackie and Toni visit her apartment, and she'd set up the laptop in the dining room so they could conduct their meeting. She was slower to move now. The baby had decided to suddenly pack on weight these past few weeks, so she felt puffy and gross. Thank goodness Jackie and Toni understood that pregnant women didn't have to have clean and tidy houses. Well, tidy ones, anyway.

Dan was now paying for a cleaner, and since he'd started putting together some of the baby gear their place was really cramped. She'd moved her keyboard to the living room, but now things looked untidy. And considering there was still a baby room to paint, and the car seat to organize, it felt like there was still so much to do. It was a good thing Jackie was organizing the baby shower this weekend.

"How are you managing?" Jackie asked.

"I'm a little achy most days. And I'm suddenly fat."

"Lucky you," Toni said.

"Only because I threw up half my body weight for the first five months."

"That's unfun," Jackie sympathized.

"I remember waddling around, and Joel, my brother, making fun of me." Toni wrinkled her nose. "Second time around was a lot easier, probably because I knew what to expect."

They swapped baby stories for a little while until the others could join for the online meeting.

It was nice when Dan was absent to have the opportunity to do this. To meet with friends, to feel their support, to have them pray for her.

They caught up with where things were at—Lincoln's newly-formed Muskoka Hearts Foundation had bought the property, and Rachel's contractor husband was gathering quotes to renovate. Jackie, Serena, and Anna were all involved in different aspects of the various legalities of setting up a registered charity and a special needs home, while Staci, Toni, and Sarah were focused on public awareness and fundraising, thanks to their profiles and fan bases. How much they could raise awareness when things were barely decided remained to be seen, but this was a long game.

The discussion concluded with prayer and a final jest from Rachel, which drew everyone's laughter, before Sarah's yawns drew Jackie's insistence that they finish.

"Are you sure you're okay? You seem weary."

"It's just been a big day. Dan will be back tomorrow night." Late, but he'd be back. Then they could enjoy their reunion, and he could opt not to go to the following day's optional skate.

She yawned again.

"I'm going to take that as our cue," Jackie said.

"Yeah, super subtle, Sarah," Toni teased.

"Thanks for coming here."

"I'm heading to Muskoka tomorrow," Jackie said, "but you'll let us know if there's anything we can do, right?"

She nodded, and closed the door. Glanced at her phone. Dan had a game tonight, but he might be free to talk now. The way she was feeling now, she'd probably be too tired to stay up late tonight. Good thing the man understood her need for sleep these days.

She dialed, but had to leave a message, which she did, then wrote one too.

Hey, love you. Hope tonight goes well. Talk soon xx

Then she stumbled back to bed, closing her eyes against a headache.

THE CHANCE TO connect with his Original Six buddies during the season didn't happen as often these days. That was the challenge of finding time squeezed between families, games, and differing time zones. So the fact so many of them 'just so happened' to be free on a weekday afternoon felt like a God-thing.

Dan was supposed to be having a pre-game nap, but he'd much rather talk to these guys. Brent Karlsson from Detroit, Beau Nash from Montreal, even former Boston-player Mike Vaughan had dialed in from over in Calgary. He'd see New York's Tim Carruthers and TJ Woletsky tomorrow night in the game, but they'd find a moment to catch up. Both had lots to share, with Tim's IVF twins, and TJ's new son.

"So, how is that amazing wife of yours doing?" Beau asked. "Maggie wants to know. And she says that Sarah and the baby are in her prayers."

"Ditto with Holly," Brent said.

"And Bree," Mike added.

Dan smiled. He still recalled the time when he'd first admitted to falling for the lead singer of Heartsong, and how the wives of these guys had instantly made Sarah feel welcome.

"The latest result is that the left side of the heart is nearly where it should be—"

"Praise God," Mike said.

"Amen." Dan praised God every day. Every hour. "God is so faithful, we keep seeing little miracles like this every time. The water on the brain they were concerned about is healing. And it doesn't look like spina bifida will be an issue anymore, either."

"That's awesome," Beau said.

Dan nodded. Beau had long supported kids' hospitals, since his nephew had died several years ago. "They're still talking about having a neonatologist team on standby, but that's tricky, as Sarah's previous surgeries means she's not a straightforward candidate for a cesarean." That, and her utter refusal to countenance more surgeries. Thank God Dr. Feldman had understood.

"Apart from that, she's doing well, getting tired, and is

looking forward to a baby shower coming up this weekend." It was a shame her family couldn't be here for that. He'd offered to pay for their flights again, but Lindy and Bek had said they'd be back for the birth in April.

"And the doctor?" Beau asked.

"Dr. Feldman has been great. She keeps telling Sarah to relax, but her blood pressure isn't coming down much. She's over it."

Brent nodded. "I remember Holly being the same. You can't keep a good woman down."

Or a busy one.

"But you do need to be careful," Mike warned. "Stuff can happen unexpectedly."

And Mike should know. His wife, Bree, had been pregnant with twins when her low iron levels led to complications that saw her admitted to the hospital early. It had been a scary time for them all.

"We'll be praying for you," Beau said. He was a father of two, after marrying single mom Maggie a few years ago, and had another on the way.

"Thanks. We appreciate it."

"Yeah, Bree said she's sorry she can't make it, but she's got a basket of awesomeness—her words—coming your way."

In the apartment that was already too small. Dan chuckled. "Tell her thanks."

"And Holl said if ever Sarah needs to get her Aussie on for a chat, then she's more than willing and able," Brent added.

"I'll pass that on. I think Sarah would love that." His lips tweaked. "That's gotta be easier than moving to Australia."

"What?" Beau exclaimed. "No way. Are you moving?"

"Really?" Brent asked. "I've actually wondered how that would work."

"No. Well, not yet. I'm just looking at post-hockey options."

"So you really are thinking of retiring," Mike said.

"My body is sore," Dan admitted quietly. He might be a veteran who got his own hotel room while on road trips, but he didn't want anyone on the team overhearing this. "And I'd rather finish on top than outstay my welcome."

"You're the best thing about that team," Beau scoffed.

"So Sarah keeps saying."

"It's good to have a wife who is your biggest cheerleader."

"Amen."

He and Sarah might not have had an easy run this past couple of years, and there had been times when she definitely hadn't wanted to cheer him on, but he knew the love that they shared was a miracle, and something that God had ordained.

CHAPTER 23

The headache pounding behind her eyes was making it hard to hear. Dr. Feldman was talking, but for once wasn't smiling, which couldn't be a good thing. Sarah leaned closer, doing her best to focus.

"...and having reviewed this, I have to admit, I'm getting a little concerned about the amount of protein in your urine." Dr. Feldman frowned. "And when that's combined with your high blood pressure reading today, it leads me to suspect you're a likely candidate for pre-eclampsia."

"I beg your pardon?"

Dr. Feldman's face wore compassion. "I'm sorry, Sarah, but you're going to the hospital today."

"Today?" No. *No, no.* "I'm not due for four more weeks."

"I know, but—"

"I've read the baby books, and I know if a baby comes this early it can have all kinds of issues." Oh, look at her arguing with an obstetrician.

"And if you continue to have these symptoms, then your baby may quite possibly end up with even more."

Her lungs tightened. Oh, if only Dan was here.

"You need to call your husband."

"But he's still in New York."

"And that means he can be here in just a few hours. Sarah, your blood pressure is getting dangerously high and so that baby needs to come out. You'll be monitored, but I think we'll need to induce you this afternoon or tomorrow."

"What?" No way. "But I haven't got my bags packed."

"Would you prefer a C-section?"

Be cut open again? "No."

"Sarah, please call Dan."

"He's at training."

"Have you got someone else you can call?"

Sarah gripped the edge of the desk. Something solid. Something real. For this moment that felt anything but.

"Sarah, you need to calm down. Unless you want me to call an ambulance for you?"

"What? No." She sucked in a deep breath. *Lord, You see this. Help!* She tried to smile, but it felt fake. "It's just I'm not ready. I haven't even had my baby shower."

"So have it afterwards. You need to go to the hospital today. This is getting dangerous."

"But I feel fine." Maybe a little agitated at times, but she was a redhead. Come on…

"Sarah, listen to me." Dr. Feldman leaned across the desk. "Your kidneys and liver can be permanently damaged if you do not get this dealt with soon. Do you want to spend the rest of your life having to give yourself needles or having dialysis just because you don't like the timing of your birth?"

Sarah stared at her. Well, when you put it like that…

"But Dan's in New York." Hadn't she said that already?

The doctor exhaled. "So get someone else to take you. Sarah, I'm concerned, and the longer you leave it, the worse this situation can get. I know you want to do all you can to give your baby the best chance possible. Please, if you don't want a C-section, and I'm already going out on a limb by not insisting on you doing that, then I need to set up the specialist team and ensure they're available, just in case."

Sarah's eyes filled with tears, and she bit her lip to keep it from trembling.

"Call him now."

She rang the numbers slowly, only to get his voicemail. She ended the call without leaving a message. "He's not answering."

Dr. Feldman looked at her steadily. "Sarah, I'm calling the hospital to book you in. If you're not there by five p.m. I'll be sending an ambulance to collect you."

SARAH DROVE HOME SLOWLY, her mind racing through what needed to be done. She so wasn't ready to have this baby now. Her parents were supposed to be coming for the birth. Now they'd be coming when the baby was weeks old! The baby room wasn't even set up properly yet; the baby shower was supposed to be this weekend. She'd intended to clean the apartment from top to bottom, but had only managed to do the kitchen so far. It was all so wrong…

She pulled in and parked, then slumped against the steering wheel. *Lord, give me strength.*

She must've closed her eyes, for the next moment she was jerking awake to the *tap, tap, tap* on the window.

Davis, the concierge, looking at her with concern. She shifted upright. "Mrs. Walton? I saw you on the security monitor. Are you okay?"

She shook her head. "I don't feel good."

"Do you need a doctor?"

"No, I've just been there." There was something she had to do. What was…?

"Have you called your husband?"

That was it. "I tried. He has a game."

"Okay. Well, let me help you get upstairs. And I think it might be good to try him again."

She tried calling once she reached the foyer, but no answer. Tried again when Davis escorted her to her front door. No reply.

"Is there someone else I can call for you?" Davis asked. "Mrs. Cash? Oh, that's right. She left yesterday to go to Muskoka."

"I'll be fine. I'll try again. Thanks, Davis."

"If you're sure," he said, as she shut the door.

She peered at the apartment. So much remained to do. But first she needed to call and leave a message. She sank into the leather lounge—oh, so comfy—and finally made the call.

"Hey Dan, Dr. Feldman told me I need to go to the hospital today to be induced." Her throat clogged. "If you can come get me, that'd be really good. I love you."

She hoisted herself out of the lounge's comfort and slowly trudged to the baby room. The room was filled with boxes, the cot that needed to be assembled, the pram that still needed adjusting, all crammed next to the spare bed. Somewhere were some nappies—diapers—and little newborn clothes she needed. Stepping carefully over the detritus she bent over and grabbed the items, then slowly made her way back to her bedroom.

She was so tired. What would she need anyway? Somewhere there was a list provided when they'd attended a hospital orientation. She reached under the bed, pulling out an assortment of suitcases until she finally found what she was looking for. Grabbing an overnight bag she slowly filled it with an assortment of clothes and toiletries, finally zipping it closed, before lying on the bed. She was so tired, a little sleep wouldn't hurt...

~

"Princess?" No answer. "Sarah?" Dan raced through the apartment. Was she even here?

No, there was her handbag. He saw a small bag of clothes in the baby room. She'd obviously been here. He raced to their bedroom, discovering her lying on the bed, a variety of suitcases of various shapes and sizes strewn across the room.

"Oh, Princess, I've been so worried."

He stroked her hair, suddenly aware of the sweaty smell coming from his body. He'd not had a chance to change since getting her phone call. It'd been straight to a cab, the team had found him the first flight, and he'd driven directly here.

"Sarah?"

She opened an eye, and he watched her face relax. "Dan, I'm so glad…" She drifted off again.

"Sarah, sweetheart, come on. We need to get to the hospital."

"I'm so tired."

Dan bit his lip. This was going to be a challenge. He could still carry his wife's pregnant form, but the bags might be a challenge as well. "Sarah, I'm going to need your help here. What bags am I supposed to take?"

She pointed at one waiting near the door. "It just needs, just needs…" She closed her eyes again, and he realized she looked a little paler than normal.

"Just needs the baby stuff, okay."

He hastily grabbed the baby bag, then swung her up in his arms, carefully balancing the bags, collecting her handbag on the way out.

"It's nice to have you back," she murmured sleepily.

"So, are you feeling okay?"

She yawned. "I'm just so tired."

"You relax, Princess. We'll get you there soon."

Once he propped her inside the Jeep, he gunned the engine. Fortunately, the traffic was minimal; peak hour was still a little way away and they made it in good time.

He parked, then carrying the bags, escorted his wife through the foyer, swiftly gaining directions to the maternity section. He followed Sarah to the monitoring room and watched as she was strapped in, and the machines began to whirr and beep. Her blood pressure was taken, the nurses looked at each other, then exited the room, but Dan could hear them outside.

"This is the one Dr. Feldman told us about. We'll need to get a rush on."

They soon returned, and Sarah was wheeled to a room, where a doctor who partnered with Dr. Feldman frowned. "Given the complex nature of things, I think we'd be better off to do a C-section."

Sarah's eyes opened wide. "No! No, I'm not being cut open."

Dan didn't blame her, having spent months in hospital after her car accident seven years ago. Half the scars on her body were from the injuries sustained from her car accident; the rest were from the surgery.

He held her hand and addressed the doctor. "We have been assured by Dr. Feldman that we can do this without surgery. Call her if you need to check."

The doctor studied the chart again. "Okay, but she needs to be monitored closely. Let's start with the gel asap."

Moved to a new room, Sarah had some gel inserted before she was encouraged to lay back and rest.

Dan didn't like the pale sheen, and this lethargy was something different. "Sweetheart, tell me how you're feeling."

Big anxious green eyes turned to him. "Scared."

He kissed her on the cheek. "Princess, it's going to be fine. You heard what the nurses said. You need to rest."

"But there's still so much to do."

"It'll get done." He'd planned to sort out the baby's room this weekend, when Sarah was supposed to be at Jackie's for the baby shower, but now he'd have to ask for help. "Sweetheart, the more you worry, the higher your blood pressure, and the more they'll insist on a Cesarean, so stop panicking." He smoothed his hand over her hair. Would his little son or daughter have the same beautiful color? Oh man, he was going to be a dad in a few more hours. How awesome.

As he prayed with her, he noticed her start to relax, the stress starting to recede, until she finally fell asleep.

"Hey, Dan. Good to see you got her here in time. How is she?" Dr. Feldman popped in, checking the charts at the end of the bed.

"She's just fallen asleep. She's been pretty lethargic."

"Hmm. We'll have to keep monitoring that. I don't know if she explained things, but her blood pressure is sky high, and I'm concerned that the baby will be in distress if we leave things for too long."

His heart fisted. *Lord!* "If… if the baby is distressed, will you have a team to help?"

"Of course. I had to make a few calls, but they're on standby." Dr. Feldman's face softened. "But the fetal monitoring is showing things are normal. Remember, the most recent scans showed there was no longer any abnormality of the heart or brain cavities. You can rest assured, because your child is coming early, we'll have a space ready in the NICU if necessary."

There was so much to absorb, so much they hadn't planned, this situation felt like it was spinning out of control. But he did know one thing. "We really don't want you to do surgery."

"I understand. We'll have to hope this induction works; if it doesn't in the next twenty-four hours, a C-section is the only possible outcome." She studied him for a moment. "You do realize what's at stake here?"

Dan must have looked blank as the doctor continued.

"She needs to deliver. Her kidneys and liver will be compromised unless your baby comes out in the next day or so."

Oh Lord, please help.

Dan nodded stiffly. It was time to make some phone calls. His wife and child needed urgent prayer.

SARAH WOKE, the dark shadows not quite hiding the room fittings. Dan wasn't here, but the steady beep of the blood pressure monitor was filling the room with assurance. The rest had helped, the overpowering tiredness from before had diminished somewhat. She vaguely remembered having some sort of cold gel inserted hours ago. She wasn't sure what effect it was supposed to have. She didn't feel any different right now.

Oh Lord... The worries from before loomed up again and she heard the beeps increase in frequency, so she tried to calm down, praying.

"Hey, Princess, you're awake."

Dan's return was so welcome. He'd showered and changed, and brought a sack of things she hoped contained food. He gave her a kiss, before settling into the seat next to her. "How are you feeling? Any twinges?"

She shook her head. "The rest was good. I think it all got to me."

"Well, you sure look better." He retrieved a long slushy from the sack. "It's mango."

Oh. How thoughtful. She gratefully took a long draught, the cold seeping into her system.

Dan settled back, a smile on his face. His smile always had a way of smoothing the jagged parts of her heart. Maybe the doctor should tell Dan to smile at her ten times a day and that might help her blood pressure drop.

"I called your folks. They're trying to reschedule their flights, and aim to be here by the end of the week."

The tears welled up. "Thank you," she managed to whisper.

"And Ange and John are on standby, in case you need anything. I'm not planning on going anywhere."

He reached across, smoothing her hair. She gently caught his hand, holding it tight. "I'm so glad."

Dan pulled out a couple of books. "Which of these do you want to read?"

They'd both been on her bedside table. "I don't know. I'll start one and see if I like it."

"Okay."

The next hour was passed in blissful quiet, the occasional slurps from the slushy the only sound. The book was okay…

Then she felt a slight pain across her middle. Wincing, she tried to sit up.

Dan looked up, his face a study of concern. She forced a smile. "I'm okay."

Another fifteen minutes passed before she felt another twinge. "I think it's starting to happen."

The book was abandoned as the nurse popped in to make a quick examination. "Well, it's good to see that the gel is working. And the fetal heart rate looks fine. But we've still got a long way to go yet. Try to rest as much as you can. You'll need all the energy you can get later."

Once she'd left, Dan looked at her, amused. "Encouraging lady, that one."

Sarah tried to smile, but it came out more like a grimace as her stomach tightened again. It felt like period pain. That was it, just think period pain. But she wasn't able to hide the discomfort.

"Sar?"

She shook her head. "It just hurts a bit, that's all."

He bit his lip. "Maybe you should stand up and move around. That's what they recommended in the prenatal class."

"I would if this silly drip wasn't attached to me."

Dan rang the buzzer, and a nurse swiftly appeared, and he explained the situation to her. She checked the baby's heartbeat, checked Sarah, then agreed, and removed the IV and monitoring strap. "You're pretty lucky to be starting so soon. Some women take hours until they feel anything."

Sarah wasn't feeling so lucky right now. She gingerly moved off the bed, Dan helping her stand. She felt so unwieldy, her stomach protruding over her feet.

⁓

DAN FELT HELPLESS. Ever since the first contraction over an hour ago, he'd watched his wife anxiously, noting the strain as she held her body rigid each time the pain tightened. She wasn't saying much, and he was trying to help, but man, this wasn't easy. Sarah would close her eyes, stand still then exhale slowly through gritted teeth. He'd seen her combat pain before, but that was nothing compared to this constant wracking of her body. Her hands gripped his in such intensity he knew another one was filling her. *Oh God, please help her.*

He knew women did this all the time, but he'd never known anyone, let alone loved them, so watching his beloved undergo such torture was torturous. She gasped, then her shoulders relaxed again. He took a moment to massage her shoulders gently. "You're doing great, honey."

She glanced up at him, wryness curving her mouth. "This is your fault you know."

"I'm really glad."

"Sadist."

He chuckled, before leaning close to her ear. "No, lover."

The smile lightened her face before another contraction hit, and she grabbed hold of the bed railing this time, her knuckles going white under the pressure.

"Try to relax, Sar."

She moaned, eyes shut tight, before a final gasp indicated the end of the contraction. "Relax? You have got to be kidding me. This hurts so much."

"Good thing redheads have got such a high pain threshold."

The glare she sent him made him smile inwardly. He checked his watch. "I think we're at five minutes now."

He left Sarah wearily propped against the bed—just as well she'd had her rest before—found a midwife then returned.

The midwife did another examination, checked the monitor, then nodded. "It's all looking good. I think it's time we move you up to the delivery room."

"Anything to get this over with," Sarah muttered.

Amen.

A few minutes later they were in a light, bright airy room with attached ensuite. The nurse briefly explained some things before leaving them to it.

Another contraction.

"Oh, that *hurt*."

"You want to have a shower, like the midwife suggested?"

Eyes filled with pain caught his, and she nodded. He moved to the ensuite, turning on the shower, helping her strip off her loose clothes.

"Don't want my hair wet."

He found a shower cap, wrapped her long hair up in a ponytail, then neatly secured the cap over her head. "I love you, Princess." He gave her a quick kiss then she stepped into the shower.

"Ohhh…"

Her groan rattled him. The hot water was too hot for him but seemed to work for her, soothing the muscles that kept cramping. He sat down on the toilet seat lid, wondering what to do now. He'd never liked being helpless, but what more could he do?

After ten minutes of the shower she looked at him. "Dan, I really need to go to the toilet."

"You want me to get a nurse?"

He grabbed a towel and carefully helped her out, leading her to the toilet. She sat down heavily.

"Sar? You want me to get a nurse?"

She was breathing heavily now. "I don't care."

Uh oh. "I'll be right back."

He poked his head out the door, relieved to see their midwife walking back.

"How is she doing?"

"She's on the toilet."

The nurse looked at him wide-eyed before rushing in. "Sarah? Sarah, you need to get on the bed now."

"I just need to finish…"

The nurse crouched down. "Sarah, that's your baby trying to come out. We don't want it born in the toilet, so come over to the bed."

The nurse glanced up at him and Dan moved to help Sarah, holding her, encouraging her as she shakily moved over to the bed and climbed into a hospital gown. He stayed with her, smoothing her hair while the nurse checked on her dilation progress, then checked the baby's heartbeat again.

"Well done, Sarah. It looks like you'll be meeting your baby in the next hour."

Dan could've cheered.

～

SARAH WANTED TO GROAN. Another hour of this? Why had she ever been excited about having a baby? This was ridiculous. The shower had helped a little, but the contractions had sped up, so she barely had time to breathe. She was so tired she felt wobbly. And Dan wasn't helping. He reached out to touch her hair.

"Don't touch me!" she snapped. She was so tired of being poked and prodded. Besides, all this was his fault. If he hadn't made her fall in love with him, they'd never be in this predicament.

Oh God.... She wanted to push, it was like she was constipated. How embarrassing to have total strangers see everything down there. She wished she'd shaved her legs.

She shut her eyes again. This pain was almost too much. She wanted to scream but didn't want to scare Dan with the intensity of pain she was feeling.

"Sarah, you're doing really well." This midwife was nice. Thank God. "I've paged Dr. Feldman. She'll be here any minute."

"Good." She wanted this baby out now. Yesterday.

The door opened and Dr. Feldman appeared. "Sarah, Dan, looks like things are almost there. Let's have a check of you, and we'll see if we need to call the neonatologist team in."

Sarah grimaced. Sure, why not? Anyone else want to see? Dan had moved down to have a look too. Why not take pictures?

"Okay, Sarah, all those contractions have moved the baby down the birth canal, and he or she is just waiting to come out."

"What about the head?"

"The head looks fine, the heartrate is perfect, so I'm not concerned. We're going to need you to start pushing on the next contraction, but ease off when we tell you, to help your baby the best way. Okay?"

She nodded. Thank God they were at this stage. She couldn't cope with much more.

"Dan, you go up and support your wife. We want gravity to help so get behind her, support her back."

Sarah felt another contraction begin.

"Okay, Sarah, push."

Gritting her teeth, Sarah couldn't stop the low whimper as the contraction lasted ten seconds, twenty, thirty… She started gasping.

"Sarah, breathe, deep breaths. Come on, your baby is almost here."

Glad for Dan's strong hands holding her shoulders she

pressed back as the next contraction hit. She tried to breathe over the pain, but it hurt, it hurt, it *hurt!*

"That's it, Sarah, well done. You can relax."

Relax? She wanted to faint, she felt light-headed.

Dan's voice came from behind her. "You okay, Sar?"

"I feel awful. This is so hard." The tears filled her eyes but there was no more time as the next contraction hit.

"Come on, Sarah, push." She tried to push, everything inside her tried to push, and she heard the doctor say, "That's it! The baby's crowning. Let's have another of those."

Well, yeah sure. Why not? The next pain hit her, and she tensed back against Dan.

P-u-u-u-s-s-s-h-h-h.

"Well done, Sarah! The head's out."

How gross did that sound?

"Come on, another couple of pushes and you'll have your baby."

"I can't do this…"

"You can, Sar. You've got this."

"So *tired.*"

The midwife moved up to the bed, wiping her face with a damp cloth. "Sarah, you're doing beautifully. You're almost there. Don't give up now." The midwife swapped positions with Dan who moved down to watch.

Oh, to be a man right now. She was never doing this again.

Sarah breathed in, expelling the air as the next contraction gripped, and pushed for what seemed like forever.

"That's the way, come on, come on…"

And with a final desperate push and a slippery thrust her body finally expelled the tiny human form, and Sarah collapsed against the pillows, listening as a tiny cry filled the room. *Thank you, God!*

~

THANK YOU, God! He was a father. Watching his wife's body do what it had been designed to do was amazing. Sarah was amazing. And now he had a little…?

The midwife quickly cleaned the tiny pink form, wrapping it in a soft blanket, before handing it to Dr. Feldman, who took some time to do some checks, then finally handed the baby to Sarah.

"Congratulations. You have a perfectly healthy little daughter."

"Perfectly healthy?"

Dr. Feldman nodded. "Thank You God."

"Amen." Dan kissed his wife, looking into those gorgeous eyes that had been filled with pain only moments before, and now were filled with rapture. "Oh, Sarah, you really are amazing. I love you so much."

She smiled at him, and they were connected, a steady stream of love vibrating between them, before the cry of their new daughter filled the space between them and Sarah looked down at the pale red fuzzy head.

"I love you too, Dan." She kissed the little babe. "And you, my sweet."

The staff, after smiling congratulations, had left the room for a few minutes. For a few minutes they were cocooned in love, a sweet bubble of bliss and answered prayers. Wonder filled.

"How are you feeling?" How many times had he asked that question over the past year?

"So much better. I can't believe it."

"You were awesome. I don't think I could've done that."

She smiled at him. "I wish you could've."

He laughed, stirring the baby. He touched her cheek. "She's so little, like a little doll. A tiny princess."

"What will we call her?"

They'd run through baby names before, but there really was only one possible name.

Sarah looked up at him, her clear green eyes dancing with delight. "Grace Elisabeth."

Dan kissed her, then his new daughter on the top of her tiny head. "Welcome to the world, Grace Elisabeth Walton."

EPILOGUE

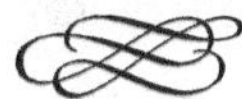

One year later

"And I want to say thank you to everyone who has turned out on this beautiful Muskoka day to celebrate the launch of this awesome initiative." Dan paused. "Many of you are aware that Muskoka is a place that holds a very special part of my heart. It's where I met my wife, Sarah—"

Sarah blew him a kiss as they were surrounded by applause and cheers, Sam's loudest of all.

"—and where I've grown in my faith, and now live with a family of my own."

"Whoo!" Sam again.

Sarah snuggled Grace closer.

"I love the fact that here in Muskoka we find respite from our busy lives, as we soak in what I like to call God's country."

"Amen!" Rachel called.

"And I love the fact that the Muskoka Hearts Foundation is supporting this incredible cause that focuses on the importance of valuing all people, including those who are often marginalized or considered broken. I believe that God is in the business of restoration, whether it be healing people's lives, or using people to make right an initiative to help the poor, or the beautiful, revamped grounds you see here today."

Dan gestured to the renovated gardens, courtesy of Damian, Rachel's husband, and his contractor connections.

"Here in Muskoka, we value community, family, friendships, all of which we can enjoy in this beautiful location. We don't always get things right, but we can trust in God that things are being made right. So on behalf of the Muskoka Hearts Foundation, and the Musko-cheers, thank you all for turning up today and for your support for this awesome cause."

Sarah covered Grace's red curls with her hand, and blew him a kiss as the applause filled the air.

He was glad-handed and thumped on the back by numbers of people, then he made his way to her, kissing her cheek before drawing Grace from her arms.

"Thanks. She's getting heavy."

"Good thing these guns still work."

She chuckled. "You were great."

"It wasn't too short?"

"It was perfect. You got your main points across, and you knew your audience. There's a lot of young children here, so you couldn't talk for too long."

She glanced around, heart full at the scene. The old Muskoka Ferns Lodge buildings had been mostly torn down, apart from a farmhouse that Damian had deemed habitable. Instead, where once broken people were virtually enslaved, children ran, and flowers bloomed.

"Okay, it's photo time!" Alexa, today's photographer, called. "Can I please have all the people involved in the Muskoka Hearts Foundation and the Musko-cheers join us here."

There was a bustle of movement, Dan protecting her as

usual. He might've retired from defenseman duties, but he'd always be her defender.

"Now after three, say cheese. One, two three!"

Sarah grinned as Alexa snapped their picture, her arm around Dan as he held Grace. This, the event to cut the ribbon for new foundations being poured for new Muskoka special care units, was making the media, both here and province-wide.

Dan, newly retired, was planning one more camp onsite, before handing the reins of running the camp to Travis, who had agreed to be mentored by Dan to learn outdoors skills and continue the legacy started by Dan and Boyd all those years ago. Dan knew he'd be too busy next year, with two children under three, finishing his studies, and working part-time for his team as a scout and mentor.

"You look like you're filled with moonbeams," Staci said from beside her.

"Aww." Sarah hugged her. "That might be one of the loveliest things anyone has ever said to me."

"It's not too corny? It sounded good in my head, but I wanted to know what it sounded like out loud. Because you do look radiant."

"It's Muskoka. How can you not love this place?" Although they may well be loving this place for half this year, Dan agreeing to clear his schedule so they could spend summer and Christmas in Australia. Oh, how wonderful that would be to be warm in December, to visit the beach, and enjoy picnics and New Year's Eve on Sydney Harbour. Or, she smirked, just enjoy creating their own fireworks at home.

"What's that look for?" Dan murmured.

"I'm just picturing summer in Sydney..." She sighed happily.

"Can you imagine flying all that way with a toddler and screaming newborn?"

"No. And considering our first child was an angel on that

flight, I refuse to believe that this next one won't be *exactly* the same. In Jesus' name."

Serena laughed, and leaned back against Joel. John had recently installed Joel as the head pastor of Muskoka Shores Community Church, John and Ange finally stepping down to take time off and travel. Toni stood with Matt, their two young ones between them. Matt's financial wizardry and business know-how had helped make this vision a reality much faster than anyone had dreamed.

Toni's art auction had resulted in a bidding war that had seen movie stars from the likes of Harrison Woods to Ainsley Beckett to NHL stars like Luc Blanchard and Zac Parotti paying eye-watering amounts. But it was all for a good cause. The special needs home would open later this summer, once the first stage was completed.

Anna and her husband Tom were chatting with Rachel and Damian, who had done so much to improve this place. Next to them stood Lincoln and Jackie, who held their newest addition in her baby-carrying sling. And James held his wife's prominent baby bump tenderly, as if he too couldn't believe the miracle found in Muskoka.

That same heated sensation that had flowed through Sam when he'd prayed for Sarah, had flowed when she'd felt an overwhelming desire to pray for Staci, and lo and behold, here they were, six months later.

Sam's laughter rippled across the ground, as Alexa smirked at him, before taking her new husband's picture. Alexa's calendars of Muskoka had helped fundraise, as had Staci's latest book, a Christian contemporary that had rocketed to the top of the bestseller charts, with all profits going to the Muskoka Hearts Foundation. The same could be said for Sarah's secular album, which had opened her up to legions of new fans, even as some had questioned why she was straying from her roots.

She wanted to respond and say, "Because God is the God

who is love," and that "God so loved *the world,*" and that if the worldly only ever saw Christians as judgmental then why would they want anything to do with that kind of God?

But she didn't, Dan's wise words ringing in the back of her head. For if God so loved the world, then He could be trusted to draw people to Himself, when the time was right, when their encounters with God were stories ready to be written.

Her job, his job, all of theirs, was to love people, and by showing how God had transformed their lives, God could touch all willing hearts with His hope and His Life.

That was the miracle she'd found in Muskoka. And that was the miracle found anywhere by people hungering for God.

THE END

Turn the page and find out more about this story...

A NOTE FROM THE AUTHOR

This book is a much-edited version of what was originally my sequel to *Muskoka Blue,* one of my favourite books I've written. Somehow along the way, I cropped the initial scenes concerning Dan and Sarah's wedding, and in doing so, found a bunch of characters (like their wedding coordinator, Serena) who each demanded their own story, which was how *Muskoka Shores,* the first book of the Muskoka Romance series, began.

But this book was always going to be centered on Sarah and Dan and about miscarriage and the challenge of trusting God in dark days. My husband and I struggled to get pregnant, and then were overjoyed when we finally fell pregnant, only to have a miscarriage eight weeks later. Later that year we attended a conference at Christian City Church, Oxford Falls, Sydney, and Pastor Phil Pringle called out to the front couples having trouble conceiving. He prayed for me and my husband, then said, "In twelve months I want you to return and show me the baby." Twelve months later, we did.

But as I wrote this, I felt God prompt me to include more than just my own story (which also included the fun of gestational diabetes and induction three and a half weeks early), but that of a couple my husband and I knew whose baby had been diagnosed in utero with a heart condition, spina bifida, and hydrocephalus. This scenario harnessed the prayers of a faith-filled church, and saw a miracle baby born, perfectly healthy, a baby whom doctors had advised to terminate. Thank you to Wendy and Michael Baker for sharing your story and allowing me to share some of that in this book. The scene when people shared about seeing visions of Sarah and Dan's daughter getting married, and God healing the baby's heart, and the Exodus 14:14 Bible verse, are all from what people shared with Wendy and Michael. God is so good. I'd also like to thank my friends Kim Jacobs for her midwifery expertise and Jenny Glazebrook, Carol W., Evelyn F. & Brittany S. for reading through this story and helping make it better.

Of course, we don't all see healing or answers the way we want or expect. Does that mean God doesn't love us? No. Does that mean God is not there with us in the midst of hard times? No. God loves us, and is with us in all things. And His promise is that He is working all things together for the good of those who love Him. Does good mean easy? No. Romans chapter 8 suggests that 'good' means being transformed into the likeness of Jesus Christ. So we can take comfort that in the middle of pain and grief and long-suffering that God still loves us, is still there with us, and is still using these circumstances for His purposes.

I hope and pray that everyone, no matter what situation you're facing, will be encouraged to trust God with all aspects of our lives. He may not answer our prayers the way we want or expect, and God showing up doesn't mean we get what we think we're going to get, but God *is* faithful, He can be trusted, and He is the God who can do "exceedingly abundantly above all we can ask or imagine."

The song Sarah wrote was the song I wrote in the hours after my miscarriage. I believe the words still hold true today:

I know You love me, I've seen Your grace so many times.
Your faithfulness surrounds me. You gave me this hope I feel inside.
I will not worry. For I know that You're always there.
Nothing can come between us because Your love is great.
Your love so undeserved. Your love stretches out forever to me.
Your love is not contained. I see the evidence each day.
Your love means all the world to me.

There is nothing I can do. To make You love me more or less.
I'm created as Your child. So You love me. Yes, You love me.

I pray that you will know God's love and let it be the full stop in your life too.

Thank you for reading the Muskoka Shores Romance series. I hope you've enjoyed getting to know the women and men of this fictionalised small town in Muskoka, Ontario! (You can see pictures of this area on my website www.carolynmiller author.com) If you have enjoyed *Muskoka Miracle*, a quick review at Goodreads / Bookbub / your place of purchase is always appreciated.

To find out more about Dan and Sarah, make sure you read *Muskoka Blue*, and the other books in the Original Six and Northwest Ice romance series for more glimpses of their lives.

And if you need more small town stories, check out those in the Trinity Lakes and Greener Gardens collections.

Don't forget to sign up for my newsletter at www.carolyn

millerauthor.com (where you can also get a free book!) and be the first to discover upcoming releases, behind the scenes details, sneak peeks, and more.

May God bless you - and happy reading!
   Carolyn

ABOUT THE AUTHOR

Carolyn Miller lives in the beautiful Southern Highlands of New South Wales, Australia, with her husband and four children. A long-time lover of romance, especially that of Jane Austen, Georgette Heyer and LM Montgomery, Carolyn loves to write contemporary and historical romance that draws readers into fictional worlds that show the truth of God's grace in our lives.

To find out more about Carolyn's books, and to subscribe to her newsletter, please visit www.carolynmillerauthor.com. By subscribing, you can also get a free novella, Originally Yours.

You can also connect with her at

ALSO BY CAROLYN MILLER

Contemporary:

<u>The Original Six hockey series</u>
The Breakup Project
Love on Ice
Checked Impressions
Hearts and Goals
Big Apple Atonement
Muskoka Blue

<u>Northwest Ice hockey series</u>
Fire and Ice
The Love Penalty
Pointe, Shoots, and Scores
Faking the Shot
Plays By the Book

<u>Three Creeks Ranch Romance series</u>
A Cameo for a Cowgirl
A Valentine for a Vet
A Second Chance for the Dancer

<u>Muskoka Romance series</u>
Muskoka Shores
Muskoka Christmas
Muskoka Hearts

Muskoka Spotlight

Muskoka Holiday Morsels

Muskoka Promise

Muskoka Miracle

<u>Trinity Lakes collection</u>

Love Somebody Like You

Tangled Up in Love

Only You Can Love Me

<u>Our House on Sycamore Street</u>

The Lost Daughter's Irishman

<u>The Fairall Romance Legacy</u>

An Irish Kiss

<u>The Greener Gardens Romance series</u>

Restoring Fairhaven

Regaining Mercy

Reclaiming Hope

Rebuilding Hearts

Refining Josie

<u>The Silver Teapot Series</u>

Not Exactly Mr Darcy

Historical:

<u>Regency Wallflowers</u>

Dusk's Darkest Shores

Midnight's Budding Morrow

Dawn's Untrodden Green

Regency Brides: Legacy of Grace
The Elusive Miss Ellison
The Captivating Lady Charlotte
The Dishonorable Miss DeLancey

Regency Brides: Promise of Hope
Winning Miss Winthrop
Miss Serena's Secret
The Making of Mrs Hale

Regency Brides: Daughters of Aynsley
A Hero for Miss Hatherleigh
Underestimating Miss Cecilia
Misleading Miss Verity

'Heaven and Nature Sing' from the Joy to the World Christmas
novella collection

'More than Gold' from
the Across the Shores novella collection

'Convincing the Circuit Preacher' from
The Courting the Country Preacher novella collection